To Marsh Cliff

Over the years our appreciation for you has grown. We look forward to many more years of success.

Best,

E. Berine Nash

Crossing the Bridge Over Troubled Water

∽

by

E. Bernie Nash

authorHOUSE®

AuthorHouse™
1663 Liberty Drive, Suite 200
Bloomington, IN 47403
www.authorhouse.com
Phone: 1-800-839-8640

©*2008 E. Bernie Nash. All rights reserved.*

No part of this book may be reproduced, stored in a retrieval system, or transmitted by any means without the written permission of the author.

First published by AuthorHouse   7/18/2008

ISBN: 978-1-4343-9062-2 (sc)

Library of Congress Control Number: 2008904647

Printed in the United States of America
Bloomington, Indiana

This book is printed on acid-free paper.

To Cydne my soulmate and backbone; to

Amiri my inspiration and my future

and to Khalil in loving memory of your enduring spirit

Contents

Chapter 1:	Was It Destiny or Just Coincidence?	1
Chapter 2:	The First Time, I Ever Saw Your Face	5
Chapter 3:	More Than Just a One-Night Stand	9
Chapter 4:	Breaking Up Is Sometimes Hard To Do	12
Chapter 5:	Meeting the Family for the First Time	15
Chapter 6:	Taking the Road Less Traveled Across the Country	21
Chapter 7:	Mechanical Failure or Failure to Communicate	27
Chapter 8:	On The Road Again	31
Chapter 9:	The Bates Motel	37
Chapter 10:	Chitty-Chitty Bang Bang	43
Chapter 11:	West Coast Meets East Coast	50
Chapter 12:	There's No Turnin' Back	59
Chapter 13:	A Reason to Return Home	65
Chapter 14:	Spending a Little Time to Reminisce	72
Chapter 15:	Time to Get Serious	77
Chapter 16:	We'll Do It Our Way	84
Chapter 17:	Reception in St. Louis	91
Chapter 18:	Getting Ready for the Move	103
Chapter 19:	The Phone Call	110
Chapter 20:	Atlanta, Here We Come	117
Chapter 21:	Home Sweet Home	125
Chapter 22:	Planting Our Roots in Atlanta	130
Chapter 23:	An Opportunity of a Lifetime	135
Chapter 24:	The Graduation Surprise	141
Chapter 25:	New Job-- Big Responsibilities	150
Chapter 26:	The Emerging Leaders	157
Chapter 27:	Slowing Down to Save the Marriage	164
Chapter 28:	EPT does not mean Exchange Personal Time	169
Chapter 29:	An Eventful Christmas in D.C.	174
Chapter 30:	Family Fun for Christmas	179
Chapter 31:	Our Loss	186
Chapter 32:	Pregnancy, Take Two	192
Chapter 33:	The Family Reunion	197
Chapter 34:	The Life Changing Trip to D.C.	202
Chapter 35:	The Ride to the Mall	213

Chapter 36:	The Call Home	218
Chapter 37:	Meeting with Specialists	223
Chapter 38:	A Friend in Need	231
Chapter 39:	The Procedure	237
Chapter 40:	The Outcome	246
Chapter 41:	Released from the Hospital	253
Chapter 42:	The Departure	262

Acknowledgements

As many writers know creating a book is a process. To some like myself it's like running a marathon. At some point you hit a wall but you've got to keep going to finish the race. This book has been a journey, sometimes painful but ultimately uplifting. I am forever grateful to my wife, Cydne S. Nash and son Amiri Nash for keeping me going after long days at work. I thank my parents Elson Nash and Thelma Nash for their enduring example of sticking to each other and making marriage work. I would also like to thank the following people who have touched my life in special ways and keep me grounded in faith and love: Cynthia Bagby, Cat Blake, Ozzie Blake, Lori Dixon, Reggie Dixon, Damali Edwards, Arlando Edwards, Cliff Harris, Kenecia Harris, Alonza T. Hill Jr, Sharese Hill, Sadie Jasper, Herman Johnson, Joyce Johnson, Pastor Noah Kaye, Tricia Kaye, John Lee, Paulette Lee, Jacob Marshall, Karen Marshall, Levelle McKinney, Buddy Moore, Carolyn Moore, John Moore, Theresa Moore, Byron Nash, Freida Baker-Nash, Loyde Nash, Barbara Nophlin, Calvin Nophlin, Burleigh Rideau, Ewell Rideau, Cliff Smith, David Smith, Joyce Clements-Smith, Vicki Smith, Anthony Stithz, Sonya Coleman-Stithz, Lisa Williams, and Stuart Williams.

I also want to thank other supporters and friends: Bridgette Allen, David Allen, Beverly Dabney, Sharon Greene, Kathy Miner, Donald McShane, David Neuwirth, Tracey Scott-Yetunde and Ayo Scott-Yetunde.

Lastly I would like to thank Elaine Watkins Smith and Lindsay Smith of Editing on Demand.

～

We were as one babe

for a moment in time

and it seemed everlasting

that you would always be mine

now you want to be free

so I'm letting you fly

cause I know in my heart babe

our love will never die.

"Always Be My Baby" – Mariah Carey

～

Chapter 1: Was It Destiny or Just Coincidence?

It was 1972 and all I could remember was that Dad (Linton) was always away from home. Whenever Dad did make it back from his long trips he would bring things back like Boston Cheesecake or knick knacks from other cities. This time he was gone a long time, almost a year, and we barely saw him.

Mom (Ewell) worked hard taking care of us – two boys and a girl. I was the youngest. I was the "brat." When Dad returned from his business trips it was a big deal. This time Dad had been in Washington, D.C. for almost a year. We were excited. This trip was important because Dad had a big question to ask us when he returned.

Not long after he arrived home did we get the surprise. The Department of Transportation wanted to relocate Dad to Washington, D.C. Dad's constant traveling took a toll on Mom and she wanted him home. Dad explained that a move to D.C. would solve the issue while giving him the opportunity to advance his career. Mom wasn't buying it and she thought it was a bad idea. We had a house, rental property and we (the kids) were well adjusted to our surroundings. Mom could not fathom leaving the Bay Area where my four aunts also lived.

After some serious discussions and cajoling by Dad, a compromise was made. We would live in D.C. for a summer. That summer we lived in Silver Spring, Maryland on the border of College Park near I-495. Like any seven-year-old, I just wanted to play with other kids. I found many children to play with in the apartment complex and when possible, I explored my new environment.

Dad did his best to appease us and to show us that the move was a great opportunity. I remember walking up the thousands of steps at the Washington Monument. Denise, Silas, Mom and Dad were all very tired but I was the Energizer Bunny wanting to see everything.

A close cousin named Spencer lived in D.C. He always liked to show other relatives around. Since we wanted to see all the sights, Spencer arranged for us to see the White House through his best friend Will. Will was a police officer for the Secret Service. He was a very nice fellow and Dad took a liking to him. Dad was a stickler for returning favors to people. One day he figured he would have the opportunity to repay Will for his good deed.

We decided not to live in D.C. because Silas, Denise, and Mom did not like the major transition. In addition, after I got lost at a department store, Mom felt the area was too unfamiliar for the family and too dangerous for me. I left the East Coast with fond memories of playing in Silver Spring, visiting the Washington Monument and going to the White House to meet Will.

As the years passed I didn't think about the Washington, D.C. experience until my college days. I was a college student who had not experienced anything outside of California. One summer I got the urge to take courses and participate in an internship. After looking at a summer catalogue, I decided to take a physical chemistry class at the University of Virginia. UVA was a great experience. I had just pledged a fraternity so I was anxious to meet new frat from the East Coast. I was also enthralled at the idea of going to a popular East Coast university. Arriving at UVA, I quickly learned my surroundings. I met some frat brothers taking summer courses and soon became acclimated to the slow southern life style.

After completing the summer course at UVA, I decided to stay on the East Coast to participate in an internship. I asked my sister Denise, who was a newlywed, if I could stay with her and her husband in Silver Spring, Maryland.

After seven months in the Washington, D.C. area, I returned to California more focused on finishing college. One day when I returned from class with my girlfriend, I was told that Will was in town for a conference. He was a great guy – funny and very personable. He hung out with us and acted just like my cousin. He was pretty nifty with the camera, asking me to pose for a picture with my girl friend.

A few months after Will left, his wife Jane visited the Bay Area to take care of her brother K.C., who was sick. Will called Dad to ask if Jane could stay at the house because she had no one other than her brother in California. Mom and Dad said it was not a problem and made sure she felt at home. In fact, as usual, being from the South, they laid out the southern hospitality. Dad remembered the White House tour and Will's hospitality when we were in Washington, D.C. He believed in making friends and extended the family comforts. Little did he know that his kindness would leave a long-lasting impression on Jane.

That summer I graduated from UCLA and felt good about life. I was pursuing medical school and had been accepted into a summer medical program at Washington University at St. Louis. It was a great opportunity to improve my science skills and increase my chances of getting into a medical school of my choice.

I attended the program with a partner from UCLA named Ed. Ed was from Los Angeles. He was a hard worker with a knack for the sciences. Although he worked hard, Ed liked to venture out and have a good time. Ed and I were roommates and quickly connected with a "mac daddy" from St. Louis named Dave. We worked hard and played hard. I was involved with someone at the time, but was not married. I didn't go to St. Louis to meet anyone so I just flirted. We all had a great time. Dave had a car, so he took us around to places like the clubs in East St. Louis.

Ed was starting to get close to a young woman who was in a program with entering medical students. She was amused by Ed's smooth, laid-back style. She quickly became the female addition to the team as we stayed up late studying or clubbing on the weekends.

Lesson 1: Sometimes people and circumstances are placed in your life for a reason.

Chapter 2: The First Time, I Ever Saw Your Face

It was two weeks before the end of the program when Mom reminded me that Will and Jane now lived in St. Louis. I didn't remember Will and Jane until Mom reminded me of the very nice woman who visited our house when her brother was sick. As usual, I didn't think anything of calling them until Mom nearly twisted my arm through the phone. The time was approximately 6 p.m. on a Thursday when I called Will and Jane.

"Hello, may I speak with Jane Moore?" I said.

"This is she."

"Hi, I'm Bentley Johnson, son of Linton and Ewell Johnson. I wanted to call you since I was in town for a summer program at Washington University at St. Louis." I talked about the program and how my parents were doing. Then she asked me what I was doing that weekend.

"Well, I'm supposed to be going to the movies with some friends down at the St. Louis Center."

"Oh," said Jane. "We'll be in that area too. Let's try to meet so you can connect with Will and meet my daughter Rikki."

"Sounds good to me, let's meet after the movie at ten."

The next day after classes and studying, we set off to the St. Louis Center to catch a movie. We had a great time talking about the program and tripping off the people. We enjoyed the movie and were just about to catch a cab back when I reminded them that I needed to meet some friends of the family. Jane told me to look out for a grey Benz in front of the movie theater. I spotted the car and introduced myself and my friends.

"Hi, I'm Bentley and these are my friends who attend the summer program."

"Hi Bentley, do you remember Will? This is my daughter Rikki, who is finishing college in this area."

"Hey Will, I remember you from coming out to Cali and hi Rikki, I'm pleased to meet you. These are my friends, Ed, Dave, Andrew and Sheryl."

I remembered Will vividly because when he came to Cali, I was with my girlfriend. Will had taken a picture of us. Our eyes met and Will said, "Hey I remember you and that bubbling brown sugar you were with." I laughed to myself.

"Do you guys want a ride back to the dormitories?" Jane asked.

"Sure it sounds good to me," I replied. "What about you guys?"

"Let's do it," said Ed.

So we all climbed into the car and squished together.

On the way back to the dormitories, we made small talk and laughed about the summer program and asked questions about living in St. Louis. Will and Jane were very talkative while Rikki was somewhat reserved. I thought she was nice. She reminded me of a school teacher. She had glasses that were rather thick and wore conservative clothes. The only thing that was not conservative was her diametrically twisted braids.

Upon arriving back at the dorm, we thanked them for the ride. I told Will and Jane that I would give them a call the next day to arrange time to visit with them since I would be going back to Cali in two weeks.

The next day I gave them a call. Jane answered the phone.

"So Bentley, what are you doing tomorrow for dinner?"

"Oh just having this wonderful dorm food."

"How about dinner at our house? I'll have my daughter pick you up."

"Sure, I'll be ready around three." I thought nothing of the dinner except an opportunity to get a home cooked meal.

Sunday came and I was ready around three when Rikki picked me up. I waited out in the lobby of the dormitory and saw a little Volkswagen Fox drive up. She got out and walked up the steps.

"I'll come down—there's no reason to come up."

I still remembered her from Friday night, she was cute and I was glad to get a change of pace from the medical program. Although I had fun at the pre-med program, there were the usual relationship games people played in an environment where hormones flew. I just wanted a change of pace and a place where I could feel at home. As we drove out to the suburbs we talked non-stop about school, life and politics.

"She's not so bad," I thought.

I had preconceived notions that she was going to be boring and conservative. Instead I found that she was quite outspoken and funny. When we got to the house I greeted Jane and Will. I also had the opportunity to meet Will's children Steffie and Tim, from his previous marriage.

They had a huge one-level house in a suburb of St. Louis. Will worked for the Secret Service and was transferred from D.C. a couple of years before. Jane moved to St. Louis a few months after Will and Rikki moved from D.C. about a year after to finish college.

We ate a delicious meal that both Will and Jane cooked. I was starting to get comfortable in their home and was glad that I called them a few days ago. After dinner we played Pictionnary. Rikki and I were a team while Will and Jane were on a team. We kept winning and made a good team together. That's when things started to click. After playing Pictionary we talked for hours. Before we knew it, it was time for me to head back to the dorm.

Our conversation on the return trip to the dorm was quite different from the one heading to the house. We talked on a more personal level. In fact, we divulged a little about our relationships with others which seemed a bit odd because, it wasn't even a date.

When we arrived at the dormitory I said goodbye. We agreed to give each other a call in the next couple of days to hook up.

Lesson 2: Never underestimate the power of parents.

Chapter 3: More Than Just a One-Night Stand

The next day we talked and decided Rikki would come to the library with the crew. As usual I tried to be the study bug at the library but it always turned out that I became the "headless horseman." Each time I got into a library, I would fall asleep with my head bobbing back and forth. I would look up from a deep sleep and attempt to play it off. Meanwhile, my buddies would play silly pranks like the game "three pointer" where they would try to toss paper balls into my open mouth. Rikki just giggled while attempting to do her work.

After studying at the library we drove back to the dormitory. Ed, Dave, Andrew, and Sheryl went to their respective rooms while Rikki and I talked. We talked for nearly two hours. At the end of our talk Rikki said goodnight but before she departed, we embraced for a passionate kiss. With only a few days left before I returned to California, passion got the best both of us. We decided to meet the next day for a good-bye dinner. All day long I could not think straight. I was in a relationship with someone back in California but I couldn't stop thinking about Rikki. As I talked things through with Ed and the others, they reminded me that I was not married and that the likelihood of me seeing Rikki after the program was nill. I took the "plunge." When Rikki picked me up, I was stunned. Gone were the glasses and conservative look. Rikki had on contacts, her braided hair was down and she wore a curve-fitting summer dress that was tastefully sexy.

"Wow, you look great," I complimented.

"You don't look bad yourself," replied Rikki.

Our conversation was light and airy. It was as if we had known each other for years. After dinner Rikki started to drive me back to the dorms. We passed a hotel and looked into each other's eyes. Rikki drove straight to the hotel and I checked into the room. We did not say a word. Only actions and passion led us into the room. The minute the door closed, we became sex-crazed animals. Clothes flew everywhere. It might as well have been a cave. Amidst the grunts and groans we moved across each other's bodies as if we had known each other for years. Somehow we knew the right positions to tantalize each other. It wasn't until hours later in the fog of sweat and exhaustion that we realized what happened.

"I've never had sex after knowing someone for such a short time," admitted Rikki.

"Neither have I."

There was not a moment's doubt. We were hooked, but I was out the next day to California.

When I returned to California, I broke the news to Rikki that I had been in a serious relationship. Rikki was disappointed and quickly thought I had taken advantage of her.

"Rikki believe me, I've never done anything like this. I really do like you and feel we have something special."

"Something special! What do you mean?" Rikki was hurt and filled with mixed emotions. "Are you going to stay with her? If you really are into me then leaving her should not be a problem."

"Rikki, it's really easier said then done. When the time is right, I will break it off."

I knew this was going to be a point of contention. In fact, when I saw Jolene she sensed something was not right. I was distant and did not seem happy to see her. Everything annoyed me.

"What's bugging you?" asked Jolene. "It seems that your trip to St. Louis made you angry. Did something happen in the program?"

"I just need time to sort things out."

She was on to something but just couldn't put her finger on it.

Six weeks after leaving St. Louis, I returned for a weekend of fun. Rikki and I acted like little kids. We went to the park, LaCledes Landing and to a concert near Ozzies. Like two teenagers we couldn't keep our hands off of each other. We cuddled, laughed, hugged and had great sex.

I knew that Rikki would ultimately ask me if everything was broken off.

"Have you broken it off with Ms. X?"

"I'm still breaking the news to her. Things like this take a while. I can say that I am no longer committed to the relationship."

In reality I knew I was growing distant from Jolene but was a wimp when it came to breaking her heart. It was the first real relationship for Jolene. I knew she would take it really hard. However, the fact of the matter was that it had to be done.

∽

Lesson 3: There's no denying a direct connect.

∽

Chapter 4:   Breaking Up Is Sometimes Hard To Do

I was at Jolene's apartment when I finally broke the news. We had just returned from a weekend trip to Santa Cruz with some of our friends.

"Jolene, I need to tell you what's been bugging me. You know when I went away for the summer."

"Yes," she said.

"Well, I met someone."

"What do you mean?"

"Well, I met someone that I believe I'm in love with."

"I knew you acted weird once you came back!" Jolene's eyes looked like she had gone mad. Her face contorted and it looked like she was spewing fire.

"Why didn't you tell me while you were there? That is so unfair and selfish!"

Tears were streaming down her face. She started to throw things out of her way as she rushed into her room. Just before she slammed the door, she yelled out.

"How could you do such a thing?"

At that point, the world seemed to be crashing in on me. I was extremely uncomfortable but it was the best thing to do. I knew the road would be rocky but eventually things would pan out. I knew that in order to be with Rikki, I had to be tested. Little did I know that a real test was coming. I talked to Rikki later that evening.

"Okay, Rikki—it's finally done. I've broken things off with Jolene"

"I'm glad you did it. You know, Bentley; she's going to make you feel guilty. It's a woman's instinct – especially when the man breaks up."

I knew it was true but felt torn. Fortunately, there was no turning back. Rikki and I started laying down the plans for the future. Since I was at home doing some post-baccalaureate work and working two jobs, I had more flexibility with my life. Rikki on the other hand was still trying to finish her undergraduate studies. We decided that I would move to St. Louis while Rikki finished school. This decision would prove to be pivotal in our relationship because it began a pattern in which we would make sacrifices one for the other.

We decided that I would leave California in December, right after Christmas. Rikki would fly to California to help me drive to St. Louis since she was on Christmas break. Up until the time Rikki arrived we talked every day. I couldn't wait to move away from the Bay Area. I was tired of the same old stuff—working at Macy's, taking a science course and working in a lab. I finally realized that home provided no real challenges because it was too familiar. There were too many opportunities to repeat the same patterns of stagnation and wonder why there was no progress.

The weeks flew by quickly. Rikki and I talked every night and wrote love letters to each other. As the days drew near to my imminent date of departure I grew a little nervous but was glad to be going away. I knew that life would change dramatically and that I would probably never return home again.

Lesson 4: Long distance "lovin'" is a hard thing to do.

Chapter 5: Meeting the Family for the First Time

Christmas was always nice in northern California. Not exactly a white Christmas but it was nonetheless a time when everyone enjoyed the sights and sounds of Union Square, Macy's, and Nieman Marcus. The stores in The City bustled with visitors and locals. I often saw friends shopping who were home from the East Coast or from the South.

This Christmas was quite different because it would be my last Christmas as a California resident. I prepared myself for what would be a journey across the U.S. The car had been tuned up by my father's friend at the Presidio army base and I had all my things packed up and ready to roll. Things didn't settle in until Rikki arrived.

Her flight arrived in San Francisco.

"That's my baby," I thought as she jetted down the runway. "Hmm I got me an East Coast honey. Yep, I got me a D.C. girl."

Little did I know what that meant. I was a California guy who dealt with West Coast women. These were women who did not really challenge me. Well, I was in for a rude awakening. It didn't happen fast but when it did it, it hit hard.

I stood at the entrance of the gate waiting for Rikki to walk in. I had flowers and a card welcoming her to Cali.

"Hey beautiful, how was your trip?"

"Oh, it was pretty good but now it's much better."

"Gees, that's all I need. My ego is going to be real big now."

Yes, I was proud and even felt like boasting a little. At this point in my life, I was on top of the world. My "baby" had come to pick me up and we would venture half-way across the nation to be in St. Louis.

I took Rikki through San Francisco to check out the sights. I loved to play the cultured tour guide. I got it from my older brother who took women to Half Moon Bay and Sausalito to romance them. In high school I would tour the honies from Berkeley and Oakland into San Francisco and Sausalito. They thought I was such a worldly person.

Rikki really enjoyed the ride through San Francisco and then through Sausalito even though she had a long trip.

"I really like the Bay Area. It's just so beautiful. I don't remember the Bay Area looking like this when I visited my uncle years ago. But I was just seven years old."

Then it dawned on us that when she was here visiting California, I was in D.C. for the summer.

"That was the summer my parents contemplated moving to D.C. My father's job at the Department of Transportation had an opening at headquarters. Gosh, that's so ironic to be in each other's back yard. In fact, that's when we met Will (your step-father) at the White House. He was a Member of the Secret Service."

When we arrived at the house, Mom greeted Rikki warmly.

"Hi, Rikki I'm so glad you made it."

Now, I knew what Mom was thinking, "So, you've come to take my son away. Let's see how nice you are." Mom would never say anything outwardly negative to Rikki. Her style was more wait and see, then, if there was a problem or issue she would take it up.

I placed Rikki's things in the room upstairs. She slept in the room next to mine. My parents were still old fashioned. They did not believe in unmarried couples sleeping in the same room. I understood their rationale and respected it.

After taking Rikki's things upstairs, we grabbed a bite to eat. Mom always "threw down" during Christmas. In fact, she fixed gumbo every Christmas Eve. Rikki arrived the day before Christmas Eve so she had a chance to watch Mom prepare the food. Rikki and Mom got along very well. They talked about girl stuff and of course Mom talked about me. They talked until almost two o'clock in the morning. It was Mom's way of feeling Rikki out and letting her know of my quirky ways.

The next day we visited my "boyz" and cousins around the Bay Area. Rikki was on display. I pranced her around town introducing her as my fiancé. I thought I was the man. The ultimate test would be taking Rikki to meet my cousin Cyndi. Cyndi is a classic Spelmanite. She has class, attitude, extremely good looks, and her stuff is together. She has the ability to intimidate other women because she can be stand offish. Well, she was ready to test Rikki.

We met Cyndi at her grandmother's house. Usually, every holiday her grandmother gives some function. This was the time when Rikki not only met Cyndi but she met a whole slew of relatives. It was the gauntlet. Sometimes my relatives could be critical without knowing it–especially the females. This time it was intentional. You know the look. In fact one of the cousins was already talking underneath her breath.

"Hmm what does this girl have that's making my cuz move clear across the nation for her?"

"Dag, she must be putting the clamp on him."

"Well, we'll make her feel like we know what's up by giving her the look."

My cousins were very cordial, but they were on the case. I was glad Rikki came and didn't trip off the looks she got. In fact, she handled everything quite well. Rikki passed all tests with flying colors.

After we left Cyndi's grandmother's, we paid a visit to my homeboy Tyrone's place. It was an opportunity for my best friend to case Rikki out. She met my surrogate mom, Mrs. Anderson, and Tyrone's sister and brother-in-law. They even had a frat brother come by and some other friends. Everyone checked out Rikki because they knew she was the reason I broke up with Jolene.

We left Tyrone's house around 11 p.m. I figured Rikki had enough meeting people and having to put on the plastic smile.

"Wow, you passed the test with flying colors. I'm sorry if my family and friends seemed trippy. It's just that it seemed unusual for me to meet someone and fall head over heels."

"It's okay, I understand the game and can play it well. You're making a big commitment to me by moving out to St. Louis. My Mom coached me well."

Rikki continued to smile while I shook my head. I was pretty amazed by her unwavering confidence.

The next day we celebrated Christmas in typical California style. It was a brisk sixty degrees with no clouds in sight. This Christmas would be my last in California for years to come. Everyone understood the implications of my move.

We exchanged Christmas gifts and assisted Mom with the Christmas meal. The other important item on our agenda was packing for the trip to St. Louis. The plan was for me to do research at Washington University (where I participated in the summer program) and move somewhere else upon Rikki's graduation. It was a good plan and I was ready for change. My success at the summer program prepared me for the possibility of doing research. I knew that I would be in medical school that next year and that Rikki would follow with graduate school.

For most of the day we packed for the trip. When it was time for dinner (around 4 p.m.), we were ready to eat. That day my brother, his wife and daughter came for dinner. It would be the first time they met Rikki. I heard the door bell ring and answered it.

"Hey Bentley, what's up, fella?" Silas asked.

"Oh, nothing much; just getting ready to head out. Hey, Jewel, hey Dominic."

I hugged and kissed them all as they entered the house.

"I want all of you to meet Rikki."

Everyone greeted Rikki warmly. One thing I can say about my family is that they embrace people wholeheartedly without inhibitions until you do someone wrong. So, as far as everyone was concerned Rikki must have been quite special for me to pack up my things and move across the country.

Dad, Silas and I piled into the living room to watch the Christmas basketball game. The women went into the kitchen to get things ready for dinner. We Johnson men were clear about gender roles. This would come back to haunt me in the near future because Rikki was not raised to fulfill the traditional female role of cooking, cleaning, and washing.

After about an hour we sat down for dinner. Dad said his traditional blessing of the food. Dad says grace so fast that it sounds like pig Latin or a bit of the Creole from his childhood. Since Dad was from Louisiana, some of his heritage came out during meal time.

We ate dinner and thoroughly stuffed ourselves. Silas and Dad went to the living room to watch T.V. for a bit and then feel asleep. I helped the ladies with the dishes. Time passed rapidly and it was time for Silas and his family to go home.

"Okay Bentley, so please call us when you get to St.Louis. You all have a safe trip," Jewel said.

Silas concurred, but he didn't understand why I was moving. I was the strange bird in the family but I didn't care. I was set on moving to St. Louis.

We quickly started getting ready for bed. We knew it would be important to get rest for the next day. We would hit the road by 8 a.m.

Lesson 5: Never put a woman in a situation where she meets all the family at once.

Chapter 6:   Taking the Road Less Traveled
              Across the Country

The next morning I woke up to the smell of coffee and cornbread. Dad always cooked cornbread when it was an important day for me. Cornbread was the breakfast of champions to me. Dad cooked it whenever I had important sports events and finals for school. Dad would always say it was the substance that stuck to my bones and made me perform better. I didn't know if it did all of those things but I did know it was surely good. It was also a symbolic gesture from Dad that he loved me very much and supported me. There are certain things that males don't do and showing affection is one of them, especially in the Johnson family.

I quickly took a shower and shave and made it downstairs to talk to Dad before Mom got up. I trotted downstairs and before I knew it, Mom was wrestling on her robe. She didn't sleep well because she was worrying about the cross-country trip.

I walked into the kitchen but realized Dad was downstairs feeding the dog. I grabbed a cup of coffee and started to add honey to the deep black Louisiana chicory.

"Hey Brat, are you ready for the trip?"

"Yeah, I think we're ready. Everything is packed up and ready to go. About the only things we need to put into the car are ourselves and the lunches mom packed last night."

"Let's review your travel course one more time," said Dad.

My Dad was a great fan of AAA's trip tick. We reviewed the course that went through Bakersfield, the Mojave Desert, Flagstaff, and Albuquerque and through Oklahoma into Missouri. It wasn't too bad and the road conditions were in our favor. By the time we finished reviewing the course, Mom and Rikki came in.

"Good morning, Rikki," said Dad.

"Good, morning Dad," Rikki said. It sounded weird to hear her say that, because we were not married yet. I knew she did it on purpose and it worked.

We all sat down to breakfast. The cornbread was just great. We ate almost the whole pan. After we finished it was time to brush the teeth and then shove off. As Rikki went upstairs to brush her teeth, Mom pulled me aside.

"You know you can always come back home. I don't want you to feel that if things don't work out, there is no place for you to return."

'Mom," I said. "Thanks for your support, but I think things will work out."

By 8:10 a.m. we were off for our trip. I took the scenic route through all my most memorable spots. I went past Sacramento Street and the Alston Pharmacy where I worked as a clerk. Then I turned up Ashby and followed the street up into the Berkeley Hills where we would get onto I-13 and then I-80. We went past the historic Clairmont Hotel. I loved that section of Berkeley. It was so picturesque and so "Californian." The view from the Berkeley Hills was like none other in the world.

We quickly passed all my old hangouts. It was like saying goodbye to an old friend. It was, in fact, goodbye for a very long time. I loved California, especially northern California. There's no place like it. It's extremely picturesque and clean. Even when it's dirty, there's a certain clarity about it. The people are nice and there's not the hustle and bustle of the East Coast. Yes, California was a great place but I was about to leave it for another world.

We edged out of the Hayward Hills and moved past Livermore. Before we knew it, we were upon the gigantic windmills in the Central Valley that generated power for the Bay Area.

"What in the world are those?" Rikki asked.

"Oh, they're the windmills or wind generators."

I knew she would ask about the windmills. To me, they were one of the wonders of the world. Can you imagine seeing hundreds if not thousands of huge propellers rotating at the same time? The whole valley was covered with windmills. Seeing them rotate at the same time made me think of Star Trek or Blade Runner. It was always nostalgic to see those windmills. They were a treasure of home just like the Golden Gate Bridge, Alcatraz Island and Lake Merritt.

Soon we hit the boring part of the trip-- the Central Valley of California. We played music and talked about life. It seemed pretty unreal that we were finally on the road. I was happy to be with Rikki and I think she was happy too. We pulled off to fill up the tank and get something to drink. The air was dry and warm. Although it was winter in other parts of the world, it felt like summer to us. We bought our drinks and got back on the road.

Just as we were getting into the groove of Janet Jackson, the car sputtered and jerked like it was choking on a piece of meat.

"Hey, what's wrong with your car?" Rikki asked.

"I don't know what's up. Maybe some water got in the fuel injectors."

I punched the car in an attempt to burn up the water but it just sputtered back. I slowed down and then pulled off the side of the road. After waiting for a few minutes, the car was ready to roll.

"What was that?" Rikki asked.

"I don't know."

"Is this going to continue throughout the trip? I thought your car had a new engine."

"The engine is rebuilt and there's nothing wrong with it. My father had it tuned up before we left."

Little did I know, that was the problem. Pops had the car tuned up with Japanese parts. Hel-lo, Japanese parts on a German car don't mix. Essentially, the Japanese distributor cap shorted out the German ignition. We didn't know this and didn't find out until much later.

We continued our journey, albeit nervously, and passed Harris Ranch where we smelled the thousands of cattle. Harris Ranch is famous for their steaks. It's a popular spot off I-5 where people eat fresh meat. We went so fast that we barely smelled the air. Our minds were set on getting to New Mexico that first night.

The San Joaquin Valley was rather desolate. I stuck behind a car for a while to keep my attention on the road and off whatever problem occurred with my car. I figured it was just bad gas. All of the sudden the car started to sputter and lose speed.

"Bentley, what's that?"

"Well, it looks like we got a batch of bad gas. My father and cousin Sam went across the country one year and stopped off in Mexico. With four horses and four dogs, they ran into some trouble with two tanks of bad gas. Their truck sputtered for miles, but once the bad gas was out, they were okay."

After telling Rikki the story, she calmed down a little bit.

"We need to buy some additive. In fact, let me call Pops to see what they did."

I pulled off at the next service station, bought some additive and called home.

"Hey Dad, we've got a slight problem with some bad gas."

"Oh," he said. "Just put in the additive and never go below a half tank. It may take a while but eventually you'll burn off the bad gas."

"Sounds good to me," I said. "We'll do that. Thanks Dad, well keep you posted."

I relayed the information to Rikki. I quickly realized my girl was a nervous individual.

"I hope this woman doesn't freak out over this car," I thought to myself. "If necessary we'll turn back and get it fixed."

We came to the junction that took us into Bakersfield. By this time it was about 3:00 p.m. The car had been sputtering and stopping all afternoon and we were quite tired. Rikki was starting to wear on my nerves with all her questions about the car. I finally suggested that we stop in Bakersfield at a Volkswagen dealer.

"Rikki, let's just stop here and get the car checked out."

"Yeah, let's do that because I'm not walking in the desert."

"Rikki, you won't have to walk in the desert. We'll do our best to get it fixed here and if necessary I can ask my father to come pick us up." She was burning me up. I didn't need her dagger poking me. Shit, I was nervous and hoped we wouldn't need the car tank removed.

That's what Dad and Cousin Sam had to do. Both tanks had to be removed and emptied out. It was a costly venture.

Lesson 6: Sometimes you've got to take time to really determine the extent of a problem

Chapter 7: Mechanical Failure or Failure to Communicate

We pulled into the Volkswagen dealership. I explained what was happening to the Service Department Manager and asked if he could check it out immediately.

"Mr. Johnson, we'll do whatever we can. It sounds like you have a bad batch of gas." "Yep," I said. "I'm familiar with the problem."

Rikki and I decided to stay the night across the street at the Motel 6. After we checked in we took a nap and tried to make light of our nervousness. We strolled around the area and got a bite to eat. We were tired and went back to the room to watch a movie.

"What should we do?" Rikki asked.

"We can't do anything until we find out what's going on."

By now, I figured that Rikki wanted a definitive answer. She did not like uncertainties or situations that she could not control. Well, I had news for her. This one was out of our hands.

"Rikki, we might as well settle in until we hear from the dealership. The problem sounds like a batch of bad gas. If push comes to shove, I'll ask my folks to come pick us up and we'll fly out of San Francisco."

"Hmmm, I dunno," she said. "I just don't want to get stuck in the desert. I swear I'm not walking."

The tone in Rikki's voice implied that the car was the problem and I was indirectly responsible. I was starting to get increasingly impatient with her theatrics.

"Look, I'm going out for a bit to get some air. Do you want anything?

"Where are you going?" she said anxiously.

"Rikki, I'm just walking down the way to the store to get a magazine. Please calm down, I'll be alright."

"Hmmm, okay, I'll see you in a little bit," Rikki replied.

As I left the room, I felt like screaming to myself.

"What the heck did I get myself into? If this is an indication of things to come, I'm in big trouble."

I walked down the street and recounted the past few months. I thought about the hundreds of letters I had written to Rikki. I thought about the phone calls every other day and great friendship that had developed. "Was this the same person?" Yes, it was but these circumstances were extreme.

I entered the drug store and went to the periodicals. Of course every title I read had something to do with relationships. Essence read, "How You Can Deal With Your Man"; Vogue read, "10 Tips for Making Your Relationship Sizzle"; and Ebony read, "Black Male/Female Relationships: How Can We Make Them Better."

"Damn, why are they reading into what's going on with me," I said to myself. "I'll just get something non-threatening like the USA Today."

I got the paper and slowly made my way back to the hotel. I didn't know what was in store for me but I did know that I would probably read the paper front to back before I dealt with my frantic fiancé.

As I opened the door I heard Rikki on the phone.

"Okay, okay, I'll take that into consideration. It should be okay," she said.

"Hey," I said, as I entered the room.

"Hi," Rikki replied, as I moved toward the opposite end of the room.

"I'm talking to Leeza, she said, "Hi."

"Please tell her I said, 'hi,' too."

Leeza was Rikki's best friend and confidant. It was in situations like these that she needed a friend to share ideas and concerns with. I thought it was good, but I was also a little leery because I didn't want someone else to influence Rikki's emotions while she was upset. I knew how friends could easily sway a person when emotions set in. I would monitor how much influence her friends had on her decisions.

When Rikki got off the phone, she was a little upset. Leeza's Aunt Henrietta died.

"They are going to have the funeral sometime early next week. We really have to get back to D.C. now."

"Okay, Rikki we'll do our best to get to St. Louis in time to fly to D.C. Keep in mind that I can't control everything, especially if its car related."

"I know," Rikki said. "But we really have to make it to D.C."

After talking for a while we finally went to sleep. I didn't sleep too well because I was wondering if I made the right decision. I thought out loud to myself while Rikki slept.

"Is this the person I want to be with? She's starting to become a pain. I really don't know. Besides, she snores hella loud!"

I chuckled myself to sleep and tried not to over analyze the situation.

The next morning we woke up, showered and got dressed for breakfast.

"How did you sleep last night Bentley?"

"Oh, I slept okay." Knowing good and well I was lying. I felt like saying, "Shoot, you snored loud and I was thinking about leaving you!" I kept my thoughts to myself and suggested that we both have pancakes for breakfast.

"Do you think the car's ready?" Rikki asked.

"Yep, after we eat we'll go check. In fact, while the food is cooking, I'll go across the street to check on the status of the car." I knew she would bug me throughout the meal so I decided to get a jump on her. As I entered the Volkswagen dealership, I asked the guy what was going on.

"Oh I think it was bad gas sir," he replied. "There was nothing else that we detected wrong. We cleaned out your gas tank."

"Great--We'll come pick it up after breakfast."

Lesson 7: Sometimes cars have minds of their own.

Chapter 8: On The Road Again

Those were the words I wanted to hear. It was music to my ears to have the service manager say nothing was wrong. Now, I could go back to Rikki with good news.

"Hey, guess what? The service manager gave the car a clear bill of health. He said they detected nothing wrong. It looked like the gas was the problem."

"Did he really say that?" Rikki asked. "Let me see the work order." One thing I realized about Rikki is that she scrutinized everything. I mean the girl would be a great detective or a lawyer. Whatever the case may be she has a highly analytical mind.

"Well, it does say, no problem is apparent. I guess we can go. Yes, we can go through the Mojave Desert."

I felt my blood boil but I didn't say anything because it would make things worse. These first few hours seemed like days and we had a long way to go.

We traveled through the desert with ease. The car hummed through the sand as we played the radio and talked about life. It seemed as if the problem was solved. In the backs of our minds, we still hoped nothing would happen but we began to feel comfortable. Although it was winter, the warm spring weather of the desert lulled us into a dreamy state.

"Where are we now?" Rikki asked.

"Why don't you look on the map? I think were close to the Arizona border."

"Yep, we're almost there," Rikki said. "Our next major city will be Flagstaff."

"Oh--remember, Mom said the weather in Flagstaff is kinda funny—like it could periodically snow."

"I really can't imagine a place in Arizona having anything but hot weather."

"Well I didn't know until Mom told me that Flagstaff was in the mountains and could experience heavy bursts of snow."

"Let's get something to eat before we hit Flagstaff," Rikki said. "Besides you look a little tired. I'd like to drive through Flagstaff."

"Okay, let's pull off at the next chicken joint and grab a bite."

We pulled off the road and marveled at the redneck drivers. We were about the only "colored folks" on the roads. It was nothing new to me. Most of my life I dealt with white people being in the majority. I did however find out that Rikki was accustomed to black people being in the majority. That was a new phenomenon to me just as white people being in the majority was new to Rikki.

"My gosh, do you think they could stare any more?" Rikki exclaimed.

"Well, we are a novelty to them, just passing through. Don't pay them any attention, just act like we've been here all along. That will trip them out even more."

We ate our food and commented about the people. It was fun, but the reality is that blacks in the United States are in the minority. Thank

God it wasn't during the Civil Rights Movement or before when blacks couldn't travel in many places without getting harassed.

"Okay, let's hit the road. We've got to make it to Albuquerque."

We hopped in the car and made our way up the highway. The car was great. It buzzed along as we started heading up the mountains. We noticed cars and trucks on the other side of the highway with their lights on and dirt on the sides. It reminded me of cars that came down from Lake Tahoe, in the middle of the winter.

"Please don't tell me we'll be going through a winter storm."

I tried not to act nervous, but it was getting the best of me.

"Hey Bentley, you're awfully quiet. Is everything okay?"

"Oh yeah, I was just mapping out our trip in my brain."

Just then, a few snow flakes hit the windshield.

"Hey look at that," Rikki said as she drove. "Snow in Arizona." As the snow started to drop I thought about the car breaking down. I kept saying to myself, "Lord please don't let this car break down."

The snow fell harder and the cars around us started slowing down. We also slowed down as the road became slushy. It was hard to believe that just a few hours ago we passed through the Mojave Desert.

"At least we made it through the desert," I thought.

As time passed and my mind (and car) started to ease up, I became more comfortable with my decision to leave California. I had it all figured out. Rikki and I would live in St. Louis until she finished undergrad, and I would go to one of the medical schools wherever I was accepted.

"Hey, let's stop and get some gas. It looks like we're getting close to half a tank."

Our plan of action was to fill up on premium gas at half a tank. That way we would burn out the bad gas. As we pulled into the gas station, I thought about my situation. I was already tired and paranoid about the trip.

"Hi, I'd like to put $6.00 of premium on number seven." The woman responded and gave me change. "About how much further do we have until we reach Albuquerque?"

"Oh, about four hours," she responded.

"Thanks," I responded dejectedly.

As we drove down the mountain, the weather cleared up. The night was drawing near and I could see the lights of New Mexico. I was relieved that we didn't have another breakdown.

When we pulled into the Best Western, we were tired and hungry.

"Hey, let's get some food before we check into the hotel," Rikki said.

"Sounds good to me; why not take it into the hotel with us?"

"Good idea," Rikki said.

It looked like we were finally on the same page.

We checked into the hotel and ate our food on the bed. Almost simultaneously we said "let's call our parents." Rikki called her mom first and then I called my folks. My father's first question was "how's the car?" He felt bad about the car but it was also my fault for not getting the car tuned up myself. Because I was the youngest, my father felt compelled to take care of me. I was his "Brat," but now it was time for me to act like a man.

"Hey Dad, things are a little better. The car didn't give us much grief today."

"Good, that's real good. Maybe all that bad gas is out of the tank."

"Yeah, maybe so," I said. After the brief conversation, I hung up.

"Well, it's time to turn in."

"Yea, I'm pretty tired," Rikki said.

We brushed our teeth and set the alarm for 7 a.m.. My mind drifted away as I recalled the day's events. It was still vivid in my mind but it didn't deter me from sleeping. I was on a cloud just floating away as I felt Rikki's warm body next to mine. Then the alarm went off.

"Damn," I thought.

"Tell me it's not 7 a.m." I hit the snooze button, but it seemed like it buzzed even louder the second time.

"Rikki, it's time to get up," I said.

"Yea okay, you go take a shower," she said.

I quickly realized she was not a morning person.

"Ok, I'll take my shower but you need to get up." I turned on all the lights in the room and the T.V.

"Hey, what are you doing?"

"I'm making sure you get up." And with that, I whisked into the bathroom, snickering all the way.

After Rikki took her shower, we ate breakfast and hit the road. The car ran pretty smoothly--in fact, we whizzed through a couple of states. We talked about our dreams together and sang to the popular beats of songs. Janet Jackson had just come out with her latest album. We sang the tunes and danced with our heads and shoulders. As we were gliding through Oklahoma late in the afternoon, I started to get a strange feeling. The car started to sputter and once again my stomach felt like it was in my throat.

"Oh I don't believe this! It looks like the car is going to give us a problem." I turned on the hazard lights and pulled the car off the highway.

"Bentley, I just don't believe this. What are we going to do? Is the car going to just break down?"

Of course I didn't have an answer and I detested that she asked me questions that I had no answers to. It really bothered me, but that was her way of dealing with being nervous.

"Rikki, why do you ask me the same questions over and over? You've experienced the car just like me. If we give it a break and then fill it up with premium, things will be okay. This time tomorrow we'll be in St. Louis."

We sat on the side of the road for about 10 minutes before we pulled into a service station. I asked for fuel additive and filled up the car with supreme unleaded. My car roared off and we were on our way. We filled the car with Janet and quickly made our way down the highway. The car gave us no problems after that and we drove late into the night. In fact, we made it all the way to the Oklahoma Turnpike.

Lesson 8: It really does snow in Arizona.

Chapter 9: The Bates Motel

We got onto the Oklahoma Turnpike at about 9 p.m. It was already dark since it was December. After we passed the toll booth and saw the sign that said "no turnoff for 35 miles," my mind started playing tricks on me.

"Oh my God, what if this car decides to break down during the thirty-five-mile stretch," I said to myself. "We'll really be up the creek."

Getting stuck in the backwoods was my worst nightmare. My mind then flashed to the movie "Deliverance." I could see some hick trying to get me to squeal like a pig and plug me in the butt. I would just have to die fighting. I then thought about my big hunter's knife sitting under the driver's seat.

"If someone comes up on me, I'll just have to carve them like a turkey," I thought to myself.

The car hummed along pretty good for thirty miles. I was just getting ready to get real comfortable when it started to sputter.

"Bentley, please tell me this car is not going to stop! I don't want to be stuck out here."

"We should be okay for the next five miles," I said. "After that I'll stop at a gas station."

The car sputtered the whole five miles. My palms were sweaty and my heart raced. I prayed to God to have mercy on me. Even my back was sweaty and it wasn't hot outside. In fact, it was pretty damned cold. At one mile to go the car sputtered almost to a stop. I pulled off to the shoulder, but kept the engine running. I could not afford to turn the car off for fear of it stalling. We rested on the side of the turnpike where there was no emergency lane. We were both very quiet as we thought the same thing. "What will happen if we have to walk a mile in complete darkness?"

After idling for five minutes, I pulled back onto the Turnpike and sputtered down the road to the next turnoff. I was extremely relieved to see a sign for a gas station and hotel. I was just getting ready to claim victory when something caught my eye. It looked like it also caught Rikki's eye.

"Hey Bentley, do you see what I see?"

"Yes, I see it but I don't care. We have to get to a gas station for help."

In front of us were scores of cars cruising down a street. Each of the cars had a confederate flag attached to it. Not a black person in sight. I followed the signs, which led me to a well-lit Texaco. People were packed outside. I got out of my car and proceeded into the gas station. All eyes were fixed on me and loud conversations became whispers.

"What'll it be?" asked the attendant.

"I'll take $10.00 of premium and some fuel additive," I said with a slight southern drawl. Then I thought about it. My car tags were Californian.

"Thanks, where's the public phone?"

He pointed to an outside phone. I nodded.

While I filled the tank, I directed Rikki to give her mom a call. Her eyes were big and frightened.

"Go ahead and make the call," I said. "After you talk to your mom, ask Will to get on the phone."

I directed her to talk to her mom so she wouldn't drive me crazy. I learned early on that a woman needs to talk to another woman when she felt in trouble.

While she quickly walked over to the phone booth, I surveyed the area for trouble.

"All it takes is for one of these hicks to get an idea in their head and we're headed for some serious stuff. I started thinking of films like "Mississippi Burning" and "Do the Right Thing." It made me think of my worst fears. In fact, it appeared this whole trip was a test of my character and on my relationship with Rikki.

"Well," I said to myself. "I won't let it get the best of me."

By the time I finished day dreaming, the tank was filled and Rikki was chatting away rather emphatically. I knew she was getting pretty upset but her mom would calm her down. "Hey Bentley, Will's on the phone."

"Thanks," I said. And with that she headed straight for the passenger's seat.

"What's up buddy," I said to Will.

"So Bentley, what's going on with the car?" Will asked.

"It really tried to stop this time," I said. "It's acting like the fuel injectors are clogged or something."

"Bentley, open up the hood and pour a little of the additive in the injectors," Will said. "It should help clear things out."

"I'll do that," I said. "We're going to stay here tonight and get an early start."

"Alright," he said. "Just call if you need anything."

I hung up the phone and got in the car. The car started up with no problem and sounded like it was ready to make it to St. Louis. I felt pretty good but was getting tired due to all of the excitement.

"Bentley, where should we stay?" Rikki asked as we passed another group of Confederate flag-toting teenagers.

"Hmmm, let's stay right here," I said as we approached a seedy-looking motel. It was right near the entrance of the Turnpike and not far from the main road.

As we pulled into the motel, it seemed that everyone peered out the door. Unfortunately, you couldn't see anyone beyond the curtains moving. A door opened and it appeared as if a rifle protruded ever so slightly through the door. I knew my mind was playing tricks on me; but when I looked at Rikki, her eyes said she saw the same thing.

"Let's just stay here," I said. "We really need a place to crash."

With that I drove up to the front office and was met by a trio of Indians.

"May I help you?" the oldest one asked in a thick British accent.

"Yes, I would like a room for the evening."

"I'll set you up with room 107. You and your lady friend will have a great time."

With that I gave him my credit card and listened to his cackling in his native tongue with his other family members. I grabbed the key and got back to the car.

"Let's just leave most of the stuff in the car. I don't want to attract too much attention." "Okay, I'll try to be quiet," said Rikki.

As we gathered a few things from the car, it seemed that all shades from the adjoining rooms moved a few notches. We saw the eyes glaring at us, watching our every move.

"I don't like this place," Rikki said. "It gives me the creeps."

"Me too, it doesn't look too safe."

I opened the door to the hotel room. It was pretty ratty. The carpet looked about thirty years old. There was an old dusty Bible on the end table, and the room smelled musty-like a dirty old man. In fact, it dawned on me why the owner said we would have a good time. The bed was hooked up to a vibrator. Lots of dirty old men made nasty love in this room.

"I'm sleeping on top of this bed," Rikki said.

"Well, I'm not sleeping at all," I said. "I don't trust those crackers one bit. Someone may try to firebomb our room or vandalize our car. You go to sleep and I'll just watch T.V."

"Bentley, you can't do that. It's too dangerous. You need to drive in the morning."

"Well I can't take a chance on these people. They may sneak up on us and then what will happen?"

"That is just ridiculous and you're scaring me by sitting there with that big hunter's knife!"

"Do you really think someone could do something to us?"

"I don't know and I'm not going to wait," I said.

I sat on the edge of the bed and Rikki called her mom because she knew I wasn't going to listen to her.

"Yes, mom," Rikki said in a desperate voice. "Bentley won't go to sleep and he's sitting here with his knife. Okay I'll calm down and I'll tell Bentley that Will's coming to get us."

Rikki hung up the phone and glanced at me. Things weren't going well between us but she wasn't going to make that ruin things. I walked into the bathroom and took a hot shower. When I returned I could tell Rikki was crying.

"Will is on his way," she said sleepily. "My mother made him come to pick us up. She thought this place was too dangerous."

"Aww, Will didn't have to do that," I said. "We could have sputtered into St. Louis."

"Bentley, don't say another word. Will is coming to get us. I'm too sleepy to argue with you."

I tried to stay up while Rikki slept. My eyes got tired but I fought hard, trying to watch T.V. Before I knew it, I was fast asleep. Suddenly there was a loud thump at the door.

"Hey, open up in there!" The voice said loudly. I jumped from the bed with my knife and ran to the door.

"What do you want?" I screamed as I peered out the peep hole. Just then, I recognized the big eyes and Cheshire cat smile. It was Will, who came to save the day.

Lesson 9: There are still places in the U.S. that are trapped in a time warp.

Chapter 10: Chitty-Chitty Bang Bang

"Man, you scared the dickens out of me," I said with a chuckle.

"Yeah, I knew I'd get you with that one. Get your stuff and let's get on the road."

I woke up Rikki and then brushed my teeth. By the time I finished, Rikki was up and chatting with Will.

"I better call Mom and tell her we're on our way," Rikki said.

"Yeah, that's good idea," said Will. "In fact, let me talk to her so she won't worry."

As Rikki dialed the phone I found out that Will hadn't been to sleep that night. He was summoned once he returned from a card game.

"Man I just drank a Coca-Cola and ate a Snickers bar. That had me wired for the whole four-hour trip," Will said anxiously. "I'm ready to get on the road now!"

We chatted with Rikki's mom for a quick minute and then made our way outside. It was still early and dark- about 5 a.m. Unfortunately, it was also extremely foggy. Will drove the whole four hours in the fog with very little visibility.

"Bentley, I need you to stay right behind me on the highway. You need to be right on my butt. We're going to gun it down the highway.

Whatever's in the fuel system of your car, we're going to get it out. If you have a problem just flash your lights and I'll pull over."

I couldn't get two words in. "Okay," I said as I got into the car.

"Bentley I'll get in with Will. He needs to stay awake and that way I can watch your headlights."

"That's fine with me."

"Its better that way," I said to myself. "We might kill each other before we get to St. Louis."

We then jumped into our respective cars and hopped on the highway.

I had no idea about the thick fog. Will said he almost ran into the back of a big rig and now I understood why. You could only see about three feet ahead of you. Will had a little BMW and he was starting to pull away.

"All right," I said to myself. "I'm on your tail."

I gunned the VW and heard the little engine hum. I was doing ninety miles per hour in the thick fog. I knew Rikki was driving Will crazy. She got real nervous in these situations so her mouth was in rare form. We flew through the fog for over an hour. Then the fog started to break. All of a sudden, my car started to get a bad case of hiccups. It backfired and sputtered. Slowly but surely Will and Rikki pulled away. I flashed my lights on and off several times until they realized what happened. We both slowed to a stop.

"What's going on?" Will shouted as he walked to my car.

"It started acting up again."

"Hey Bentley, you've got to just gun it. It may seem like it will stop but apparently that's when the debris is getting caught in the injectors. The force of the engine should just kick it out. Let's start out again but this time, don't worry about the sputtering. Just increase the speed if you have a problem."

We took off like gangbusters. Once again we hit ninety. I was feeling pretty good because it seemed that Will knew what he was talking about. Besides I thought if the car stopped now, I would have someone else who had my back. I did not want to get stuck on the side of the road with just me and Rikki. If that happened, we would not endure as a couple. I would just have to pull out the car iron.

The morning sun was starting to burn through the fog. It was easier to see the back of Will's car and visibility was such that I could see the other side of the road.

"Pow, pow, pow," went the engine. It started to sputter much worse than before. The car lurched back and forth as the speed steadily decreased. I quickly flashed my lights but Will and Rikki didn't see them. Apparently, they were deep in conversation and didn't notice that I was drifting further and further away. My car slowed to a crawl as I continued to flash my lights like a sailor sending Morse code. They finally recognized I was not close behind and stopped their car. Will quickly put his car in reverse and sped backwards down the highway. Just like a special agent. I think that's why we felt safe with Will. No one would mess with him.

Will and Rikki both walked out to check on me. Meanwhile I fiddled with the starter.

"Hey guys, the alternator is dead."

"You're kidding," Will said. "Here let me check it out." Will fiddled with everything he could imagine. He opened the hood and fiddled with the injectors. He looked at the starter and even the battery. Nothing appeared to be wrong, but the car would not start.

"Well, we've got to get this thing towed." Just as he said that we noticed a tow truck on the other side of the freeway. All of us frantically waved the guy down. He passed us but money must have been on his brain. The guy slowed down and crossed the median. Before we knew it he was standing right beside us.

"What's the problem?" he said in a country drawl.
"The car's dead," I told him.
"Can you tow us to the next town?" Will asked.
"Well, sir I'm actually on another run. So I'll just have to come back," the guy told Will.
"Why don't I make it worth your while and you can be a little late for that other run."
Will then pulled out a fifty-dollar bill. The guy's eyes lit up.
"Let's hook her up!" he said.
The guy quickly hooked up my VW. He told us to follow him. The guy was flying! I never saw a tow truck driver drive so fast with a car on the back.
"That fool is going too fast," Rikki said. "At the rate he's going, that car will fall off the back. Don't get too close to him"
I didn't say a word but I was a little worried. My car swung back and forth as it barreled down the highway. All of a sudden the, tow truck driver pulled over to the side and came to a halt.
"Now what?" Will exclaimed.
We all jumped out of the car and met the guy between our cars.
"Mr., I'm sorry but you won't believe this," the guy said. "My truck is out of gas."
"What!!" We all said at the same time. "This is unbelievable," Will said. "Where's your gas can? I'll go down the road and fill it up. You guys stay with him."

Will took the cans and some money and took off down the road.

"I don't know if we'll make the flight to D.C.," Rikki said. "I really wanted to make Henny's funeral. Leeza is going to be pretty upset."

"Oh, we'll still make it," I said. "We've come this far and nothing has stopped us."

Time clicked by slowly. We made small talk with the guy, but we were starting to worry about Will. All of a sudden we saw him pass us on the other side of the road. He couldn't get through the median like the tow truck because his car was too low. So, he kept on down the road until the next off ramp 15 miles away. Will finally drove up next to us.

"Damn, the next exit is pretty far away. That's why it took so long," he said.

He gave the guy the gas can and threw us a couple of Snickers.

"Thanks Will." We both said in unison.

The guy started up the truck.

"Follow me to the next turnoff," he said.

We all jumped in Will's car and sped off. The guy turned off about eighteen miles down the highway. Not far from the turnoff was a VW dealership. He unhooked the car.

"Sorry about the inconvenience," he said. "Your car will be okay here. Charlie and the guys will take good car of it. I'll probably see one of the mechanics this evening and I'll tell them to look out for your car."

"Thanks," I said.

After thirty-five minutes, the guy took off to get his other call.

"Let's unload just your essential things," Will said. "Jane and I will come back to get your car. You've got a plane to catch."

We quickly unloaded some essential things and placed a note on my car.

"Now hold on and close your eyes," Will said.

Will got on the highway and pushed the car to almost one hundred miles per hour. I liked the thrill of speeding past cars. I also liked the fact that if someone pulled us over, Will had a badge. Rikki, on the other hand, closed her eyes to not think of the danger of the car possibly rolling over.

We made it to Will and Jane's house in record time. We ran into the house to check on the departure time of our plane. By the scheduled time of departure, we had about thirty minutes to get to the airport.

"Hi, ma" said Rikki.

"Hi, Jane," I said.

"I've got to go to the bathroom," Rikki said. "Could you please check the schedule of the plane?"

"Will do. Where are the phone books?"

"Check the drawer near the breakfast bar," said Rikki as she closed the bathroom door.

I looked up the number and called the airline. I listened to the recordings for a brief moment and quickly pressed 0 to speak to someone.

"Hi, we're scheduled to leave on Flight 906 to Baltimore at 9:15 a.m. Is that flight on time?"

"No, sir that flight has been delayed for three hours due to the heavy fog," said the operator.

I exhaled deeply and felt an overwhelming sense of relief. We would make it to D.C. in time for the funeral.

I told Rikki about the delay. She was very pleased. It gave us enough time to take a shower and get something to eat.

"Come let's take our shower," Rikki said as she entered the bathroom with the towels and underwear.

"Uh, you can go ahead of me," I said uneasily.

"Oh, are you afraid of what my Mom and Will would say? Do you think they're going to get you? Well, I can tell you that in this house you are an adult and that's how they'll treat you."

I was flabbergasted. Nothing like that could go on in my parents' house. They frowned upon unmarried couples sleeping together. So taking a shower together in their house would send them over the top. I reluctantly took a shower but every minute I looked at Rikki's body I felt guilty.

After the shower, we grabbed a quick bite to eat and headed out to the airport. Will and Jane gave us a ride. After dropping us off, they were going to pick up my VW three hours away. We were clean, happy and quite tired from our cross country expedition. However, it was just the beginning for me. My next adventure was meeting a host of family and friends from Rikki's hometown of Washington, D.C.

∽

Lesson 10: Make sure you know your mechanic.

∽

Chapter 11: West Coast Meets East Coast

We boarded the plane at the St. Louis airport. We were both excited about the prospects of spending our first New Year's Eve together in D.C. The flight was rather uneventful but I was starting to feel a little nervous about the prospects of meeting so many relatives and friends, especially under the circumstances. We were going to the funeral of her best friend's aunt.

"So Rikki, who's going to pick us up at the airport?" I asked.

"Oh, it'll be my girlfriend Leeza. She's the one whose aunt passed away."

"I see, do you think we should get someone else since she'll be under so much duress?"

"Don't worry about it; this will actually ease her mind. She's very high strung so getting away from the crowd at her house will be good for her. Remember, Leeza is married to my cousin Neal. His father is my mom's brother."

Just then, the flight attendant announced that the plane was beginning its descent into National Airport. I looked outside the window and saw the beautiful snow covering the ground of Northern Virginia. This brought back memories of when I lived in D.C. but under very different circumstances. Now, I would actually get to know people of D.C., not transplants who often carpet bagged into the city for school or stints in Congressional offices.

The plane eased onto the runway. Just as it touched down, Rikki leaned over and put her hand around my arm.

"I'm so glad you're spending this time with me after our terrible trip across the country. I know you'll like everyone and they'll like you. This is going to be the best New Year ever!"

I was starting to feel at ease with my decision to move across the country and then to spend the New Year in D.C. with Rikki's family. Although it was a test of my commitment to her, I already felt a strong sense of belonging to her. I squeezed Rikki's arm and gave her a kiss. It filled us both with warmth that would spill into the evening. The plane came to a halt at the gate and folks started to deplane.

As we walked through the gate, I could see people peering into the doorway looking for loved ones. I smiled as I tried to pick out Leeza. Just then I heard a voice scream.

"Hey, Rikki!" It was Leeza. She was about 5' 9" with long black hair. She looked like a cross between Sally Richardson and Sheila E. In a West Coast city she would be considered a Hollywood type and one would expect a stand offish attitude. Well, Leeza was hardly that. Leeza was talkative, bubbly and slightly goofy.

"Wow, how refreshing," I thought.

Leeza hugged Rikki and then me like she had known me for years. She then led us to the car. The two friends talked non-stop. I listened intently as I tried to imagine all the friends and family the two discussed. As we exited the parking lot, someone cut Leeza off.

"What the heck are you doing?" Leeza screamed out the window and simultaneously honked on the horn.

"Yeah, you're about to get your butt beat," Rikki screamed.

"Oh boy," I thought. These two were in rare form. It was my first experience of the D.C. crew. They had no fear of expressing themselves and definitely had no fear of reprisal. The white man who cut them off quickly sped away in fear.

"Dag, you guys are too much. I see when you get together the world better watch out!" The two of them laughed and told me stories of their escapades in high school. This seemed to ease the worry lines in Leeza's face. We quickly passed from Virginia to D.C. and then to Maryland. The feeling in the car was warm and spirited even though we were in the middle of winter.

"We're almost there," Rikki said. "It's the second house on the right." We pulled into the driveway behind a car that looked just like Leeza's.

"Doesn't that car look familiar?" said Leeza chuckling. "I bought mine shortly after Granny got hers."

Granny was Rikki's grandmother. Correction, she was everyone's grandmother. Judging by the tone in everyone's voices, she was warm and very loving. By the time Leeza turned off the engine, Granny was at the door.

"Hey you youngin's, do you need some help?" Granny asked. Granny was a petite woman who looked like an older version of Rikki. You could tell that she had been quite striking in her younger years. She had outlived two husbands and even an older son. Granny was in great physical and spiritual condition. She was definitely the matriarch and rock of the family.

"Granny, this is Bentley."

"Hi Ms. Jones," I said as I gave her a big hug.

"Bentley, you can call me Granny. You don't have to be formal around me, Sugar. Rikki and Jane have told me so much about you that you feel like family. Bring in those bags and let me feed you."

As I lifted the bags, I got a waft of the food Granny prepared. Rikki gave me a forewarning that Granny cooked the best food and expected everyone to eat. It wasn't a problem because her food was quite good. She was a short order cook during the old days.

I followed Rikki up the stairs while Leeza and Granny went into the kitchen.

"She likes you already," Rikki said. "Isn't she great?"

"Yeah," I said. "I wish I'd had a granny like her when I was growing up."

"Well, now you have one," Rikki smiled. "Just put the bags on the bed and let's go downstairs to get something to eat."

Just before we went downstairs I popped a question.

"Hey Rikki, will Granny mind if we sleep together in her house?"

"Oh, Granny is totally cool. She knows what's up and mom told her how serious we are. Otherwise, she wouldn't think about letting us sleep together in her house," Rikki said assuredly. "Okay, I would hate to get on her bad side by being presumptuous."

We went downstairs and ate like there was no tomorrow. Granny fixed us smothered chicken, string beans, mashed potatoes and her famous coconut cream pie. While we ate, Rikki caught up with Granny on the lives of family members and friends. I listened intently as I tried to imagine the faces and figures. They talked for nearly two hours and then went to bed. I was waiting for this moment because it had been nearly three weeks since we made love. There had been so much stress driving cross country that we couldn't think about it. I liked the challenge of making love to Rikki in odd places. It was a challenge because Rikki was a screamer and she did not want her grandmother to know she was doing the "nasty." I rode her like a stallion while she covered her mouth and screamed into a pillow. Every muscle contracted and twitched with bursts of energy. We expended every ounce of movement left in our bodies.

The next day, we prepared for the funeral. This is where I would meet all of Rikki's friends, even one of her old boyfriends. The day was cold, gray and dreary. It was the type of day that exuded sadness and misery. But there really was not much sadness at all. The attention was focused on me: what I looked like, where I was from and if I measured up to the standards.

"Hi Rikki, girl it's been a while. Where do you live now?" asked a bubbly Halle Berry look-a-like named Alex who gave me a quick going over.

"Oh, I live in St. Louis with my fiancée Bentley," said a confident Rikki.

"That's right, I heard from Leeza that Bentley moved from California to be with you." "Yep," I said as I wrapped my hands around Rikki's waist and gazed into Alex's eyes.

I knew that Alex was checking me out, from my big brown eyes to my tight weight lifters thighs. This chick was a home wrecker.

"So, Bentley what part of California are you from? L.A.?" asked Alex.

"Nope, I'm actually from Oakland, as in the land of Huey Newton and M.C. Hammer."

It was the standard response I gave people since M.C. Hammer was a popular rapper and dancer at the time. He helped put Oakland on the map.

"Well, welcome to the East Coast and I hope you have a chance to hang out with us after the funeral. Our crew will be at Leeza's house."

I smiled and nodded because I knew that's when "the crew" would really check me out. "See you later Alex," said Rikki, as she pulled me away to find seats close to Leeza.

"She is a total trip," Rikki whispered to me. "Alex is a spoiled brat who tries to get other women's men. Alex thinks she's all that since her father is a doctor and gets her everything she wants. That mentality spills over to other things in her life, like career and love life. I can't stand her. One day she'll get hers and it's not going to be pretty."

We sat behind Leeza and her husband Neal. Neal was Rikki's first cousin. It was one of those situations where the best friend is introduced to the cousin and then the rest is history: marriage, kids, home. The service was brief, which was typical for a Catholic funeral. After the service everyone went to the cemetery. On the way to the cemetery, the true colors of Rikki's friends came out. Yes, they represented D.C. well. They were directing traffic and making sure everyone made it to the burial site. It almost reminded me of a few years back at the Black Beach Party in Norfolk. Although everyone was very respectful of the elders, they did not let the mood destroy the spirit of seeing family and friends. At the burial site, the priest said a few inspirational words before lowering Leeza's aunt to rest. The crew then got ready to head off to Leeza's house.

Leeza's house was a typical D.C. cape cod on a tree lined street. All the homes were well kept and most of the neighbors were long-time residents. As we approached Leeza's house, we could see fewer and fewer parking spaces. The street was lined up on both sides. A few kids played outside in the cold while a few of Leeza's friends smoked on the front porch. We parked quite a way from Leeza's house. As we walked up to the house, Rikki gave me a little nudge.

"Now, things are going to be a little crazy in there. I anticipate folks will be in rare form since they don't know you and especially since you are from California. It's an aberration that someone from the crew dates someone who is not from D.C. – let alone someone who is from California. I'm one of the few who ventured outside of the typical places like Atlanta."

"Oh, so I guess they'll have a ball with me."

"Don't worry; just have fun."

"I'm not the least intimidated by scrutiny. I know that my heart is with you and nothing else matters."

I could tell I said the right things. Rikki was really paranoid about me meeting her friends and fitting in. More importantly, Rikki didn't want one of her friends to alienate me or try to "snatch." Although she liked her buddies, she was well aware that some of them had no one steady in their lives.

We had a good time talking and joking with her friends. My easygoing ways blended in with the East Coast flavor. Rikki's friends grilled me on my intentions with Rikki and I was pretty honest. I wanted to marry her at some point. My answer surprised many but pleased all. By the end of the evening I was accepted into the crew.

The next day I had to pass the next important test: meeting Rikki's father. Thelonius B. Jasper- was a native Washingtonian. Although he was not born into the D.C. upper class, he moved himself into it. He held leadership positions throughout the city. He was a well-known politician and business man. Thelonius was a dapper dresser and connoisseur of cars and art. He would drill me on my lineage and then drill me on my education. Lastly, he would drill me on my intentions with his only child Rikki.

"Whatever you do, don't act like you're scared of him," said Rikki. "Once he knows you're scared, he loses all respect. He believes a man should be a man."

"Okay, so this is going to be like pledging again. It's not a new feeling for me. I know how to jump through hoops." As we pulled up to Thelonius' house, my hands started to sweat. The house was a D.C. brownstone near the embassy of Ghana. Outside he had two rare Mercedes and a convertible Jaguar-his prize possession.

"Bentley!" Thelonius said with a booming voice. "How are you?"

"Hi, Mr. Jasper, I'm doing fine, now that I've finally met you. Rikki has told me so much about you."

"Well," said Thelonius. "I'm sure I've met your standards, now it's time to check you out. Hi, sweetie," Thelonius said to Rikki. "I hear you had quite a cross country trip. I hope the trip was worth it and this young man lives up to your expectations."

"Oh Daddy, I'm so glad to see you too and yes Bentley lives up to my expectations. Let's stop the surface talk and get inside, it's much too cold."

With that, we walked into the house. As I entered the house I saw what many would consider to be a museum. Thelonius had a beautiful home full of paintings from world renowned African and black artists. The home looked and felt like the Huxtables from the Cosby Show.

"So, Bentley from what college did you graduate? You must be a Morehouse Man."

"Well, not exactly. I've always wanted to attend Morehouse but I got too busy with UCLA. UCLA is a pretty good school, but you don't have the same interactions or camaraderie as Morehouse."

Thelonius didn't have much to say about UCLA. He seemed relatively impressed that I graduated from the school.

We talked all night. By the end of the night, Thelonius was convinced that I was committed to his daughter. I didn't oversell myself. My answers were straight from the heart and my plans were to be a physician, with Rikki by my side. Although I didn't outright tell Thelonius, my intentions were pretty clear.

We returned to Granny's house late. We traveled from the Gold Coast to the Beltway via 16th Street and Georgia Avenue. Rikki showed me where she lived a few years back in Silver Spring, MD. I then showed Rikki where I lived with my sister in Silver Spring.

"Man, what a trip. I had no idea we lived so close to each other a few years ago."

"Gosh, we could have come across one another in the grocery store or on Metro. Maybe it means we were just destined for each other."

"I think it means we were destined for each other, but at a later date."

As we headed back to Granny's house, I started thinking about our new beginning as a couple in St. Louis where I made a conscious decision to start a new life. I didn't quite know what was in store but I did know that the rapidly-ending D.C. trip meant my life would soon take a dramatic turn.

Lesson 11: Meeting family and friends can work to your advantage.

Chapter 12: There's No Turnin' Back

When we returned from D.C., we slowly got into a groove. I took post-baccalaureate courses to prepare for the MCAT while Rikki finished her undergraduate coursework. We both worked for a minority student academic preparation program. Rikki served as an assistant administrator. I worked as an assistant instructor. To save money, we moved into Rikki's mother's house. It was a big home with over six thousand square feet of living space. Some days you couldn't tell who was at home. However, living in another man's home started to get on my nerves. I was raised to be self-sufficient. I anticipated some opposition from Rikki but knew it was time for me to move out of the house after six weeks.

"Hey, sweetie," I said, after getting undressed for bed. "I need to start looking for a place to live."

"You have a place to live. It's right here."

I started to feel uneasy because I knew a fight was coming.

"Sweetie, I'm sorry but I think I'm wearing out my welcome. You probably don't understand, but it's a man's thing. You see, a grown man is not supposed to live in another man's house. A couple of weeks are okay because you're in transition but an extended period of six weeks or more is a bit much."

"Oh, so did Will say something to you? If he did, my Mom will put a lid on it. This is HER house," said Rikki.

"Please, that's not the case at all. In fact that would cause a MAJOR problem. I'm not trying to jeopardize my relationship with your family. It's better this way. Trust me," I said emphatically.

We turned off the light and jumped in Rikki's bed. I could feel the tension in Rikki's body. I held her tightly and kissed her neck. We lay perfectly in the fetal position, both wondering how this issue would play out.

It only took me a week to find a place. It was near the university in a gated community. The large one-bedroom apartment had a lot of character. It seemed larger than usual with no furniture. This was something I would have to live with. I just had my clothes, dishes and an air mattress. It didn't bother me because it was my place and no one could dictate what went on except Rikki.

It took Rikki about four days to finally ask me when I would do some decorating.

"Hey Bentley, when do you plan to buy some furniture and linen?"

"Oh, I don't know. I'm in no big rush since we are not sure what we're going to do after you graduate."

"I see but I think you should do a little something since I'm staying around here."

"Okay, okay, you can bring some things over to fix up the place. I don't want you to feel unwanted."

"Thanks, sweetie. Our place will look great in no time." With that she gave me a quick kiss and exited for class.

"Wow," I thought to myself. "I just had my first lesson in getting railroaded and didn't know it."

After a few weeks, the place looked great. It definitely had a woman's touch, but it was still masculine enough for me. We were hitting our stride. Rikki stayed over my place quite a bit. More and more of her clothes hung in my closet. I was starting to learn more and more about Rikki. Some of it was not all good, especially the housekeeping issue. I was very meticulous, while Rikki was quite messy. I tried not to be a Felix Unger, but sometimes the unmade bed or the clothes on the floor really irked me.

"Hey, Rikki could you please pick up your clothes! I don't want to see your dirty draws."

"Yeah, yeah okay Mom, I'll do it before we head to the university."

"Alright, you know how that drives me crazy."

Rikki smiled, walked into the kitchen and made her lunch. She tried to brush me off when it came to cleaning the house because she knew I would eventually get tired of her and clean things up. However, slowly but surely she started to do it on her own because she knew it was the right thing to do.

We had a nice routine. Rikki would stay over my place during the week while I stayed at Rikki's parents' house on weekends. We worked together and went to school together. Rikki graduated from Washington University in the summer with not much fanfare. Our summer jobs were an extension of our academic year jobs. I also continued as a lab assistant to a brother named Dr. Jerry Mathis. I met Dr. Mathis while taking his Cell Biology class. He was a cool straight shooter who became my mentor. It was the first time I had connected with a professor. His style was direct yet laid back. He didn't take any stuff, but he offered words of encouragement. It was also the first time

I took a class from an African American professor. This was something I really liked.

I navigated my way through Washington University with great support from Dr. Mathis. Everyone supported me and Rikki. We were seen as an up and coming young couple with tremendous potential. The administrators made us feel at home and encouraged us to work as one. The young high school students looked up to us as mentors socially and academically. They dreamed of the days when they too could work with their loved ones. We were wonderful role models for children who often saw none.

One day, a group of teenage girls asked me when I would marry Rikki. They told me they overheard Rikki talking to some other women about marriage and how she was ready to settle down.

"So, Mr. Bentley, when are you going to give Ms. Rikki her ring? We know Ms. Rikki is ready to marry you so you can tell us when it's going to happen. We promise not to tell her."

"Oh yeah, like I can tell you all something. My business would be all over the summer program. I can see it now: 'Mr. Bentley plans marriage to Ms. Rikki in the fall.'"

"Mr. Bentley plans marriage for Ms. Rikki during the fall."

"I promise you all will be the first ones to know when I pop the question, okay."

That night, when we returned to my apartment we had a message from Rikki's mom to call right away. Since it was a Thursday night, we decided to drive over to see what was going on. As we entered the house we could feel the excitement. We weren't quite sure what it was but we knew something was up.

"Guess what," announced Rikki's Mom. "Will got a special assignment to London."

Everyone was so excited, initially. Rikki hugged her mom while I shook Will's hand. We all went out to celebrate.

"Well when do you guys have to move?" Rikki asked her mom.

"Hmmm, it looks like we'll only have six weeks to get ready. They want us there by the end of the summer."

"That is ludicrous!" Rikki exclaimed. "How do they expect anyone to move in that short period of time?"

"Well," said Will. "They don't expect us to move anything. In fact, they'll move everything for us. I don't have to lift a finger at either end of this move."

The next couple of days were filled with mixed emotions. With her mother leaving the country, Rikki reflected on her life. Although she was practically living with me, she still had her own place—well, her mother's place. With her mother gone in a few weeks, Rikki had to think about the seriousness of our relationship. She was not accustomed to being dependent on anyone except her mom. The thought of her mom in England made Rikki realize how much she'd miss her. Life in England was a great opportunity, but what a price they had to pay.

Rikki was quite preoccupied with her Mom's imminent move. I did what I could to relieve her anxiety but I couldn't quite understand her feelings. I had never seen Rikki so dumbfounded. She was happy for her mom and Will but it would mean she would be left alone with me. That was not a problem, but there was so much uncertainty in our lives. After dinner, I returned home. The minute I walked into the apartment, the phone rang.

"What do you think we should do, Bentley?"

"We'll focus on our future."

"Let's concentrate on moving to either Atlanta or D.C. Very soon I'll know something from either Emory or Georgetown for school. Both places are nice and we can concentrate on our careers."

"That sounds like a pretty good plan, but how will I know you're really committed to our relationship if we're not married?"

"Please don't start to pressure me on getting married now. We've got a good understanding that we'll get married but we've never placed ourselves on a deadline."

I could see the creases on Rikki's face even though we were on the phone. The silence was deafening. I knew she was upset, but she was too tired emotionally to put up a fight for now. Just then my phone beeped. I was receiving another call.

"Hold on a minute, sweetie; let me get that." It was my mother. Her voice was pretty serious.

"Bentley, we need you to come home as soon as you can. Your father is scheduled to have surgery in a couple of days."

Lesson 12: Relationships are not always fun and games.

Chapter 13: A Reason to Return Home

The next day I was on the plane. This episode momentarily distracted me from Rikki. My mom's words kept ringing in my ears.

"Bentley, we need you to come home as soon as you can. Your father is scheduled to have surgery in a couple of days."

Before I knew it, the plane was over the San Francisco Bay. It was still one of the most beautiful places I had ever seen. The plane hovered over the seascape and slowly glided over the bay. As we got closer to the runway, things started to speed up. Just like the pace of my life. I would have to make some major decisions soon, but not until I discussed them with my folks. The plane hit the ground and the large flaps shot up to slow down the large bird.

"You have now arrived in Oakland. Please do not unbuckle your seatbelts until the plane comes to a complete halt."

Of course by now the impatient white men had already unfastened their seatbelts and sat poised to capture their things in the overhead bins. Their quest to beat everyone to the punch amazed me. Even in the face of danger, they still had to be ahead of everyone.

I departed the plane leisurely and looked around for a familiar face at the gate. No one was in sight. I passed smiling faces but no one looked familiar, so I continued to the baggage claim area. Outside the baggage area I looked for a familiar car of one of my family members. I saw no one. I knew someone would show up at some point. The Oakland Airport was notorious for not letting drivers wait for their passengers, so everyone had to wait for their rides to circle around the terminal. As my mind drifted to pleasant thoughts about Rikki, I was startled by two loud little voices screaming at the top of their lungs.

"Uncle Bentley, Uncle Bentley!" they said excitedly as the Volvo station wagon approached the nearby baggage claim area.

"Hi, Jordan and Amber. Hey, sis." I was so glad to see them and gave them big hugs and kisses. "Well, how's Dad?"

"Oh, he'll make it, but his leg will never be the same. Dad will always have a slight limp. He's in the hospital now. Do you want to stop by Kaiser or should I take you to Mom's?"

"Let's stop by the hospital. I know Dad will like that I came directly to his bedside from the airport."

We headed to Kaiser to visit Dad. The kids were very chatty and excited about the possibility of seeing him. They didn't seem to mind the hospital atmosphere, since their Dad was a doctor and they spent many a day in the hospital visiting him. He was an older medical student and now resident so he spent quality time at the hospital with the kids.

"Hey, where's Grandpa?" asked Amber as she climbed on the desk to the nurses' station. She was an exact replica of Denise, but five times smaller.

"Well," said the nurse. "Your Grandpa Johnson appears to be doing better. I think he's up to receiving company, especially his grandchildren. His room number is 1456."

The little feet took off down the hall and burst into the room before Denise and I could leave the nurses station.

"Hi, Grandpa! We came to see you and we brought a present – Uncle Bentley!"

"Hey, how's everybody doing? Wow, this is like a mini family reunion," said Dad. "I'm so glad you all came to visit me. Hopefully, I'll be out of here shortly. My leg is feeling pretty good but my body feels a little weak."

We stayed with Dad until 9 p.m. My niece and nephew were fast asleep by the time we left. Dad was also fast asleep. His leg hung high to balance the flow of blood. One by one, as we left the room each of us kissed Dad on the cheek. He slept so hard that we didn't wake him. On the way to our parent's home, we talked while the kids slept. We caught up on our lives and our older brother's life.

"Well, how's Silas doing?"

"He's actually doing pretty well. He's gone in business with his father-in-law. They now have a host of group homes throughout the Bay Area. Silas is the chief operating officer, so he's got to manage all of them. He likes it a lot because he's not working for "the man," but working for THE MAN- his father-in-law. We laughed at that because his father-in-law was a wealthy guy who was not shy about people he didn't like. He did, however, like Silas and the way he interacted with and motivated the staff. Silas was definitely in line to be the "heir apparent."

I knew sooner or later Denise would ask me the big question.

"So Bentley, what's up with you and Rikki? You know we haven't seen you since you left to live in St. Louis. Mom and Dad were flabbergasted as was everyone else. Do you really love her or is something else going on?"

"Oh, she's definitely the one. We are both love struck. At some point, I think we'll get married."

"At some point! You know our family doesn't take well to shacking up. What are you waiting for? I know you don't have cold feet! Shoot, you live in St. Louis."

We had to laugh at that one because it got pretty cold in St. Louis. The statement made me remember the time I had to wrap the car battery with a blanket because it was so cold.

"I don't see why you use waiting as an excuse. You've gone this far and might as well take the plunge. When you do take the plunge, just remember it's a commitment for life."

For the rest of the drive to our parent's house, we sat quietly. This gave me a while to reflect on Denise's statements and my relationship with Rikki. I thought over and over about our future. It was time to settle down. We were Catholics and did not believe in "shacking up."

"This confirms it. It's time to get married."

When we arrived at our parents', I told Denise and the kids goodbye. It was late, so they dropped me off and continued home. I rang the doorbell. I could hear Mom walking down the steps approaching the door.

"Bentley is that you?"

"Yeah, Mom it's me. Come on and open the door. It's cold out here."

My mom opened the door and I gave her a kiss and a big hug. The living room was the same, but it didn't have the books and papers near my father's chair. The dining room was also the same – clean as a whistle.

I dropped off my things in my old room and met Mom downstairs.

Crossing the Bridge Over Troubled Water

"Do you want something to eat, sweetie? I have some oxtails with some potatoes and carrots in the refrigerator."

"Yep, Mom I'll get it. Why don't you go back to sleep? As soon as I get a little of this good food, I'm going to bed."

"Alright, honey, I'll see you in the morning."

I zapped my food and pulled out a *Jet* from the side of my father's chair. He always loved to read *Jet*. I stayed up for about an hour then went to bed. I slept quietly and peacefully in my old bedroom. I was awakened by the smell of bacon and biscuits. Mom was preparing my favorite meal. I could hear the clanging of dishes and my mother's voice talking on the phone to Aunt Annie. Aunt Annie lived virtually around the corner. She was my mother's favorite sister and my godmother. I dragged myself up and made my way downstairs for coffee.

"Hey, honey. My, you look tired and skinny. Have a seat while I get you some coffee. By the way, your brother is coming over."

"Oh, I figured that," I said. "Whenever you cook biscuits, he somehow shows up out of nowhere with HIS bottle of Uncle Steve's Syrup."

"So how's Rikki?" Mom asked. Are you guys doing okay?"

"All is well, Mom. We're doing pretty good. The real issue we're dealing with is that her mom and step father are moving to London.

"Oh, so what are you two going to do?'

"Well, I think we're going to get married at some point."

Thinking about getting married made me a little uneasy. I left a pretty serious relationship to be with Rikki. I loved Rikki but didn't know if I was ready to take the plunge. None of my buddies were married. I would be the first one.

Just then I heard Silas's footsteps. Silas was ten years older and about a foot taller than me. He was the spitting image of my dad. The front door clicked open as two large feet hit the front foyer.

"Hey, where's my little brother?" Silas shouted. "Man something smells good in here. I've got my bottle of Uncle Steve's syrup to soak up with those biscuits."

The three of us ate breakfast and talked about old times. We would all visit Dad later that day. After breakfast Silas and I walked around the corner as Mom cleaned the kitchen and got ready to visit the hospital. During the walk, Silas inquired about my relationship with Rikki.

"So Bentley, what's up with you and Rikki? Is she pregnant or something?"

"No man, I'm just diggin' her. I don't know what it is, but I believe she's the one. It's the same way Dad met Mom and how Sis met Morrelle."

We laughed about the pattern of our familial relationships. Our parents started out as long distant lovers and ended up as husband and wife. It was a great testament to the power of our family. No one had divorced and no one had any major problems with their marriages. The percentages were working in our favor and the love Rikki and I shared was definitely going to last.

The next day, the whole family visited Dad. His leg was feeling much better and his spirits were normal. Based on the prognosis of the family and his general sense of well being, he would be out in no time. This was the first time that sickness affected the inner circle of our family. Everyone responded with such composure and strength. This made me feel much better about leaving California and the tight inner workings of the family. I thought sooner or later they would have to know my plans for marrying Rikki. However, I would not give them enough time to change my mind or influence plans for the wedding.

I stayed two more days in the Bay Area. Dad was released the day everyone visited his room and was on track to rehabilitate his leg. The color in his face was back to normal and he was eating Mom's good food. I made a few rounds to different relatives' homes to inform them of Dad's recovery. On the way to my favorite cousin's house, I detoured around Lake Merritt because of the infamous "Festival at the Lake." I forgot the magnitude of the festival and how many hoodlums and hoochee mamas it attracted.

Lesson 13: There is no real reason to shack up.

Chapter 14: Spending a Little Time to Reminisce

Everyone was out in rare form, including all the "macs" and "mackettes." Drop top cars were circling the lake with loud music and plenty of TLC's "Scrubs." Women were pushing their baby carriages with "short-shorts" and extra large hoop earrings. It was all very colorful, loud, festive and definitely OAKTOWN. I felt an urge to get out. Before I proceeded, I called my favorite cousin, Cyndi.

"Hey Cyndi, I'm down at the festival, why don't you come down to meet me."

Cyndi suggested a place and quickly got off the phone to meet me. She knew it was a pretty rare thing to catch me between women and jobs.

While I waited for Cyndi, I walked around the festival entrance. There were scores of people milling around checking out each other and the scene. Five lines of people flooded the entrance to the festival. It looked like the opening concert to Budweiser Superfest. People were dancing to the beat of Sheila E., who was now on stage at one of the venues. Her drums could be heard blocks away. This made the crowd of people at the entrance even more anxious to get in. I saw a number of friends and acquaintances. My close friends were surprised to see me and the acquaintances could not believe I lived in St. Louis. Within minutes, I caught a glimpse of someone I dreaded seeing. It was an old flame named Felicia. She saw me at the same time and started heading my way. She was what I called a "bubbling brown sugar." Her skin was a radiant mocha brown with a tint of red. She was petite with the body of an aerobics instructor. The Eastbay winter never did her justice but the summer absolutely matched her personality and the curves of her body.

"Well, well, well, I never thought I'd see you here Bentley," said Felecia. "I thought you were in St. Louis living with the new love of your life."

"It's good to see you," I said.

I had to quickly assess my rebuttal to Felecia. I didn't want to confirm nor deny that I lived in St. Louis because I also didn't want her knowing my business.

"Well, it's good to see you too, Bentley," said Felecia as she embraced me. Her thirty-six-D bust pressed against my chest. She was not overly flirtatious but she was direct in what she did and what she wanted. I embraced her but immediately felt a sting of guilt run through my body. Like any male I felt an urge to "game" Felecia. In an instant I remembered episodes of sexing Felecia down on the beach, in the car, in her grandmother's room and on the living room floor of her mother's apartment. Yeah I felt this was a close encounter of a dangerous kind.

As my mind drifted for an instant I was jarred back to the present time by my cousin Cyndi. "Hey you two, I know you're not starting anything up again. This is just a friendly reunion, right?"

It was perfect timing. Both Felecia and I knew what was racing through our heads. We quickly separated so Felecia could hug Cyndi. I was grateful for my cousin's arrival. She always had a knack for pulling me out of compromising situations. Felecia left but made it a point that she wanted a call from me later.

After Felecia left, Cyndi and I entered the festival. We hung around the concert venues grooving to the sounds of Sheila E. and Maze. We danced like there was no tomorrow. The two of us were more like brother and sister than cousins and everyone could tell. We looked like each other and in many ways thought like each other. Cyndi was my closest confidant and it was time for her to know what was going on with me.

"So Bentley, what's happening with you and Rikki? I know you wouldn't leave the Bay Area for nothing. You were in a pretty serious relationship and before we knew it you broke off that relationship to live with Rikki. Was it that good?"

I had to laugh. I had heard that question time and time again. Everyone thought I was "whipped." In fact, that was not the case at all. I explained the familial and intuitional bond between me and Rikki. It was much more than a physical attraction. I had many women who fit the California bill – tight body, exercise enthusiast and into hair. No, this attraction was like the "Age of Aquarius." It was guided by the stars and a "guttural" instinct that drew us together like magnets.

Once I completed the monologue about my feelings for Rikki, Cyndi knew this was it. I would marry Rikki. Cyndi saw me like this once before and that was with my first girlfriend. This time it was much more mature and guided by principles that would assure longevity. Cyndi was happy for me but also a little leery. This was the first time she could not stare down the woman affecting my life. Cyndi had a way to cut straight through any woman involved with me. It was her protection mechanism. Some saw it as jealousy but she saw it as a way to shield me from the foolish games. As we continued to walk around the Festival, Cyndi schemed on how she would get to Rikki to let her know that eyes were watching. We stayed for about three hours talking to old friends, nibbling on good food and laughing about old times. I cherished this conversation with my cousin because I realized that very soon I would have to confide in Rikki as my wife.

When I returned to my parents' home I checked in on my father, who had just returned home. Dad was propped in his favorite chair reading the Wall Street Journal. In addition, he was figuring out the next time he could jump back out on the golf course. His leg was feeling much better and the doctor suggested he take daily walks to loosen up his limbs. Dad briefly chatted with me before he drifted off to sleep in his lounge chair. I then grabbed something to drink before I placed a call to Felecia. It was something I had to do, to set the record straight.

"Good evening, may I speak to Felecia?"

"Well, well, well, if it isn't Mr. Bentley the world traveler," said Mrs. Timms, who was Felecia's grandmother. "I thought you were gone for good. Sure, I'll get Felecia for you."

"So when are you going to stop by the house? I want to hear about what you're up to these days."

"Okay," I said. "I'll be sure to stop by to see you Mrs. Timms. That's when I'll fill you in on my latest developments."

"That'll be nice, honey. It was nice talking to you. Let me go get Felecia." With that, Mrs. Timms laid down the phone and called out to Felecia. I could hear them whispering in the background. Felecia picked up the phone.

"Hi, Bentley," said Felecia.

"Hey Felecia, it was nice to see you today."

"Yeah, it was nice to see you too. So are you stopping by tonight or what?"

I chuckled to myself. I always liked Felecia's directness and the ease with which she told me things.

"Yep, I'll be by in a few. Do you want anything from the store?" Yeah, can you bring me and grandma some frozen yogurt?"

"Will do. I'll see you in a minute."

I hung up the phone, not believing how easily I fell back into a routine. It was as if I had not left the Bay Area. My relationship with Felecia was one like the typical high school sweetheart. In a fairytale world I was destined to marry Felecia. However, things weren't happening that way. I followed my heart rather than my mind. My heart said Rikki swept me off my feet while my mind said I needed to be practical and stay home with Felecia. I was in a quagmire. So much was going on. I had to admit, it was a bit conflicting. Life had its contradictions and this was definitely one of them. I put on my jacket and headed out.

Lesson 14: Before you marry, get over old relationships.

Chapter 15: Time to Get Serious

The next day, I headed back to St. Louis. I felt a heavy sense of relief due to the conversations I had with family members and because of the night before with Felecia. I shook my head as I recalled our brief encounter. Felecia greeted me at the door with a big smile and a big hug. We talked for about two hours, recalling our high school days and the current state of affairs. Both of us were in serious relationships, but we had not resolved our feelings for each other. We both agreed that love would always be present, but that life did not destine us to be together. We parted ways with one last passionate night filled with memories of the past and an amicable separation that would push us into the future. As the plane lifted off, I smiled, gazed into the clouds and envisioned that last long hug at Felicia's door. We were good friends that held onto memories like the Senior Ball. Our lives would move on as we hung onto a past that led us into adulthood. I drifted off to sleep remembering the past while hoping for the future.

The plane arrived in St. Louis in no time. As I walked off the plane I looked for Rikki. She was waiting for me at the gate. I felt a little guilty about the night before, but quickly dismissed the thoughts.

"It was needed," I said to myself. "If last night didn't happen, I would always wonder what if." With that turned off, I brushed off the guilt and focused on Rikki.

"Hey, sweetie, I surely missed you," I said.
"Gosh, I missed you too. It seemed like a lifetime."
"Well, I'm here and we need to start planning."
"For what?" asked Rikki.
"For our wedding."

Rikki was stunned and a little bit overwhelmed. I could tell I caught her totally off guard. Just a few months before, she had written me off to concentrate on personal development. Most of the men she had dated were domineering or overly needy. I was neither. In her mind, I was ying to her yang. Sometimes I let her control situations while other times I considerately led the way. This was one of those times.

"Well, what are you going to say?"
It wasn't your typical proposal.
"Here's a little token of my appreciation."

I pulled out an engagement ring. The centerpiece of the ring was shaped like the symbol I drew that represented our love. It was a triangle with a heart based in the middle. At the center of the heart was a small diamond.

"Oh, it's beautiful. I love it—and yes, I will marry you."

We walked hand in hand through the airport. I knew the implications of my words and the destiny it would create. In my mind, we were now inseparable. No homeboys or girlfriends would pull us apart. The two of us were interdependent. It sounded like a simple plan, but the devil was in the details. As we drove home, we discussed possibilities for the wedding – having it in D.C., having it in St. Louis, having it in Atlanta. It all seemed pretty overwhelming. Rikki then realized that within the next few months her mother would be gone to London.

"Bentley, do you know that my mom will be in London while we plan for the wedding?

She'll have to communicate with me from overseas to finalize our plans. In addition, she and Will will need to travel pretty far for our wedding. I propose that we have the wedding here in St. Louis before they leave for London."

"Hmmm, that will be pretty quick, but hey let's do it. That'll settle our problem in terms of the location, but what about all our friends and family on the East and West Coasts?"

"I've got it," said Rikki. We can have a reception in California and D.C., that way we can share our happiness with family and friends on both coasts."

"Damn, you're good. That's why I'm marrying you!"

We both chuckled. That was just one of the reasons I loved Rikki. My attraction to her went beyond physical and mental. It was deeply spiritual. During our many conversations, we discovered that we shared a commitment to the Catholic faith. We both went through twelve years of Catholic school, blessed sacraments and lots of penance. In addition, we loved our families. Much of our existence circled around family gatherings, reunions, holidays and birthdays. Rikki loved to celebrate birthdays. This was something I didn't particularly like, but could understand. It wasn't that I disliked birthdays, but they weren't big deals to me. Rikki forewarned me of her love of her birthday parties. Thus, she put me on notice to always throw her a party.

For the next two months everyone planned for change– moving to London, getting married and for us, a life together as one. I was still pursuing medical school but I decided to obtain my master's degree to enhance my academic record and to make connections with a small medical school in Atlanta. I was accepted at Emory University in the public health program. Based on my acceptance and Rikki's previous experience living in Atlanta, we decided to relocate to Atlanta after the wedding. Now everyone was preparing for a move. The days flew. Slowly but surely, Rikki started to move her things into my apartment and differences started to arise. I was somewhat of a "neat freak." I liked things in order. Rikki however, was not very orderly or neat. She liked to lay things down and spread them out. She was also much freer with her expression of self. In other words, she liked to walk around the apartment naked. I was more conservative when it came to things like that. I liked the freedom to keep things straight, the freedom to sleep during my own hours and the freedom to eat whenever and whatever I wanted. The life and habits of bachelor-hood were about to be over. My "freedom" was slipping away. On the one hand, I didn't mind living with Rikki but on the other hand, I couldn't stand to waste energy on frivolous things.

"Why can't she just pick up her clothes," I thought as I walked around the apartment cleaning up. "She knows that irks me to no end."

Rikki was at her night class as I tidied up the apartment. It was the daily routine since I came home around 6 p.m. Since I was "Felix Unger," I usually inspected the house as soon as I entered the door. After I inspected the house, I gave it the white glove treatment. Generally speaking, I was an uptight guy when it came to cleanliness. On the exterior, I appeared to be a relaxed West Coast guy, but on the interior, I was a perfectionist with little tolerance for dirt, dust or clutter. Just as I was putting the meatloaf in the oven, a key jiggled the front door.

"Hey, sweetie, I'm home," said Rikki cheerfully. Rikki entered the apartment with her briefcase and additional items from her mother's house.

"How was your day?" I laid out the plates and silverware. My mind raced and wondered, "How would my boys view me now? I feel like Mr. Julia Childs."

"Oh my day was pretty good. I missed you at lunch."

"I had to catch up on some lab work and prepare lesson plans for the science program." In reality, I could have seen Rikki during lunch but needed time to breathe.

Rikki put her things away and changed into sweats. By the time she returned, I had everything on the table. We ate and talked about the day and plans for the wedding. It was a nice quiet evening. As we were finishing dinner the phone rang.

"I'll get it," said Rikki.

"Be my guest."

I could hear Rikki talking to someone in a stern voice. I didn't know who she was talking to but I had an idea.

"Bentley, one of your girlfriends is on the phone. I told her if she called here one more time, I would hang up on her."

My stomach dropped. I knew who was on the phone but I tried to play it off. Periodically, I would call one of my old flames in Cali to see if I still had my touch. Jeanna was one of those smart, down to earth L.A. hot mommas who knew all of my hot buttons. She even knew the hot buttons on the phone. Jeanna told me that if I ever left Rikki, I was hers. Since she was already a successful pediatric resident, she had no ties to anyone. Her only request to me was that I be her stay at home dad to her children.

Although I was often tempted by Jeanna's proposals, I was a bit intimidated by her success.

"Shoot, if she was that open to me, she might drop me like a light bulb," I thought.

I quickly regrouped myself and chatted briefly with Jeanna. I told her it wasn't a good time to talk and that it might be best if we chatted another time. Rikki followed me wherever I went to listen in on the conversation. It wasn't like she had far to go. After I hung up, Rikki lit into me D.C. style.

"What the heck do you think you're doing? I'm not some fool you can treat any old way. We're getting ready to be married and you're playing games with me! Bentley, you need to straighten up." Rikki was almost crying.

I could see she was hurt.

"Oh Rikki, that's just one of my friends. Obviously, she means nothing to me because I'm here with you. Can't I have a friendly conversation with someone from Cali?"

"Don't even go there, Bentley. With friends like that, our marriage will be short-lived. How can we develop trust for each other with your little friends calling our house? I'm not having it! I wish she was here so I could kick her butt."

I liked Rikki's spunk. She was a seasoned fighter who had been around the block. Her last two relationships ended because the guys had cheated on and disrespected her. Rikki was not going to enter a marriage like that. She invested a lot of feelings into this relationship and she was going to make it work. I vowed not to let anything get between us. I caressed and cajoled Rikki so she would feel at ease. After giving her a glass of wine, I rocked her to sleep, whispering ever so gently in her ear. I assured Rikki she was my only one and that no one would come between us. In the back of my mind, I questioned my commitment. I didn't know if we had the chemistry. She was a bit bossy and demanding for my taste but she knew exactly what she wanted. I had never been with anyone with so much spunk and direction. It was an East Coast phenomenon and I liked it. For the moment, I resigned myself to believing that everything would be all right. I guided Rikki to bed and we slept soundly in each other's arms.

Lesson 15: Avoid the monkey wrenches before getting married.

Chapter 16: We'll Do It Our Way

The next day, we made plans for the wedding party. The women in Rikki's office overheard us talking about the wedding. They had a wonderful suggestion for the two of us. The women would give Rikki a bridal shower, while their husbands would give me a bachelor's party. When Rikki heard of the idea, she was delighted. Since neither of us had close friends in St. Louis, two separate parties in one house would be great. That Saturday, we drove to her supervisor Champagne's house. Champagne was a bubbly woman from Tuscoloosa, Alabama. She was a slender woman with curvaceous hips and full lips. Her personality was both bubbly and LOUD. As we walked up the steps we could hare Champagne talking to the other women from the office.

"Girl, that Rikki is going to like this cake. You know it looks like the REAL thing."

We looked at each other and chuckled, then rang the doorbell.

"Oh, oh, I think that's them." Champagne opened the door and gave us a big hug. As we entered the house, we were immediately struck by the smell of ribs and seafood. In addition, we heard loud music and loud voices. There were a lot of people in the house. All of them were colleagues from work.

"All right, Sugar," said Champagne, as she turned to me. "You head on downstairs, Willard's got you covered. Your little Rikki Poo will be in good hands."

I gave Rikki a smile and a wink. I headed downstairs for my bachelor party. As I walked downstairs, I could hear familiar voices. I entered the basement and was immediately embraced by Willard. It stunned me because Willard was not the most affectionate person, or at least he didn't appear to be. Willard was a colonel in the Army. He was one of the best attorneys in the military and had a mean streak that matched Napolean. His only apparent weakness was his wife Champagne who knew how to make him melt.

"Hey, fella, how are you doin!" said Willard as he gave me a bear hug. "Come on in, we've got good drinks, beer and advice for you."

For the next hour, Willard sponsored a wonderful experience for me. This was not the typical bachelor's party. It was like a "rites of passage" for marriage. Willard had the guys give short testimonials about marriage. In the case of the person who was not married, he testified on the success of his parents' marriage. Everyone was encouraging and sincere in their advice to me. One person, Dr. Mathis, my former professor and mentor, shared this with me: "Marriage is one of the best institutions in life. When you find your soul mate, life is so complete. You can face challenges knowing that your better half has your back. Remember that even in disagreements, your wife has your back. It is an inherent quality for women to protect their husbands and nurture their families. Don't forget that important point. A lot of brothers get caught up in their woman's nagging or slowing them down. No, your wife is often nagging you because she's trying to spend time with you and preserve your family."

Willard concurred with Dr. Mathis, as did the other guys. This was a bachelor's party like no other but it was done in a way that fit me. I was not one for all the naked women or exuberance of the male ego. I wanted to hear the core of marriage and I got it. It was the best experience and party I ever had. Willard enjoyed himself, too, as did Dr. Mathis. They both knew that I would take marriage seriously and honor Rikki for the rest of my life.

After the bachelor and bachelorette parties, everyone came together to sing songs, dance and eat trays full of crawfish. We held each other's hands and listened to the funny stories of seasoned married couples. No one degraded the institution of marriage, instead they propped it up as a way to develop personally and professionally. This was not the way we envisioned our bachelor and bachelorette parties. No, this was an unusual way to spend the final days of single life. Although it seemed strange, it was typical for us. We liked hanging around more mature couples. This was one of the best evenings we had spent together and it confirmed our love for each other. There was no hesitation. We knew it was the right decision to get married. When the night was over, we went home to gossip about the evening. We loved to compare notes after an event. We laughed and mimicked those attending the party. When I finally started nodding off, Rikki stared at my face. She then sobbed silently thinking about the happiness in finding her soul mate.

"Yes, this is going to work," she said to herself. "I've got a brotha that will love me through thick and thin."

Rikki snuggled closer to me. I hugged her closer to my chest.

The next few days, we prepared for the wedding. Rikki made sure all of the blood tests and paper work were in order. I checked on guest accommodations while Jane checked on reception details. Everything was in order. I purchased the wedding bands while Rikki and her mother put the final touches on the wedding dress and head piece. It didn't seem like much to do since it was not a formal ceremony, but it was enough to make us both nervous.

"Hey, why are you trippin'?" I asked Rikki.

"Oh, I know you're not talking about me. You're the one that's been pacing the floors at night like some dead man walking."

"All right, all right-- so, I might be a little nervous."

We both reflected on the nuances of our nervousness. This wasn't a big deal, but it made us pause to think about personal reactions under stress. Our actions were not against each other, they were just aggravating tendencies that were out of the ordinary.

My parents flew in from California for the ceremony while Rikki's father, stepmother and aunt would arrive in time for the reception. My parents stayed at my apartment, while Rikki prepared at home. Since we were getting married by a judge, our ceremony would be in his chambers. My mother and father were proud of me. As I starched and ironed my suit, shirt and tie my parents smiled at me and reminisced about their lives. After my clothes were ready, I took a cool shower. The temperature was supposed to reach close to 100 degrees, and I was determined not to burn up in the suit. I put on plenty of deodorant and baking powder. I then finished in text-book record speed. This allowed me time enough to relax as my parents got dressed.

Meanwhile, Rikki was having the time of her life. She felt her bridal headpiece was not fitting properly, her makeup didn't look right and her undergarments were too tight. All of this made her nervous. Rikki didn't like this type of pressure. It was all self-inflicted. Rikki was such a perfectionist that one strand sticking out would cause her to re-think her hairdo. She was starting to feel ill because she was so worked up. Everything was getting on her nerves.

"Mom, would you please come here and help me with this bridal piece? It's just not laying right."

"Alright, honey," said Jane. "It's going to be alright. I know you're getting all worked up but there's no need to be. You look MARVELOUS!"

Jane adjusted the headpiece and told Rikki a few secrets about how to look good under pressure. Rikki laughed at her mother's suggestions, made a few adjustments and was ready to go.

"All right Will," yelled Jane. "I want you to get the car ready and make sure the air conditioning is cold because I don't want my baby to sweat before the ceremony."

Will grumbled then walked away to prepare the car. He didn't want to get any one riled up on this special day. He was usually pretty argumentative but today he was relaxed and very cooperative.

The drive to the courthouse seemed to take an eternity. Rikki looked outside the window and thought about her future. She thought about owning a home, having children and eventually grandchildren. Her life flashed before her eyes.

"Why am I moving so fast?" said Rikki to herself. "I need to concentrate on today and savior the moment." As they approached the courthouse, Rikki could see my Volkswagen. In fact, she saw me. I was standing near the doorway looking for her. Rikki stared at the way I anxiously waited for her. My brow furrowed because I was getting impatient. However, the lines ceased to exist when our eyes met. I waved and blew her a kiss. Rikki was slightly embarrassed.

Will dropped Rikki and Jane off in front of the courthouse. I helped both of them out of the car and tightly held Rikki's hand.

"Okay, are you ready?" I said as my hand trembled so lightly.

"I'm re- ready," Rikki stuttered as we walked into the courthouse. Everyone greeted each other with hugs and kisses. By the time the greeting was over, Will walked in and directed everyone to the judge's chambers."

"Alright, Judge Whitmore is ready for us. It's going to seem a little quick since he's on recess from the trial. He's a good guy, so don't worry."

As we walked into the Judge's chambers, we saw the walls were filled with articles, plaques and commendations. In addition, we saw golf trophies, plaques and even a putting green. His huge mahogany desk and leather chair engulfed the room. There was barely enough space for everyone to fit.

"Okay, where are the soon-to-be newlyweds?" asked Judge Whitmore with a booming voice. Everyone turned around to see a rather short man who looked nothing like the impression they had of Judge Whitmore. He was quite inviting. I shook his hand and passed on the marriage licenses.

"I take it these are valid," quizzed Judge Whitmore. It was his way of making a funny.

"Yes, I sure hope so," I said with a light chuckle as I scanned the room looking at everyone's eyes. I was not in a mood for laughter. I was a bit too nervous for that.

"Okay," said Judge Whitmore. "Let's get started."

Judge Whitmore breezed through the short ceremony. Will took pictures, while Jane and my parents looked on with starry eyes. They were all thinking about their marriage ceremonies and the warm fuzzy feeling in their hearts. After the ceremony, I thanked Judge Whitmore by giving him a check for his services. Will took a few more photos before Judge Whitmore made an announcement.

"Excuse me, but now you all need to do me a favor. Those folks out there need to know where I've been for the last 20 minutes on recess, so please come out with me through this door." Everyone looked at each other and said, "Okay."

As we entered the courtroom, a look of bewilderment went over the eyes of the audience as we filed out in front of the Judge's court bench.

"As you can see," said Judge Whitmore to the audience, "I'm really not a bad person. In fact, I'm a pretty good person. During the recess, I married this young couple. Please give them a congratulatory round of applause." The audience clapped for us and gave us a big roar. It was like a scene out of L.A. Law. We were ushered out during a murder trial to be showcased by the judge-- only in America.

Lesson 16: A small wedding can work.

Chapter 17: Reception in St. Louis

After the wedding, we took pictures with our parents in front of the courthouse. Everyone then changed clothes and went out for dinner at Union Station.

"Hey, baby, so how do you feel?" asked Rikki. Feeling that I was being set up if I didn't say the right thing, I replied assuredly by leaning over for a long embrace.

"I feel great. I'm really happy to be married to you. Now, let's get ready to get some food and party at Union Station."

By the time we changed clothes, our parents were calling to say they'd meet us at the restaurant. I kept twirling my wedding band around my finger in disbelief. It was a nervous twitch that I had developed in the last few hours. I had never worn a ring or any other jewelry. My perception of men wearing jewelry was not kind. In my mind, they were either thugs or gay. It was an unfair assumption, but I was pretty conservative when it came to those kinds of things.

We arrived at Union Station feeling like a couple on the "Newlywed Game." It seemed as if everyone knew we just got married. It must have been the glow. We were both giggly and overly affectionate. While we waited on our parents, we rode on the paddle boats. It was a cute sight.

We splashed water at each other and at other couples. We were the life of the party. Just as we were getting ready to finish the ride, we heard a loud familiar shout. Will rushed to get a picture of us. He wanted us to pose in the paddle boats.

"Now that's what I'm talking about," he shouted. "There's a whole lotta love in that boat!"

The folks around the pond cracked up. We were definitely an entertaining family. After we got off the paddle boats, we met everyone at the restaurant. A few close friends and associates joined us. Everyone in the restaurant looked at us like celebrities. Our table was decorated in a Caribbean theme with figurines at the head table that matched our attire. Guests everywhere were nibbling on hors d'oeuvres and drinking champagne. When we walked into our section everyone started clapping. I could feel Rikki's hands getting warm. She was embarrassed and happy at the same time. I squeezed her hand to let her know it was okay to be embarrassed. It seemed by that gesture, non-verbal husband/wife communication began. Rikki squeezed my hand back and fell out laughing.

"Okay, okay you guys got us!" I yelled. "I never thought all of you would be here. We anticipated a quiet evening. Instead, we got a wonderful party!"

Everyone burst out laughing and clapping. We sat down at the table designated for the newlyweds. Since it was a small party of people, we had the opportunity to chat with everyone who attended. We ate chicken fingers and shrimp while drinking Long Island Ice Teas. The group shared great stories of successful marriages and failed relationships. We laughed the whole night long while Rikki and I glanced into each other's eyes. The night ended late as we closed the place down.

For the next two days, we prepared for the big reception. Rikki's father and stepmother were scheduled to arrive as were her aunt and mother's best friend. In fact, her mother's best friend Casey arrived two days early to coordinate everything. She arranged for the band, decorated the mansion and choreographed the evening's events. Casey was extremely detailed, so she left no stone unturned. She even made sure that the in-laws were color coordinated.

We were a little nervous about Rikki's father's arrival. This would be the first time her father met my parents. It was not the best of situations, because he was totally surprised by the course of events and didn't have the opportunity to really check out my pedigree or to give his consent. This didn't matter to Rikki since she didn't quite see things eye to eye with her father. In her mind his impression didn't matter because she was now married.

We traveled out to the airport to greet her father, stepmother and aunt. This was done to curtail any awkwardness later on during the day. As we headed out on the expressway I asked an important question.

"Alright Rikki, how should I handle your father? I know he's going to test me but I want to know how far I should go without offending him."

"Oh, just be yourself. He's like the big bad wolf. He talks a whole lot of trash but if you hang with him, he'll back down."

With that, I was my charming self. I greeted Rikki's father with a "brotherly" handshake and gave Rikki's aunt and stepmother kisses on the cheek. There was, however, an awkward moment when I went to kiss Clementine, her stepmother. I accidentally kissed her on the lips. She wasn't offended; in fact, she was the one who turned her head acceptingly. I brushed it off because in some families, like my sister's, this was an ordinary thing. As we walked through the airport, I noted that people were looking at us like we were stars. It was because of the confident Hollywood look of Rikki's relatives. Clearly, representing a flavor unlike the Midwest, they were bold, beautiful and black. They were the epitome of black upper class. Their bags were Louis Vuitton, the shoes were Bally, and the purses were Chanel and Coach.

"So where are your parents?" Thelonius asked. "Are they staying in the same hotel as the rest of us? I would like to have a drink with your father while Clementine and Irma go shopping with your mom."

"It sounds good to me and I can arrange that," I said. "I'm sure my dad would like to take you golfing. Since his retirement a few years ago, it's become a favorite pastime."

"Oh," said Thelonius. "I didn't bring MY golf clubs so I won't be doing much golfing." "It's okay," I said. "You can use mine. I insist. In fact, I can rent a bag while the three of us go out on the course. We should probably make it a foursome since I know Will wants to play." "Oh that's right," Thelonius said sarcastically. "Jane and Will do live here."

"Yes Daddy, remember I told you that. They'll be here for another two weeks and then they're moving to London. Will got a promotion and his job will move them to London for a few years."

"Well, well, well, they are moving up in the world," said Clementine in a sly fashion. "You know Black folks can do just about anything they want to do."

As we came to the car, I opened the doors and the trunk for my new in-laws and aunt. I packed their bags with the precision of a UPS packer and carted everyone off to the hotel.

"So, how do you like living in St. Louis?" asked Thelonius as he turned on the car radio looking for a jazz station.

"Oh, it's not bad, but it's a little slow. I really want to live in Atlanta where both Rikki and I can go to graduate school."

"I see," said Thelonius. "What's so special about Atlanta? What about D.C.?"

"Well, Atlanta is an up and coming town for young black professionals. We want to catch the wave and settle into the area for a while. Eventually, we'll settle into D.C."

"Hmmm," said Thelonius as he zeroed in to the jazz station of his choice. "That sounds like a pretty good plan. I know some of the folks in Atlanta, like Coretta and Joe Lowry. If you guys need anything let me know. I can make some phone calls."

"Thanks, Dad."

It sounded a little weird but it was music to Rikki's ears. She knew her father always wanted a son he could take to ball games and talk to about men stuff. For me, it was interesting and awkward because I also knew Rikki's step-father and considered him a father-in-law as well.

After her father, stepmother and aunt settled into the hotel everyone went out for dinner. This included Rikki's grandmother who everyone called "Granny" and Rikki's mother's best friend Casey. Casey was the reception coordinator. She knew party planning inside out and for the last week worked with Jane to coordinate the reception. Casey was the detail queen and liked to be in charge. We were all having dinner at the hotel so we could go over the reception.

"All right, come come," said Casey as she ordered everyone to the table for dinner.

"The kids are on their way and I want all the parents to sit together in the booth while the kids, Granny and I sit at the adjoining table."

The parents complied and filed in one by one. Meanwhile, we arrived on time. The other thing I could not stand was tardiness. Being on time was not exactly one of Rikki's attributes. She arrived on time when she felt it was important.

"Hi everyone," we said. We hugged and kissed all family members then sat down at the head of the table. Everyone was in a festive mood. We ate chicken, catfish and hush puppies. It was a good southern meal for a Midwestern town.

After dinner, I suggested that we all head to Twins on the south side of St. Louis. The men perked up with this idea because we could talk loudly, drink and listen to some old school jazz. The women were less excited but nonetheless open to a good time. Will, the consummate party animal, assured the visitors that it was a great place and they would enjoy the atmosphere. Mom gave me a stare down, which meant I was being inconsiderate.

"Alright mom, what did I do?" I asked after she pulled me aside where no one else could hear.

"Boy, don't you know that women get a little tired after long meals and long days? We like to go out sometimes, but springing surprises on us is not too cool. Besides, we have a full day tomorrow with the reception. Now, this is your first lesson on being a good husband. Be considerate to your wife and think about her needs first."

I became a little flushed in the face. "Okay, okay," I said rather flippantly. "I was just trying to provide us with a little post meal fun. After the reception everyone will leave so I thought this would be a great opportunity to do something spontaneous."

"Honey, you'll have plenty of time for spontaneity, just make sure you're considerate to your new wife when you want to go out or you'll never live it down."

The drive to the south side of St. Louis took us through the many neighborhoods of the city. We drove through beautiful Forest Park, which was lined with colonial brick and frame homes. As we started edging closer to the southern side of town, the homes and streets looked older, darker, urban and poor. There were more liquor stores on the corner and folks hanging out. As we pulled up to the area close to Twins, you could see rows of cars lined up and a stream of people coming in and going out of Twins. Twins was not much bigger than a corner store, but it had a deep corner lot that was rather deceiving. The outside looked like a dive but once inside, you were in for a treat. We parked the cars next to each other down the block from the club. As we started walking down the street, a group of teens sitting on a porch screamed out, "Hey, you want us to look after your cars? We know you're not from around here."

With that, Will motioned for the young men to come over to him. He talked to them for a short minute. We could all see them shaking their heads and Will pulling out his badge and slowly motioning toward his holster. You could see the eyes of the young men get big. They got the message. Will nodded his head and they went back over to the porch.

"What did you say to them?" whispered Jane as Will approached the group.

"Oh, I just told them I was good friends with the area commander and if I found any piece of our cars missing I was going to have the commander lock them up."

This seemed to calm down the visitors and further impress upon Jane the benefits of being married to a man of the law. Will swaggered over toward Twins with the authority of someone who knew the joint and everyone in it. We followed him into the dark, somewhat loud, wall-to-wall filled club that was the hottest ticket in town.

"Beep! Bop! Tap, Tap, Tap," went the sounds of the saxophones and cymbals.

The sounds coming from the band were crisp and loud. This was the place where Louis Armstrong made his first appearance in St. Louis. The crowd clapped and screamed as the two saxophonists played tit for tat with each other. Of course the sounds were striking but even more pronounced was the identical appearance of the musicians. These were the famed St. Louis Blanchard Twins. They were just returning from the Grammy Awards, where they received an award for Best New Recording Artist in the jazz category.

"Man!" I screamed. "These guys are awesome. I almost have to pinch myself. I almost thought I was in New York."

Rikki nodded in agreement. It made no sense to speak at this club. The place was just too noisy. We tried to find seating by inching through the crowd. It was a futile attempt. No one really budged. We enjoyed the music for about 20 minutes and then I suggested to Will that we go home. I knew my mother was tired and claustrophobic. Crowded places like this actually made her sick. I motioned my parents and in-laws to the door while I held onto Rikki's hand. I could tell that she wanted to go home. We were now a married couple and Rikki wanted to enjoy me. As I led Rikki out of the club, I caught someone staring at me. I wasn't quite sure who it was but I didn't have a good feeling about it.

"Hey Rikki, do you know that guy in the black blazer standing near the bar?"

"Oh, brother. Yeah, I know that creep. He's the guy I dumped about a year ago to be with you. Remember, I told you about him."

"Oh yeah, now, I remember." With that, I stopped in my tracks and gave Rikki a passionate kiss. It left Rikki stunned and dizzy.

"Go 'head, Bro!" screamed one of the musicians. "I know what you're going to do when you leave this place!"

With that, we were out the door and into the summer air.

"Damn Bentley," said Will. "I didn't know you had it in you. You'll be the talk of most offices in the morning. Of course the talk will be coming from all the women who wished their men would do the same."

I laughed. Rikki was still a little embarrassed but pleasantly surprised that I could be so spontaneous. It was one of the things she loved about me. I was never afraid to show my affection for her. It made her feel secure and appreciated.

As we drove back to the hotel, my father was starting to drift off while my mother was wide awake.

"Hey mom, how are you feeling?"

"Oh, I feel better now that I'm out of that crowded club. It was a little claustrophobic but I really liked the music. Those guys were great."

"I'm glad you liked them."

I squeezed Rikki's hand. She was starting to drift away into dreamland. She could feel my warmth flowing through her hand. I knew she couldn't wait to lie next to me. I pulled the car into the space in front of my parents' suite. They ambled out of the car and into the room. I then parked the car in front of our suite. My heart thumped as I nervously swiveled the wedding ring around my finger. I couldn't believe I was married. It was just a few months ago that I had broken up with my old girlfriend and now I have a wife. What seemed like an odd turn of events was beginning to be a family tradition. My father did something similar before he met Mom and my sister did the same thing with Morrelle. It was love at first sight. Being with Rikki gave me an overwhelming sense of joy.

"Mrs. Johnson, let's go pop the champagne and celebrate our first night as newlyweds."

"That sounds good to me, Mr. Johnson. I wonder what that other Mr. Johnson is thinking right now."

"I know exactly what he's thinking and I hope you're up for a little night time fun."

We headed inside the suite. Rikki lit a few candles while I opened the champagne and grabbed two glasses from the kitchen. By the time I arrived to the bedroom, Rikki had changed into a satin negligee that immediately aroused my attention.

"Don't you look delicious," I said. "I can just eat you up like some cotton candy." I immediately stripped off my clothes and jumped into the bed.

By early morning, we didn't want to budge. Our bodies ached and the pajamas and sheets smelled of hot sex on a warm summer night. I turned over to avoid the small ray of sun coming through the window. I was a light sleeper who awakened upon any sign of light in the morning. Rikki on the other hand, slept like a rock and snored like a sailor.

"Damn," I thought. "Maybe she'll grow out of that terrible habit. She sounds like a wild boar." The noise was pretty loud and obnoxious. "I wish I would have known this earlier."

Just as I was getting ready to drift back to sleep, the phone rang.

I shot up from the bed to answer the phone before Rikki awakened.

Crossing the Bridge Over Troubled Water

"Uh, hello."

"Hey, Brat your mother has breakfast for you newlyweds."

My Dad was quite chipper. He was the ultimate morning person.

"Hey Pop, my wife is still sleep. Could you please save some breakfast for us? We'll come over after she wakes up."

"Oh sure son, you know I understand. It took your mother twenty years to come around to waking up with me. Oddly enough, she's now reverting back to sleeping late."

Dad got a kick out of that. He liked to laugh at his own jokes. It was another curse that I inherited. I chuckled at my Dad's call and his amusing early morning ritual. It was something that was ingrained in me.

I stayed in bed, thinking about my new life as a husband. I nervously twirled the wedding band on my finger. It was hard to believe; I was actually married. Rikki slept long and hard. She had a low grade snore that sounded like Fred Flinstone's trademark snore that blew the rooftop off their stone home. I had never slept with a woman who snored. It was a peculiar thing. The snoring reminded me of my dad's snoring. It was one of the things that became an inside joke for me and my siblings.

As the time edged closer to 10 a.m., I nudged Rikki to get up.

"Hey sleepy head," I whispered in her ear. "It's time to get up."

I kissed Rikki ever so softly on her forehead, nose, cheek and ears. She loved the way I woke her up. Early on I learned that if you wake up a person with a greeting and a kiss, their day would go much smoother. As Rikki woke up, she saw the smiling face of her newlywed husband.

"Hey handsome," she said with morning breath. "How's my husband this morning?"

"Oh," I said holding my breath. "I'm doing pretty good now that my beautiful wife is awake. I thought you were going to sleep all day."

"Not a chance," said Rikki. "This is our special day. Tonight we party like some REAL newlyweds."

Lesson 17: Always tell your wife she's beautiful even when she has morning breath.

Chapter 18: Getting Ready for the Move

We got dressed and hung out in my parents' suite. We ate biscuits and eggs and drank mimosas. It was a fitting way to start the day. After brunch, we hung out at the mall looking for accessories for the reception. The day seemed like a dream as we walked hand in hand wherever we went. People smiled at us as it was obvious we were newlyweds. After strolling through the mall, we returned to the hotel to take a dip in the swimming pool. Neither one of us felt stressed because the day went by quickly and smoothly. As night quickly approached, the phone in the suite started ringing.

"Are you guys getting ready?" asked Jane. "Casey and I are going over to the mansion with Ewell. The caterers are going to meet us there. Please don't be late. Casey wants the two of you to greet people as they arrive. We're going to have an official greeting line."

"All right, all right," said Rikki. "I promise we won't be late." As soon as Rikki hung up the phone, Thelonius called.

"Take your time, you're the guest of honor and should be fashionably late," he said. "Surely your mother doesn't expect you to be on time. Hey, Clementine, please tell Rikki that she shouldn't arrive early."

I got a kick out of all of it. This was the life of Rikki as she grew up. Her parents were exact opposites in many ways and she was a combination of both of them. Her mother was prissy and used exact manners, while her father was a bit ghetto, yet exuded a manner of aristocracy. This sometimes volatile combination was the essence of Rikki. All of it represented a combination that was unfamiliar to me.

After calls from her best friends, cousins and uncles, Rikki got ready and eventually left on time. Her mother's influence and wisdom usually won. It was the gentle nature of her mom and ultimate guilt that Rikki felt if she let her down.

"See, see I told you I can make it places on time. I'm not bad at all."

"Don't speak too soon. You have plenty of time during our marriage to be late."

I parked at the rear of the mansion and we entered around the back. We could hear the clatter of dishes and moving feet as people were getting ready.

"Oh here they come," said Casey. "The darlings of the evening. Don't you look absolutely dashing," she said to me. "And Rikki, girl you looked like you stepped out of Essence. Where did you get that dress?"

We responded with laughter and witty comebacks. It was the way in which we played The Dozens with each other. Casey went over the evening program and walked us through the events. She then asked the three-piece band to start playing music as people entered the giant foyer.

"Smile everyone, the fun is about to begin." We greeted everyone like ambassadors at an Embassy event. We spent no more than a minute with each person making them feel as though they were the most important being in the room. We were great actors and everyone knew it. In this case, it didn't matter because it was all for show and fun.

Casey's script was perfect and we followed it to the tee. The toast, the first dance and the cutting of the cake– right from the book of etiquette. The night ended as I cut the groom's cake for everyone to take home. The evening was perfect. All three sets of parents were happy, the guests were happy and most of all, we, the newlyweds, were happy. As the last couple left the mansion, we looked around the beautiful interior filled with preserved wood and ornate chandeliers. The house looked and felt like old money. The cabinets, fixtures and furniture looked like something in a Restoration Hardware Catalogue. The crystal, curios and mirrors all looked stately. This placed embued class.

"You know," I said as I hugged Rikki. "I want us to have a house like this one day where we can build our dreams and raise our children."

"Well," said Rikki. "I know we can do it because you have the determination and pockets full of money to make it happen."

I had to laugh at that because Rikki was being sarcastic about my frugal ways. She knew I could hold onto a buck. We walked out the rear and jumped into the Volkswagen to embark on the beginning of our journey as a married couple.

All three sets of parents left St. Louis within the next few days. We went from having multiple families present to no one at all. When everyone left, especially Jane and Will for their relocation to London, the world for us was pretty lonely.

"Wow, I guess we can't go over Mom's for dinner."

"Nope, we're left to fend for ourselves."

Although I said this jokingly, I was quite serious. Now was the time when we would have to focus on each other. We had to prepare for our relocation to Atlanta and the close-out of our projects and relationships in St. Louis.

The young kids participating in the high school program threw a going away party for us. We were the closest thing to a soap opera for the high schoolers. They loved the vibrancy, ingenuity and fresh perspective that we gave them. In addition, they liked the personal support and recognition we gave. We motivated the students to think beyond their local perspectives and accept a more national view toward school and life.

For the next few weeks, we packed our goods and held a weekend garage sale for the outdated items. In addition, I sold my coveted Volkswagen. It was a hard decision but I looked forward to looking the part of a married man, and the souped-up VW represented the single life. We were coming close to two weeks before the actual move. To keep us ahead of the game, Rikki traveled to Atlanta to find an apartment. Since she attended Spelman for a couple of years during her early attempt at college, Rikki was familiar with the Atlanta landscape.

"Okay, sweetie, I'm ready to go to the airport."

"Sounds good, do you have all the numbers of places you're going to visit and the number for my buddy Tyrone?"

"Yes," Rikki said sheepishly. "I have all the numbers."

Rikki was getting excited about the trip. It would be the first time she returned to Atlanta in eight years. In many ways, leaving Atlanta represented a failure to Rikki but returning with a husband and a bachelor's degree meant she was now in good standing. As a member of the Black elite, Rikki was not about to be "clowned" upon her return to Atlanta. Many of her friends still lived in Atlanta and they would wonder what she had been doing.

"Yes," Rikki thought. "They are going to be in all my business. That's okay because now I have the confidence and the man to do whatever I want."

Crossing the Bridge Over Troubled Water

Marrying me was a departure for Rikki. She usually dated only men from D.C. This was also true of her girlfriends. So, when she announced that she was marrying a man from California, her friends thought she was crazy. It also made me even more mysterious to her friends. California represented an abstract place and surely there couldn't be a Black person of worth outside of L.A. Rikki kissed me goodbye and walked down the landing toward the plane.

"This is going to be a great move," Rikki thought. "All the places we can go and old friends to meet will make this a wonderful place."

It was that optimism and renewed sense of interest in life, that I gave to Rikki. As she thought of me, her stomach fluttered as she started to daze off when the plane rose for takeoff.

Meanwhile, back in St. Louis, I was starting to feel nervous about marriage. It seemed whenever I was alone, temptations started to drift my way. Sometimes it occurred on the street or in the mall. This time it occurred while I was at home cooking dinner.

The phone started to ring. I thought it was Rikki. I looked forward to hearing her soothing voice. As I picked up the phone, I envisioned her sitting on a couch at her girlfriend's house chilling in some shorts and sipping ice tea. I picked up the phone and was surprised by the voice.

"Hello."

"Well, well, well," replied the sultry voice. "You can run, but you can't hide. I got your number from your Mom, who told me the news." I was taken aback as I tried to recall the voice since I was clearly thinking about Rikki.

"Uh, what do you mean hide," I stammered. "I'm not hiding from anyone."

"Sure, so, you were going to leave Cali, get married and not give me a chance to persuade you to think differently?"

I then recognized who it was. JT was a shining star medical student at Stanford. She had the look of a petite Jane Kennedy with a mind like Oprah Winfrey. JT was a tremendous academic who studied hard and played hard. During our college days at UCLA she and I had the hots for each other. We would study late and make passionate love after returning from the library. I messed around with JT for a couple of years. We were great friends who never became lovers. We often kidded about getting married but were never a couple. Our sexual exploits and pushing the limits were always hot on the agenda.

"Sooo, Bentley where's your wife?" JT purred like a kitten.

"Woman, you are real lucky she isn't here. You are really trying to make a brother's life difficult."

We laughed, but JT knew it was something she loved doing – especially to me. With me, JT felt she always played second fiddle. She didn't think it was intentional but she wanted to know my TRUE feelings for her. Somehow, my marriage brought out her TRUE feelings. She was pissed. My marriage hurt JT and she felt that in many ways I didn't consult her first, at least as a friend. What JT didn't know was that I had consulted many people – my siblings and my cousin Cyndi – about me and Rikki.

We talked for about forty-five minutes. It was a pleasant trash-talking conversation that brought back good memories. We didn't decide on a next time to talk. It was an open door policy. The end of our conversation was a bit awkward.

"JT," I said. "I want you to know that I will always love our friendship." I spit out the words with no remorse. In fact, I spit them out so fast that I stunned myself. They also stunned JT.

"Ummm, Bentley, I will always love, you too."
With that, we both said goodbye and hung up the phone.

∼

Lesson 18: When you're married, old girl friends have got to go.

∼

Chapter 19: The Phone Call

After the phone call, I was drained. I felt an uneasy tension in my mind like I did something wrong.

"What did I just do?" I asked myself. "Did I just cheat on my wife?"

I nervously laughed it off and chalked it up to something that all newlywed couples went through. My thoughts were broken by the sound of the phone again.

"Oh shit," I thought to myself. "Who is it this time?"

I composed myself before answering the phone.

"Hello," I said.

"Hi, honey, how are you? I hope you had a good day, we had a great day."

For the next forty-five minutes, we talked about Atlanta and our prospects for housing. Rikki assured me we would be close to Emory University. She talked about the changes to the area and the people she met. She was so proud of her ability to find us a home that she didn't sense the hesitation in my voice. I felt guilty about my conversation with JT, but I was not about to bring it up with Rikki. I hung up the phone and prepared my lunch for the next day. For the next two days,

I had the same routine – come home from work, heat up the food and box things up. I knew my time in St. Louis was short.

When Rikki returned from Atlanta, she was quite excited about the prospects for a new beginning. She couldn't wait to share her expert skill at selecting a new home for the two of us. There was something very romantic and "fantasy-like" to the move. To Rikki, it was a dream come true. As soon as she entered the apartment door, she pulled out the brochures.

"Hi, honey, I missed you," she said as she kissed me. "You are going to be so excited about our new apartment in Atlanta. It's actually in Decatur, but you know what I mean."

Before I could get in two words, Rikki opened up her folder and pulled out the brochures. She described each apartment in detail while strongly advising me of the one that made the most sense. I knew where this was heading and quickly assured Rikki that SHE made the right choice and that everything would be okay with the apartment.

"Baby, you did a great job. I'm glad you spent the time to select our new home." Rikki felt reassured that SHE made the right decision while I KNEW I made the right decision to let her feel empowered. Rikki had never met a man so confident in himself to let her feel empowered.

Now, it was my turn to show progress. I led Rikki into our bedroom where I had stacked the packed boxes and neatly cast aside the trash. But she thought some of those items were not trash.

"Oh Bentley, you should not have placed these folders in the trash. In addition, those old mugs are a part of my collection. You'll need to get a new box to place these items. They are going with us."

I was a little miffed because the items were clearly junk. I knew my wife was a pack rat but I did not know the full extent of it. I decided to pick my battles. I would eventually throw away her things a little at a time so she would not miss them.

Over the next week, we said good-byes to friends in St. Louis. The kids in the summer program were ending their term and were quite emotional about us leaving. We mentored many of them and they were shining examples of what it meant to be young, gifted and black. For many of the youth, we represented the first time a young black couple spent quality time discussing the future, embracing our culture and hearing them out. The professional staff at the university was also sad for our departure. The president of the university dropped by for the first time to tell Rikki that she heard through the grapevine of our effect on the high school students. This meant a lot to Rikki because she thought highly of the president. She was not only her soror, but she was one of the most respected black administrators in the country. As the party came to an end, the director of the department, who also was a black woman, instilled what she thought were a few words of wisdom to us.

"Now I know you believe Atlanta is the Mecca for black people. It's a good place and I should know because I grew up there. You are going to be little fish in a big pond. The attention you get here is not going to be the same there. There are too many well educated black people who are on the ball. If you ever feel like coming back home, we will always have a place for you."

We felt flushed and before Rikki could reply with her lightening quick tongue, I said a few cautious words.

"Well, Dr. Wilson, we'll have to take what you said into consideration. We may not be the shining stars of Atlanta, but perhaps we can learn from the folks that are the stars. We will take our wonderful experience here and apply it wherever we go."

With that, I gave Dr. Wilson a hug, while looking at Rikki and giving her a wink. I knew my wife was seething, but I would temper her until we got home for the "debrief."

"Dr. Wilson, we'll keep you informed of our activities in Atlanta and we will definitely let you know if we need any of your pull to open doors."

I said this to boost Dr. Wilson's ego, since she did provide the opportunities for us in St. Louis.

Later that evening as we were cooking dinner, I started the conversation about the day's events.

"Wasn't that a wonderful party they gave us?"

"Yes, it was wonderful except for those comments Dr. Wilson made," said Rikki. "She always has to have the last word to pull somebody down. She basically said we can't compete with the Black Intellegencia of Atlanta."

"Now, now," I said. "She was just trying to prepare us for the inevitable."

"Which is?" asked Rikki.

"Which is a wonderful place where black folks are on the ball," I smiled.

My comments calmed Rikki down. We did however, talk about the perception of competition in the black Mecca. We talked about the notion of competition being counter culture to those of African descent and how the vestiges of slavery tried to get blacks to compete rather than compliment one another. We vowed not to fall into the trap of pulling down fellow brothers and sisters, especially those trying to climb up the ranks. We called our operational plan to work with other blacks the "collective operative." This notion was based on the premise that if black folks didn't work together, they would be left behind economically, politically and socially.

Rikki enjoyed these deep conversations with me. This was one of the qualities that attracted Rikki to me. I was an intellectual who also respected her intelligence. In addition, I cleaned up after myself. As I cleared the table and washed the dishes the phone rang. It startled me a bit, given my conversation with JT while Rikki was gone.

"I'll get it," said Rikki.

Just then my stomach dropped. I wondered for a split second what I would say if JT asked to speak to me.

"Hello, hello, is anyone there?" With no remorse Rikki hung up the phone. "That's the second time this week that someone has hung up on me."

"Hmmm, perhaps someone has the wrong number."

Rikki rolled her eyes. She had a suspicious feeling that another woman was the culprit. She experienced this problem with a former boyfriend so she knew all the "signals." Rikki thought it could have been my ex-girlfriend. Rikki had stolen me from her and didn't care about anyone else's feelings. She was now married to me and she was going to keep her man.

The apartment looked pretty empty, except for the plaid couch and matching chair. These items along with my VW were to be sold. I composed an ad in the paper to sell the items. It was short and to the point.

"Moving Sale - Great Deal - Car & Living Room Furniture - One Day Only - Call 314-872-9455."

I always got a rush from selling things. I had sold a BMW and two VWs within the last three years. This was one of my trademarks. I didn't stay attached to things for an extended period of time. I was, however, convinced that I would stay with my wife forever. Divorce was not an option.

The next day, the phone rang off the hook. People called and came by most of the day. By lunch time the furniture and the car were sold.

"Well Rikki, it looks like we sold all that we needed to sell. We have some money in our pockets that will last us about three months until I find a job in Atlanta. Let's have some lunch and then head out to pick up the rental truck and car carrier."

We ate lunch on the front steps of the apartment. A couple of neighbors came out to say goodbye. It was hot outside, but it was not unbearable.

"I'm going to miss this place. We made some good friends and really established ourselves as a team. I want to do the same thing in Atlanta."

"We'll do just fine in Atlanta," said Rikki. "We'll have degrees and experience to be one of those power couples."

It had a nice sound to me. I knew we had the potential to rule because we were both driven but not egotistical.

We finished our lunch and left to pick up the truck and car carrier. It took us a while to get everything settled with the car carrier because the wheel mount was tricky. In addition, the rental car company wanted me to feel comfortable with the car attached to the 14-foot cargo van. After completing our transaction, we headed back to the apartment for our final night in St. Louis. Since it was the last night, we wanted to spend the final night right. With just the mattress sheets and no lamps we lit candles around the apartment bathroom and bedroom. We took a shower together and opened a bottle of wine as a treat. As I started to feel the buzz, I gently kissed Rikki on her ear, watching as she started to close her eyes. I then nibbled on her neck and started to slightly lick her neck and move down her chest to her breasts. Rikki started to breathe heavily as she arched her back, releasing herself for me to explore every sensitive junction in her body. Before we both realized it, we were moving in symphony with each other almost like doing the Cha Cha." When we both climaxed, our wet bodies lay pressed up against the shower stall until Rikki realized she was sprayed with water.

"I guess we need to take a shower all over again," said Rikki. I soaked her with soap and rinsed her off. We then dried each other off, brushed our teeth and lathered up with cocoa butter. We then cuddled up tight and went to sleep.

Lesson 19: Communicate your differences before going to bed.

Chapter 20: Atlanta, Here We Come

I rose the next morning with the roosters. I shot right up and jumped into the shower. Rikki was stone cold asleep. She let out a gentle snore that indicated to me there was no getting up any time soon. After the shower I put on my clothes. I slowly stroked Rikki's forehead while bending down to kiss her temple. I knew the slow sensitive way to wake Rikki was the best thing to start the day off right. Rikki smiled slowly. Before she could open her mouth I held my breath. I knew the first word out of her mouth in the morning was enough to kill a fly. Her breath put the S in STANK. After she uttered those first few words, I smiled and told Rikki I would walk to the store to get coffee and donuts for the trip while she took her shower.

The outside air was already humid at 6 a.m. I didn't mind. I only minded if ants or mosquitoes bit my legs. This usually happened in the evening. For some reason, as I walked everything was accentuated. I could hear the birds chirping loudly and the dogs barking at sirens. I realized how St. Louis had grown on me. It was an odd place because the blacks here were politically, but not really socially, progressive. They were not as sophisticated as their northern counterparts in Chicago. St. Louis had its' own rhythm that grew on you—it was part blues, part jazz and a dose of golden oldies.

I bought the coffee, donuts and fruit and headed back to the apartment. The air was thicker as the sun emerged and the temperature rose. I loved this part of the morning, as everything seemed to come to life, yet was still not busy. I recognized a few early risers watering their lawns or exercising and acknowledged them with a wave, smile or a nod. For many, if not all it would be the last time I would see them. When I arrived back at the apartment, Rikki was just finishing her hair.

"Hey early riser—how are all the chickens?" Rikki asked.

Rikki always asked this question because I always got up before the morning's light.

"I'm doing okay and I've got breakfast in the truck. Let's get going."

I stuck out my arm for Rikki to hold onto. This marked the beginning of another chapter in our life.

We were embarking on an exciting time to be heading to the "Modern Day Black Mecca." I started the truck and headed out of the apartment complex. Before I went out the gate, Rikki jumped out to take the apartment door key to the manager's office.

As she got back into the truck she said, "Bessie told me to tell you to treat me right. If not, she'll put a hex on you."

I chuckled, "Yea, she knows I'll treat you right—only if you treat me better." With that, I started the truck and headed out I-70.

This was a familiar scene for us—moving to another part of the country. It was already eighty degrees at 7 a.m. and the humidity made it feel like it was ninety degrees. We were headed in the opposite direction of the busy morning traffic. We didn't miss that aspect of St. Louis. However, we would miss the homey feeling from the older friends who had adopted us. I thought about the people we met and the contributions they made in our lives. I learned a lot from my mentor,

Dr. Mathis. He was one of the few black biological sciences professors I had as a mentor. He was a family man with deep faith from Jackson, Mississippi. I remembered his exact words about marriage, "You are getting ready to join the best institution."

In addition, I learned a lot from Willard and Champagne. Willard and Champagne were funny. Champagne had nervous energy—so nervous that she had to work two jobs. Willard was a super chilled attorney who was sarcastic yet prophetic. They also were one of the first couples we knew to adopt twins. Twins that Willard absolutely adored.

"Yes," I thought, "St. Louis provided a great learning experience for us. It made me grow up and it provided me with the opportunity to meet my wife."

I went into auto pilot mode. I turned on the radio and took in the Missouri scenery. Rikki was starting to snore and I was entering the "B" zone, as I called it. This was the time in which I contemplated life's issues. I switched the stations until I got to oldies but goodies.

"Me and Mrs. Jones, we got a thing going on..."

The song made me think of JT and the fact that she wouldn't be able to find me in "Hotlanta." In some ways I didn't want her to find me but in other ways it boosted my ego to have a little honey on my tip.

"You fool," I thought. "Why would you give up a good thing to fool around with that little honey?"

My retort to myself was, "because she's fine and she's successful." Yeah, it was pretty funny but I was not going to let it get out of hand.

As I headed into my sixth hour of driving, I pulled off the freeway to gas up the truck. "Hey, sweetie," I asked Rikki. "Do you need to take a potty break?" I gently nudged Rikki who was half asleep.

"Yeah," said Rikki. "I need to make a pit stop and get something to eat. By the way, I'm ready to drive."

I pulled the truck into the gas station and filled up the truck. As I looked out across the little town, many of the white town residents looked at me with some dubious distinction—as if a young black male should not have been in their town. I was often amazed how White America perpetuated the stereotypical myth of Black men. It was the badge I would always have to carry.

I watched Rikki as she came out of the bathroom and paid for the snacks and gas. I was becoming more comfortable with Rikki each passing day. Rikki returned to the truck and I handed her the keys.

"All right Pa," said Rikki. "I'm ready to roll."

Rikki took the keys, adjusted the seat and mirrors and revved up the engine. She took a look at the car as we were pulling out of the station. Rikki drove about four hours until it was time for dinner. We found a nice little restaurant that served down home food. I had a chicken dumpling dish while Rikki had liver and onions. During dinner, we mapped out our plans for the next day. We caught up on the local news and watched local people as they came into the restaurant. The people in this little town of Tennessee seemed less surprised by our presence. In fact, they seemed downright comfortable with young blacks. It provided me with some relief that I didn't have to be so guarded in this area. In fact I noticed a number of black, Latino and Asian couples.

"It has to be a function of the University of Knoxville," I said. "These people are a little too cool. There is no other way for this mix of people to be around here."

We therefore decided to camp out in Knoxville. Although we didn't know a lot about Tennessee, this felt like a safe place. We pulled out our meager bags and bought a few snacks at the vending machine. Once we obtained the room, Rikki immediately took to the bathroom for a long hot shower while I listened to the ten o'clock news. The regional news in the Southeast was no different than the Midwest. They had their share of kidnappings, robberies and the growing problem of youth violence. I tried to find Atlanta news, but to no avail. While I waited on Rikki, she called her parents to let them know how things were going. I decided to do the same thing. My mother and father were happy to hear my voice. After getting off the phone with her mom, Rikki chatted briefly with my parents and promptly got into bed. Meanwhile, I jumped in the bathroom and then quickly joined Rikki in bed. We both slept hard as rocks.

As usual, I woke up with the chickens. I went running and quietly packed away the bags. By the time I finished it was 7 a.m. I gently woke up Rikki who slept so hard that drool dripped off the side of her mouth.

"Hey, sweetie, "I whispered, "It's time to get up."

Rikki slowly woke up and stretched as she looked out the window. The sun was rising to partly sunny skies. According to the news, we were headed into a summer thunderstorm. This would be a trend as we prepared for the summer weather of the Southeast. This morning, we showered together. Like many women, Rikki loved to shower with her husband. She liked to watch me shave and have me wash her back. In addition, she loved to see me blush as she teased me about my hard body. I, on the other hand, hated to take showers with Rikki. Although we were married, I was nervous about my body. It was like my "Johnson" had a mind of its own. All Rikki had to do was brush up against my middle section or start to rub my washboard stomach. My Johnson would stand at attention.

"Oh well," I said, "at least I know it works on a regular basis."

After sharing the shower, we dressed, checked out and found the nearest McDonald's. "I'll have a sausage, egg and biscuit sandwich with a large coffee. She'll take an Egg McMuffin with a small decaf coffee and a water to go," I said.

"Oh so, you think you know my taste," said Rikki sarcastically.

"No," I said. "It's just because we've been through this before—remember our trip from California?"

We chuckled, paid for our food and headed back to the truck. I took the downhill trek of Tennessee like a champ. I wheeled the truck with great ease and comfort. The clouds were starting to hover as the sky started to darken. We could hear the deep growl of thunder. Miles away we could see the lightening brighten the sky. Rikki started to fidget in her seat. She hated lightening. Ever since a wall she leaned on as a teenager was "struck" by lightening, her left side often tingled. The memory of that feeling gave Rikki a heightened sense of concern when there was a thunderstorm. I held out my hand to Rikki. She squeezed it tightly, hoping to dissolve the thunderous rain clouds. Rain started to pepper the windshield. Within a matter of minutes, the rain covered the truck's windshield. I slowed the truck almost to a stop until the rain passed.

"Damn, these southern rain storms are a trip," I said. "I can remember similar storms as a kid when we took trips during the summer to visit my aunts in Houston."

"Yeah," said Rikki, "It does get pretty bad in the Southeast. I can remember the storms from my days at Spelman."

I pulled the truck back on the highway. My average speed was fifty miles per hour. The steady rain prevented me from going faster than fifty-five, plus I had to contend with Rikki's nervous comments. By the time we arrived in metro Atlanta, five hours had elapsed. It had been a long trip, but we finally made it. I started to feel relieved but I also felt anxious because we needed to unload the truck. We pulled off to get something to eat in Marietta, Georgia. One of Rikki's girlfriends from D.C. lived in Marietta. During our brief break at Chick Fil-A, Rikki

Crossing the Bridge Over Troubled Water

called Romaine. I overheard the two hens cackling. They talked briefly about the trip and how we would get together at a later date. I stretched my weary body and walked out to the truck to check on the vehicle. Everything was solid. Nothing was out of place. I felt relieved. I hadn't touched the car for the whole trip. As I walked back into the restaurant, Rikki met me at the door.

"Is there something wrong?" inquired Rikki.

"Nope, I was double checking. I wouldn't want us to make it this far to have the car fall off."

We ate lunch inside of Chick Fil-A, and watched our surroundings. It was almost like being in another country. The accents were thick. In this particular part of town, Air Force personnel mixed in with civilians. Blacks were either from the immediate area or were from up North. The whites were definitely from Georgia and many were flat out rednecks. We started to feel this was not a place for us to hang out too long. We felt like we stuck out like sore thumbs. In fact, everything about us read "damn Yankees." I was amazed at how slowly people moved. It was as if everyone thought it was Sunday. The workers moved slowly and the customers moved slowly. You could tell if a patron was from outside the area because they rushed into a line and looked impatient as the line took at least twice as long as it would take in northern areas.

Rikki finished her sandwich about the same time as I did.

"Well, I guess we've got to break in some of the folks around here," said Rikki. "If everyone moves this slowly you know I'll have to jack them up."

I knew my wife liked to talk stuff. This could lead to some trouble in the South.

"Alright Ms. Big & Bad, don't start complaining when you find a swastika on your car." Rikki rolled her eyes and began to say something else but then she thought about it. I always encouraged her not to sweat the little things because they could manifest into larger problems. Rikki knew I was right, but her aggressiveness tried to take over. In her mind, white folks were always trying to get past Blacks or better yet, trying to keep Blacks "in their place."

Growing up in D.C. provided Rikki with a different perspective than mine. Rikki's life was filled with Blacks in positions of power. In fact, her Dad's good friends were Stokley Carmichael, John Lewis and Andy Young. Her life, especially during the seventies was filled with notions of Black power. Rikki's sense of pride and fearlessness came from true empowerment. Not many Blacks could claim her sense of self worth. This is what attracted me to Rikki. She would never sell her soul and she had a personality that would challenge anyone. I, on the other hand, was easy going—unless provoked. My mentality was shaped by a West Coast notion of liberalism mixed with a Catholic notion of selflessness. The seventies and the Panthers didn't affect me, because my Dad told me they could be trouble. I was determined to change my personality and to make sure my children would be instilled with their mother's strong personality.

We headed east on I-285 toward Decatur. On the road, we passed the more austere suburbs of Atlanta. From the highway, we could see new homes being built. Those exiting into these areas were Black. We were starting to feel better about our decision as we approached our new chocolate city.

Lesson 20: Road trips are opportunities to communicate.

Chapter 21: Home Sweet Home

As we entered Dekalb County and approached Decatur, both of us were starting to get antsy. This would be our new home – the "Black Mecca." We would join a host of other black professionals -- young and old -- who were searching for a place to call home. I turned off on Memorial Drive and was immediately stuck in traffic. People were coming home from Sunday church services and Sunday shopping. Our turnoff was in a quaint area called Avondale Estates. The area leading to our apartment was lined with great spruce trees and five-foot shrubs. I started to like the area already.

"What a beautiful area," I said.

We passed a little business district that included a pizza parlor, a veterinary clinic and a laundromat. The houses that surrounded the apartments were old, stately and well kept.

"Wow, this area is pretty amazing, real quiet and clean. I wonder what's up with that." "I don't see too many blacks around here."

"No," said Rikki. "This area is still old school."

Although the Atlanta metropolitan area had a lot of blacks, Avondale Estates had its own niche. It was a quaint and sleepy town that looked "controlled." As we approached the apartment building, we passed a police car sitting at the light. The white officer, who had on reflective glasses, turned his head toward us as we passed him. Immediately, I knew what he was thinking. Before he gave it a second thought, I waved at him. This was my way – a southern way – to break the tension. The officer waved back and nodded to Rikki. I knew this would not be the last time I would see him.

"What was that all about?" asked Rikki. "You know that brothers need to be careful with the law—especially in the South."

"I was just letting the officer know that I was cool and respected him."

"There it is," said Rikki. "You'll need to turn in that driveway where you see the little fountain and beautiful flowers. I'll need to get the keys at the front office."

I turned into the driveway near the front office. Rikki got out and went to the front office. I scoped out the area. I noted the pool, laundromat and general maintenance of the area. It was a well-maintained property with southern charm. It had all the basic amenities—nothing was fancy. Many of the residents had lived there for several years.

Rikki hopped back into the truck. I backed up the truck with the attached car slowly. I didn't want to hit anything in the apartment complex. As we turned around the complex, we could see some of our future neighbors looking out of their windows. I came to our building.

"Is this what you anticipated?" asked Rikki.

"I think it's even better. I can't wait to see the inside."

I parked the car in front of our building. I put on the emergency brake and jumped out to pull the car off the trailer. Meanwhile, Rikki excitedly ran up to our new apartment to look at the inside. She opened the door and stepped inside. There was a note with a basket. "Welcome to Avondale Estates Villas." The basket contained knick-knacks for the kitchen with cheese, sausage and crackers for two. Rikki was really excited now. She really felt at home in this apartment complex and comfortable with her decision. For the next two hours, we unloaded boxes from the truck. Since we didn't have furniture, unloading was not a problem. After completing the move, I took the truck up the street to the drop off station. It was only about a half mile away so I decided to walk back while Rikki prepared our inflatable mattress for sleep. Walking back, I noticed that not many people were on the street. In fact, it was a little eerie. Then I remembered it was Sunday early evening and people were either back to church or inside eating dinner.

"This is definitely the Bible Belt; they don't even sell liquor on Sunday," I thought while walking into the convenience store to get some sweets.

I was a little cautious about Avondale Estates even though it was a sleepy town. I knew that many of the people in the South were polite on Sunday, but if you crossed the line any other day, their true colors would come out. In some ways, I felt at ease in the South because the racism was more blatant. Unlike their counterparts in the North and West, the prejudiced whites of the South didn't hide behind a veil of liberalism.

"I would rather see it coming than to deal with a subverted racist smiling in my face and claiming to be my friend," I thought. "The South is going to be a whole new experience, but I think I'll like it."

I returned from my walk to a nice dinner on the table. Rikki pulled out some of our nice china and candles. We broke open a bottle of wine and reminisced about our trip.

The next few weeks were busy. I found two part-time jobs while going to class in the afternoons. I adjusted well to graduate school. I was popular and well-liked by faculty and students. In addition, I was co-director of a popular math and science program that served Atlanta's inner city youth. I loved the program and the youth who participated in it. They were just as much a motivator to me as I was to them.

Meanwhile, Rikki found a position at Morris Brown College as the director of off-campus housing. Her no-nonsense demeanor mixed with her D.C. attitude and East Coast flair made her a hit with the students. Although they were not accustomed to her straight talk, they appreciated her honesty and guidance. And her style impressed students and staff alike.

Our home life was a challenge. I cooked, washed and cleaned. Although Rikki liked that I did it all, it irked her that I constantly picked up behind her. In addition, I was the money manager. I was meticulous and an avid saver. Rikki, on the other hand, believed that you didn't need to take anything with you to the grave.

"Rikki, you've got to pull back your spending. The bills are stacking up and if we're not careful, we'll be in deep doo-doo. I don't want to spend our hard-earned pennies on some trivial stuff."

I know Rikki was sick of my mouth. I sounded too much like her father. Deep down she knew I was right, but she wouldn't submit to my nagging ways.

"You know what, Bentley?" Rikki asked with a tone of resentment. "You were attracted to this stylish woman so I don't know why you're tripping. I told you I was brought up to live each day to its fullest. You plan too much and are way too cautious. We'll figure out those bills."

I looked at Rikki incredulously.

"There is no way under the sun that we can live this way," I said.

I was so mad that I was shaking. I was getting ready to say something that would make Rikki cry. I felt it didn't matter because I had to tell Rikki how I really felt.

"You know Rikki, you are acting just like a ghetto snipe. You buy material things with designer labels that you can't afford."

Rikki rushed out of the living room. On her way out she screamed at the top of her lungs. "So now you're calling me a ghetto snipe!"

She slammed the bedroom door. I knew this was a big fight, but I had to say something that would result in some change.

"Somehow, someway we'll get over this," I said to myself.

The next couple of days we said few words to each other. I was always one to hold onto anger for days while Rikki was one to NEVER say she was sorry. Eventually, we sat down and worked things out. I agreed to back down on some of the budget things and Rikki agreed to assist with the things at home. I then started to work three jobs – the one at Emory, the job at Macy's and another internship at the Centers for Disease Control.

Since I was more than half way through the program, Rikki decided to obtain her masters in education from Georgia State University. Rikki went to class in the evenings after work twice a week. At the pace she was going, the program would be complete in three semesters.

Lesson 21: Being a newlywed is like being a rookie.

Chapter 22: Planting Our Roots in Atlanta

Over the next year, we barely spent time together except on the weekends. We worked during the day and took classes at night. With a busy schedule on opposite ends of the geographic spectrum, we needed another vehicle and could only afford something in the range of $1,000.

"Hey, Rikki, this commuting thing is killing me. I either ride my bike or catch the bus to school and work. I need to purchase a little knock around to maximize my time."

"You know my theory," said Rikki. "Just get the car."

I knew what that meant—budget the expense and buy the car. I shopped around for a couple of weeks and settled on a Subaru wagon. I bought the car from a good old boy from Lawrenceville, Georgia for $950.00. Things went pretty well for about a week until I took the car to get it registered. The title came up faulty. I tried to reach the seller several times, but was miffed. All forms of communication were met with a big NOTHING, NADA, NILL. I was furious. I filed a claim against the guy and reported him to the county sheriff. I tracked down the Subaru dealership where he worked, and reported that the guy was giving the company a bad name. By the time I was through, the man was ready to return the money and fix the car.

The two of us passing each other in the night was finally getting to us. I quit my evening job at Macy's while Rikki cut back on the hours at Morris Brown. We moved from the apartment at Avondale Estates to an apartment closer to Emory. The change cut the monthly rent from $450 per month to $250 per month. And I really didn't need a car anymore. I could walk to school. The financial burden was finally letting up. I felt relieved and I also felt the extra time could be spent focusing on my master's thesis. My thesis advisor was the woman who recruited me to the school while another committee advisor was the director of minority health for the Centers for Disease Control. The last person on my committee was a young professor from California. My thesis was a project that focused on the delivery of healthcare and social services around an elementary school. The school was in the city of Decatur, but it was on the wrong side of the railroad tracks. When I first visited the area, I walked there to get a true sense of the surroundings. As I walked across the railroad tracks, the area changed. I saw people hanging outside of old unkempt houses. There were areas with dirt roads and no sidewalks. The "business district" consisted of abandoned buildings, an auto shop with old cars, and an old laundromat. I walked past the District and nodded at the neighbors who eyed me. I stuck out like a sore thumb, so I decided to take a chance to divert the attention.

A little boy on a dirt bike flew past me and I yelled out, "Hey, are you headed to Second Avenue School?" The little boy nodded.

"I'll give you five bucks for a ride!" The little boy stopped on a dime.

"I'll take you to Second Avenue," the little boy screamed back.

I hopped on the bike and the little boy stood on his pegs on the back wheel. The little boy directed me to go straight down the street for three blocks. We came upon a school that was nicely landscaped with red bricks that looked relatively new. I stopped the bike and pulled out a crisp five-dollar bill. The little boy smiled and asked me if I needed a return ride from the school. I said no, but mentioned I would catch him the next time I came to Second Avenue.

I entered the building and talked to the receptionist. She asked me to sit down to wait for the principal. Mr. Jones, the principal, was close to retirement. He was a former Army staff sergeant who ran his school like his company. The students and school were orderly. Although the students were from the lowest rung economically, they did not feel that way when they were at school. In fact they all followed Mr. Jones's motto, "When the students come to school, this is their sanctuary."

Mr. Jones studied me for a brief moment and then asked a series of questions designed to give him an understanding of my motives for studying his school. After forty-five minutes of discussion, he told me he was glad to have me on board. He then gave me the name of three parents. They were all officers in the Parent Teachers Association and would be my ambassadors. One of the teachers offered to take me to the bus stop on the other side of the tracks. I took her up on the offer and headed home. As I headed home, I looked at the kids and schools that were on the north side. These kids had the "stable" home environment and the additional resources to get higher grades. The kids on the south side were the exact opposite. Single parent homes, multiple people in homes and a general environment of poverty were the status quo for the south side. When I arrived home, I cooked dinner and thought more about the community on the south side. I could not believe the differences in the communities. The Southside was a step back in time. It was a rural mentality in an urban setting. I felt this project would be more than just a master's thesis. It was going to be a calling.

When Rikki arrived home from work, I had everything ready. She was in the apartment less than two minutes and I couldn't wait for the question.

"So how was your day, honey?" asked Rikki.

"Oh, it was pretty cool. I found a forgotten community in Decatur. In fact, they call it South Decatur."

I talked about South Decatur through dinner, dessert and up to bedtime. I was so excited about the area that I dreamed about it. The next few months I experienced the intricacies of the Second Avenue students, parents and broader community. I conducted door-to-door interviews with members of the PTA. In addition, I talked to social service agencies and the public health department. I found the gaps in services and assisted in establishing a network of health care and social services for the Second Avenue students and their families. The network I established matched premium health care in the white community. I won over the PTA of Second Avenue along with the director of public health policy of the United Way. On top of the success I was having with the Second Avenue project, I held an office in the student government and found time to teach kids golf on the weekends. Rikki had her own successes. The dean of the School of Education liked her research so much that he suggested that Rikki work with the famed African historian Asa Sumpter. Rikki was so successful in her research and coursework that she earned an assistantship with Sumpter for a semester. We were becoming quite the couple. The success and popularity we had at our respective institutions were gaining the interests of our college administrators. It was much like our success in St. Louis, but on a much larger scale.

Lesson 22: Be open to change; you can't plan for everything.

Chapter 23: An Opportunity of a Lifetime

As other graduate students at Emory University were preparing to work at the Centers for Disease Control, I was considering a special offer from a major urban renewal initiative of the former president of the United States. He was one of the most popular presidents and my work at Second Avenue captured the interest of one of his aides.

"Bentley, the work you've done at Second Avenue is a part of what we would like to achieve on a much larger scale," said Alice Browner. Alice worked with the former president as a domestic policy advisor and she followed him back to Georgia to work at his center.

"The work I did was special, but the people I worked with defined the community and the project. The key was gaining the trust and respect of the parents and the principal."

My words confirmed what Alice had heard from the many people she interviewed about me. Unbeknownst to me, Alice had me scoped out by a few folks. She knew about my high school, college life and political affiliation.

"All in all he's a solid guy who would be a great coordinator for the project in Decatur," thought Alice. "His only problem is that he's an outsider looking in."

I finished my interview with Alice. In her mind, it was a done deal, while I wondered if I made the cut.

After the interview, I drove to Georgia State University to pick up Rikki. She was just getting out of her afternoon class. I waited in the car lot across the street from her building. As I looked at the students coming from the building, I thought of how far we had come.

"Hey dream catcher," Rikki said as she approached the car. "It looks like you've been day dreaming."

"Yeah, it's been one of those days when everything has been hitting me at once."

"Well what are you talking about?" said Rikki as she pecked me on the lips. Her face started to crease. She thought I was going to drop a bomb on her. I started the car and kicked it into reverse. On the way home, I told Rikki about the opportunity I was offered. Rikki was pleasantly surprised, but more importantly, she was proud of me. The job was a giant step for me but it was an even more important step for us as a couple because one of the requirements of the position was to move into the city limits of Decatur. I thought it was important that we live in South Decatur.

For the rest of the evening, we talked about our options and opportunities for the future. We talked about living in Decatur and raising a family. By the end of the evening, we were both excited about the prospects of living in Decatur. The opportunity to work for the former president was the icing on the cake. To assure I was ready, Rikki prepped me on the questions I should ask Alice Browner before I accepted the position. We both felt good about the answers. This marked the next phase in our lives. We paid our academic dues and were looking for the social and economic reward.

"Bentley," asked Rikki. "Do you remember what Marva said when we left St. Louis?" "Oh yeah, how can I forget it? She said once you leave St. Louis you're going to be a little fish in a big pond. The success you had in St. Louis will probably not transcend to Atlanta."

"How wrong she was," said Rikki. "We've done more than she would have imagined and we didn't have to force it."

"Yes," I said. "We're a pretty dynamic duo."

The next day, I went to class and attended a meeting with my graduate advisor. My advisor was instrumental in getting me to attend the school. Whenever I saw her, I got a little nervous because it was like she saw right through me. Katie Kavanaugh was a long-time professor at the School of Public Health who was way before her time. Her specialty was behavioral modifications for populations susceptible to AIDS. This gray-haired white woman with horn-rimmed glasses was from California, but was a fixture in Georgia politics.

"So Bentley, what kind of offer did Alice give you?" said Katie.

I was a little stunned at first but I knew she asked out of concern.

"They offered me 33K per year and told me I had to live in the city of Decatur. The salary is not bad, but I'm researching the benefits." Katie gave me an incredulous look.

"Bentley, you know I am an employee of the university. I have a pretty good idea of the benefits—just ask me."

I felt pretty stupid, but didn't let on.

"Okay, Katie so you got me. Please tell me what benefits are available to Emory employees."

Katie in her motherly tone gave me the breakdown of the health benefits, retirement and the added bonus of education benefits such as earning another degree and having a child's education paid through the university. Katie loved being a teacher in class, especially loved being a teacher in life. I realized I was getting schooled, but didn't mind.

"Bentley, I think you should go for the position, but keep in mind that it will be a challenge."

I acknowledged Katie's wisdom. I shook my head and listened. Katie's reasoning was right on target. For the next two hours I relaxed before taking off to the interview at the Presidential Center.

When I arrived at the Presidential Center, I was totally "chilled." I was about fifteen minutes early and took the opportunity to check out the people going into the center. As I entered the front door, the receptionist, an elderly black woman, asked my name.

"Hi, I'm Mr. Johnson"

"Oh you're Mr. Johnson. We're glad to see you. Alice and the first lady are looking forward to meeting you."

I smiled and tried to play off how surprised I was to have the first lady in my interview. I took a seat in the suite where the receptionist directed me. While waiting, I viewed the pictures on the wall of the former president in action—using his diplomatic skills to win over people and countries. Just as I was starting to day dream, the doorknob started to turn. I became acutely aware of who was entering. Two women came in. I was familiar with both of them—one was Alice Browner while the other was the first lady. I stood up to greet both of them. For the next hour and a half I was in "the zone." I felt totally comfortable talking to both of them about my outlook for Decatur and ways in which I believed I could get the community to get behind the center's new initiative. After forty-five minutes, the first lady left and said she looked forward to working with me. When she left, Alice congratulated me on a good interview and then wanted to talk salary. Once we got past the salary issue, everything was good. I agreed to start in two weeks. Alice shook my hand and welcomed me on board. As I walked past the receptionist, I told her good night. She quickly responded with a wink and "good night sugar and welcome on board."

Crossing the Bridge Over Troubled Water

The drive back home was relatively quick. I drove quickly along Ponce de Leon Avenue past Fernbank Museum and the Fernbank School. I loved this drive home because it was so scenic. The large pine trees and southeastern foliage made midtown Atlanta a beautiful place. What made Ponce de Leon even more special were the large homes that were built by the famous southern architect Neil Reed. As I turned left on North Decatur Drive past Katie's house, I immediately thought about her words of wisdom. I chuckled to myself and made a mental note that I would follow up with her the next day. When I pulled into our apartment complex I saw that Rikki was home. I couldn't wait to share the news with her. I was quite excited. To me this meant we could finally start to live like adults rather than living like students.

I turned off the car and pulled my bag from the back seat. I said hello to the neighbors and headed up the steps. As I pulled out my keys, I could smell the aroma of something cooking. The scent was Cajun but also Italian. My senses were now heightened. The sound of Stanley Clark and Chick Corea played loudly in the background. As I walked in the door I saw a beautifully decorated table with a full setting for two. The wine and water glasses were on the table as were the salad bowls and bread plates. I was hungry before I started the drive home but now I was definitely starving.

"Hey, sweetie," said Rikki as I walked through the door.

"I made a pasta dish that includes your favorite ingredients."

"Wow!" I said, "This looks and smells great. Everything is beautiful."

We pecked each other on the lips. I laid down my briefcase in the front closet and took off my jacket. Rikki then went to the kitchen to serve the food. While she served up the food, I changed my clothes. By the time I was finished the candlelight dinner was on the table.

"Baby, this is great. What a wonderful treat as a homecoming."

Rikki smiled. She knew the dinner was a hit. In fact, she even amazed herself. This was not something she was accustomed to doing. Most of the men she had been with in the past were not gentlemen and wouldn't really appreciate what she did.

"Well, tell me about your day," Rikki said.

I talked for about an hour and was pretty excited. This new job meant we could move out of the apartment and into a single-family home. Rikki was beginning to see herself in a new home. Although I was not quite ready to move, it was nonetheless a shared goal. The big issue for us was to decide where we would live, since the requirement of the position was to live in the community of the project.

"I'll get my cousin Sonya to show me around South Decatur for a place to live," said Rikki.

"Sure, go ahead."

Lesson 23: No matter where you are, people watch your actions.

Chapter 24: The Graduation Surprise

I didn't think Rikki would find a place, so I wasn't worried. I thought we would live in an apartment in downtown Decatur until we found a house to really suit our needs. Little did I know how fast my wife could work, if she put her mind to it. By the end of the week, we were scheduled to sign a contract for our single-family home.

The next day I completed my paperwork at human resources. It was a place I visited many times in the past, thinking I could get a real job at the university to pay for school. For some reason, I could never get a job at the university. It was as if the H.R. department knew I was a graduate student and wouldn't hire me. So I savored the moment when I arrived as an employee. I completed the general paperwork for health insurance and retirement. In addition, I listened to an overview from a H.R. specialist. All in all, I felt right proud to work for Emory University. After completing the paperwork, I went to the School of Public Health to see Katie. Everything was winding down at school, students were completing exams, graduation robes were coming in and the school was preparing for a flood of guests from around the globe.

"Hi Claire, I was looking for Katie. Did she come in today?" Claire was Katie's longtime assistant. She kept everything in order for Katie. In fact, she could probably run Katie's programs.

"Hey, Bentley, she's on the road in the northwestern part of the state, but I anticipate she'll be back by early evening. Is everything okay?"

"Oh yeah, it's all good. I just wanted to share a little good news."

"You must mean about your job," smiled Claire. I could only smile.

"My, my, word gets out very fast. Yes, it is about the new job. Please tell her that she was right about everything."

Claire then whispered to me, "Are you ready to receive the award during graduation?"

I looked stunned. "Ahh, yes, you could say I am ready to receive the award." I had no idea what Claire was talking about. I tried to play it off. After leaving a note with Claire and chatting with some of my classmates, I decided to head home. All the way home I replayed the conversation with Claire.

"She did say I would receive an award, right?" I asked myself rhetorically. I would tell Rikki the story when I arrived home, to see what she thought of the story.

As I returned home, I thought about my parents coming out for the graduation. I knew they would be proud of my accomplishments at graduate school and the news of my new job. I knew my Dad wanted me to attend medical school, but I had other thoughts. Medical school was now the last thing on my mind. I had received my acceptance letter from Emory's School of Medicine. It was an important accomplishment but I was no longer impressed. In fact, I thought that owing $100,000 from medical school plus the $40,000 for grad school was too much. In addition I talked to my brother-in-law, who told me the profession was not what it used to be. With a clear conscience but without a clear plan, I moved forward with my life and wife.

Crossing the Bridge Over Troubled Water

When I got home, I decided to cook dinner for Rikki to reciprocate the great dinner she had fixed me. I cleaned up the house, put on some smooth jazz and started to grill some salmon in the little habachi on the back porch. I dreamed of purchasing a nice southern home with a big yard and trees for our kids to play. I heard Rikki coming through the door.

"Hey, sweetie," I said. "How are you?" Rikki paused before answering as if she was holding something back.

"I'm okay."

"You don't sound okay. What's up?"

"It's my damn supervisor," said Rikki. "That woman is crazy. I think she's jealous of me because she tries to sabotage everything I do."

"She's just mad because you're smarter than she is and more beautiful," I said while massaging Rikki's shoulders. "Let me pour you a glass of wine and you can take it with you while you change your clothes."

"Now that's a plan," said Rikki.

I opened a bottle of Californian wine and poured two glasses. While pouring, I decided that I would not tell Rikki about the graduation award. It was time to focus on her issue, not mine. I finished cooking the salmon, cous cous and asparagus. In addition, I had sour dough bread and key lime pie for dessert. Since we lived so close to the DeKalb Farmer's Market, I could pick up romance foods anytime. Rikki returned from changing her clothes. She had on a silk robe that revealed the cleavage of her breasts and outlining of her nipples. I could feel my Johnson enlarge with blood. It was as if someone had opened the flood gate.

"Well, let's have dinner because I know who's going to be for dessert."

We both laughed and finished off the wine. That night Mr. Johnson would have the opportunity to do his thing while Rikki released her stresses.

The next day I woke up thinking about graduation and talking to my parents. My parents insisted on staying at a hotel for graduation. One of my cousins worked for Marriott and she gave my parents a complimentary room every time they came into town. My dad was everyone's favorite cousin, so he received the hook-up wherever he went. Atlanta and the history of the Atlanta University Center really attracted and amazed my father. He was grateful for the success I had at Emory University, but was more impressed with the mass production of black professionals and scholars from Morehouse and Spelman. Although I was graduating with a good job at the prestigious Presidential Center, my father still believed he could steer me to Emory's School of Medicine if I re-applied the next year. At my father's request, I deferred my admission into medical school for a year. It was strange to him that I decided not to attend med school given all the headaches I'd been through to get admitted. In his mind, now was the time for me to live *his* lifelong dream.

Rikki and I picked up my parents from Atlanta Hartsfield Airport. We decided to meet them at the gate since the airport was so big.

"Hey, Mom; hey, Dad."

I gave my mom a hug while Rikki hugged my dad.

"Hey kids," said Dad.

I gave my dad a handshake, since he never hugged men. I thought it was a little odd, but never questioned it because men in Dad's era did not show emotion. I took my parents' bags and placed them on a rented cart. The four of us then proceeded to the parking lot. Although my Dad had never lived in a "chocolate" city, he loved them. In his mind, the self-esteem of a child would increase four fold if they saw blacks in positions of power.

"So what's happening in the "chocolate" city?" Dad asked with a chuckle. "What's up with the mayor? Is he ready to make a run for Congress?"

Dad knew all the right questions and often knew the answers as well. It was his way of testing a person's knowledge about an area.

"He's all good," I said. "We're vying for the Olympics. If we get it, the economy will be boasted significantly. The Olympics would put this city on the map and the mayor would probably make a run for Senate." I chuckled at how fast those facts rolled out of my mouth.

"I see you've been keeping up with what's happening."

We drove around town and took my parents on a tour of the city. We also ate at The Beautiful Restaurant where my dad saw the wall of fame, which highlighted all the civil rights leaders who had eaten there. After eating a late lunch we drove to our apartment and Rikki convinced my parents to stay at our apartment for the evening rather than stay at the hotel. We were all quite tired and called it a day by 8 a.m.

I woke up early the next morning on graduation day. I decided to take a run to clear my mind and to think about the day. I loved the mornings because I owned the streets, especially if it was still dark. As I put on my shorts, T-shirt and running shoes, I heard my Dad getting up for coffee.

"Good morning Dad."

"Hey son, where do you keep the coffee?"

I went into the kitchen to pull out the coffee and coffee maker. I also pulled out the honey and Half & Half that Dad liked to put into his coffee. I then proceeded to get out the cereal, wheat bread, bowl, coffee cup, silverware, and cloth napkin. Dad wanted to be treated special when he was at his children's homes. I knew dad's m.o. and decided to accommodate him. Once I got Dad straight, I ran out to North Decatur Road and jogged toward downtown Decatur and headed to South Decatur. When I arrived to the area that would be my home base, I visualized what it would be like if it was developed. I really liked this area. It was a country within a country.

"Hey, Mr. Johnson," said a little kid riding on a bike.

"Hey, Michael, what are you doing up so early?" I knew exactly what he was doing up so early. He was a runner for the local drug dealer. Each morning, he would make a pick up on his bike. Michael made good money for his family. At ten years old, he made more money than his mother and didn't have to work half as hard.

"All right Michael, I'll see you next week."

I looked at my watch. It was time to head back home. I said goodbye to my new home for the moment and thought about the task at hand, which was to graduate. I ran back through downtown and past Katie's house. Although I didn't see Katie, I did wave to the house thinking that she was the one who gave me the opportunity to succeed. I coasted into the apartment complex parking lot. I returned to the apartment where my father was reading the paper and sipping his coffee. We talked for about an hour before the women got up. For the next hour, everyone was busy eating breakfast and talking about the logistics of the day. Rikki and I used the bathroom at the same time while my parents got dressed. My parents showered the night before, so they were ready to move in the morning. After we got dressed, we hurried to the car. The apartment was only five minutes away from campus, but with traffic it could take forty-five minutes.

"I'll take the back roads and we'll get there in no time," I said.

I navigated Rikki's car through the residential area and into an area where the graduates were lined up. I stopped the car near the School of Public Health and got out.

"Okay Rikki, you can park on campus near the building where I used to work. The sticker on the car will allow you to park in the faculty lot. This will get you closer than the other folks."

I gave Rikki a quick peck on the lips before I was off running with cap and gown folded over my arm.

"See you Mom and Dad!"

I was still lightening quick and before they knew it, I was inside the building. Rikki put the Volkswagen in first gear and was off to the parking lot.

I arrived just in time to get the directions from the assistant dean.

"Okay, Bentley," said the dean. "You will lead the group by holding the class banner." I was stunned. I nodded and let the dean continue. My buddy Graden elbowed me in the ribs and whispered in my ear.

"You should have told me about handling the school banner. You're just full of surprises." I did not say a word because I knew he wouldn't have believed me. I talked to a few of my classmates and exchanged numbers and addresses.

"Okay students, let's line up," yelled the dean. "We're getting ready to march through the yard."

I lined up front and grabbed the school banner. It was a salmon color with white letters and blue outlining. You could barely see me. I walked in with the distinguished speakers and school administrators. I walked past my parents and Rikki. They were all very proud and I could feel their eyes locked on me as I passed and approached the stage. Like the other banner bearers I dropped off the banner behind the stage before lining up with my class.

The speakers were all fairly mundane except for Bishop Desmond Tutu. His daughter was graduating from the School of Public Health, and he pointed this out. His speech was a testament to the struggles he overcame during apartheid and the challenge of HIV and AIDS in his country. After his speech the school presented the special awards.

"This year's Humanitarian Awardees are Maxine Bilstein and Bentley Johnson," announced Emory's president. Both students exemplify the essence of our public purpose to the community."

Both of us approached the stage and received our awards. We shook hands with president and Bishop Tutu. I was especially happy and honored to meet Bishop Tutu. Although I was normally not star struck, I wanted to have Bishop Tutu's autograph on the back of my award certificate. At the end of the ceremony I made sure that Bishop Tutu signed my certificate. After I returned to my seat, I was beaming. It was one of the best moments in my life. I turned to look around for Rikki. When I saw her, I gave her a wink. The rest of the ceremony was a blur. I barely heard any more speeches. At the end of the ceremony, I threw my hat in the air and screamed. My colleagues did the same. I then made my way to Rikki and my parents. I introduced my parents and Rikki to a few of my professors and classmates. Each person said they were so proud of me and that they looked forward to hearing great things about me. I beamed and expressed gratitude at having been given the opportunity to succeed.

When everything was over we went out to dinner at the Atlanta Fish Market. It was the first time that my parents had been to an upscale restaurant in the new South. My father was amazed at the level of sophistication and new money. He glanced around the room and just smiled.

"I'm glad you guys moved to Atlanta. There are so many opportunities for young blacks.

I gave my father a nod and smiled. After dinner, we headed back to the apartment. My parents prepared for their return to California while Rikki and I reminisced about the day. Rikki talked about the speech by Desmond Tutu while I mentioned the sidebar comments by my fellow graduates. We finally went to sleep around midnight.

The next day, we took my parents to the airport. Just before getting dropped off, my father imparted some wisdom.

"The two of you are doing a great job. It always takes two to make a marriage work." That phrase stuck in our heads. Our success was based on teamwork.

Lesson 24: Success is easier with a good partner.

Chapter 25: New Job-- Big Responsibilities

On the way home, we passed through South Decatur to look at the area.

"Wow," said Rikki. "I still can't believe this area. It looks like the country."

"Even though the area looks rural, don't be fooled. We are still in a city."

"It has so much potential," said Rikki. "The people here just don't know or have the vision."

We drove around the area to check out our soon-to-be neighbors. We noted those houses that were in good shape and those in disrepair. On our way to the apartment, we talked about our vision for the area.

For the next two weeks, I relaxed, played golf, lifted weights, and rode my bike. It was a tranquil two weeks that gave me an opportunity to put things in perspective before I began my job. It helped me realize that medical school was not the best thing for me. I talked to my advisors and mentors at the School of Public Health. They all said to use my experience and intuition to get the job done. I was starting to get excited about The Metropolitan Project because this job would require intuition and experience. A long article came out in the Atlanta-Journal Constitution about the project and the former president. I was in the article along with the three other coordinators. It was the first time I had seen my name in the paper in the context of a professional position. The interesting thing about it was that I had not officially started. I sent the article to my father who could not believe it. My father then told several relatives that I was working for the former president. I felt good, but was nervous because everything was starting the next day.

I woke up at 5 a.m. on Monday morning. I took a quick jog through the neighborhood and appreciated the sleeping world. My second wind kicked in as I coasted along North Decatur Road. It was just me and the animals darting down the street. Occasionally, I would see someone picking up their paper from the porch. If I made eye contact, I would wave to them and wish them a good day. I headed back home as the sun rose and eased into the apartment complex. By now, the birds were chirping and the paper man was coming through. I caught the paper and opened up the front page. On the front page, I read an article with the headline, "The Metropolitan Project's Befuddled Beginning." I was flabbergasted. My heart started to race as I thought about the first day. As I walked into the house, Rikki sleepily emerged from the bathroom.

"Honey," I said with an anxious tone. "We're in today's paper and it does not look too good."

Rikki yawned and acknowledged that she somewhat understood what I was talking about. Then she went back to bed.

I decided to cook bacon, grits and toast for breakfast. While my grits heated up, I read the rest of the article. I could not believe that I was going into a controversial job. Everyone in the region was aware of the initiative. With the fame of the former president, the project was bound to gain international recognition. After breakfast, I took a shower and put on my suit. By that time, Rikki was slowly waking up. I gave Rikki a kiss then picked up my lunch and headed out the door.

"I love you, sweetie. I'll call you during the middle of the day." I headed out the door in my favorite navy blue suit and black leather bucks.

I headed down Scott Boulevard and onto Ponce de Leon Avenue. The traffic was heavy but tolerable. As I took a left toward Little Five Points, I saw the sign for The Presidential Center. Upon entering The Presidential Center, I gazed at the flags representing all the countries that had worked with the Center on democracy issues. I parked my car in the employee parking lot and headed to the front door with the first day jitters of a kindergartener.

"Why hello, Mr. Johnson," said the older black woman who worked the front desk. "I knew you would be joining us. My name is Phyllis" I smiled and responded, "I'm glad to be here, but I know the real work is just beginning."

Phyllis called my supervisor, Mr. Mack Benson, to the front. I exchanged pleasantries with Mr. Benson and headed to the back office.

"So are you ready to get started?" asked Mr. Benson.

"Yes, I am."

"We will meet the first lady and her advisor for Decatur, Mr. Aaron Brooks. Mr. Brooks will oversee your work. They are waiting for us in the first lady's quarters."

Mr. Benson and I headed over to the first lady's quarters. We met with Mr. Brooks, a short, Morehouse-looking man with a wispy moustache and piercing eyes.

"Hello Bentley, I'm pleased to meet you," said Mr. Brooks. "The first lady will come out in a moment but before she meets you, I want to be very clear that you should consult with me before talking to the first lady. I will handle any correspondence you need from her."

I was a bit miffed by Aaron Brooks but I complied because of the first lady. Aaron Brooks was an Atlanta native who had the right pedigree. He had graduated the same year as Spike Lee and he felt every bit as famous although no one knew him outside of Atlanta. Aaron was able to gain the confidence of the first lady because his boss was a confidant to the former president. Aaron had his hands in everything and wanted me to carry out *his* plans.

When the first lady came out, I quickly arose. She had a stately air about her. I had never met the Queen of England but now understood what it was like to be near royalty. The first lady was friendly, witty and funny. She immediately took to me and gained my trust. I knew, however, there would be a problem with Aaron Brooks. As I left the meeting with my marching orders Aaron Brooks made a sly remark.

"I'll call you tomorrow morning so you can move into the community center."

I didn't reply, but I did look at Aaron incredulously. The community center Aaron mentioned was old and dilapidated. Aaron had been a board member of the community center for years and he figured this was the best way to fulfill two needs. He could finally get the center renovated with the Metropolitan Project money and he could be seen as the hero in the community.

I headed back to my cube at the Presidential Center and reviewed the conversation with the first lady and Aaron Brooks in my mind.

"Somehow I need to stay clear of Aaron Brooks so I don't become his puppet." I said to myself. "I do not want to get caught up in the mess of the community center and the personality of Aaron Brooks."

I jotted down the list of the neighborhood hell raisers and ventured off to make appointments with them. I figured they would give me the true "skinny" on Aaron Brooks and his relationship with the Decatur community.

My first appointment was with Joan Liptrot. Joan asked me to come to her house the same day. She wanted to know my background and to gain more insight on how the president's project would help her help the black children who lived on the other side of the tracks. When I drove up to Joan's house, I had to take a deep breath. In the front of her house was a sculpture of a rising phoenix. I heard Joan believed she was the savior of South Decatur. I knocked on her door and heard Joan talking to her husband.

"Elmer, I'll answer the door."

I could hear her mumbling as she walked to the door.

Joan was a retired preschool teacher who had a weakness for Bailey's N'Cream. Joan had cloud-white hair that stood out like the bride of Frankenstein against her brownish-red skin. She wore a car coat and furry pink slippers. She was like a lifelike character out of the muppets.

"Mr. Johnson, I'm so glad you could make it. Would you like to have a cup of coffee with Bailey's?" she said swirling around her cup.

I declined the Bailey's offer, but asked for some coffee. I looked at the Liptrot family pictures as Mrs. Liptrot went to the kitchen. The Liptrot family consisted of three children—two daughters and a son. The son was an army veteran with post-traumatic stress disorder. One daughter had a family of her own while the youngest daughter stayed at home with her parents. She was the cause of Mrs. Liptrot's desire to change the local school system. Joan Liptrot felt her daughter's demise started and ended with the school system. From the elementary school to the high school, Joan felt the teachers isolated her daughter and intentionally crushed her confidence. As a result, Joan was on a mission to protect black children from the inequities of the school system.

Crossing the Bridge Over Troubled Water

Joan walked into the living room with coffee, cream and sugar while I gazed into the Liptrot family pictures.

"That picture right there is my husband and me on our fifth wedding anniversary," said Joan. "We were in Savannah, Georgia. Savannah was the best vacation place for black people at the time. In fact, it was one of the few places we could go without getting harassed."

We exchanged stories. By the end of the evening, I felt I knew Joan pretty well and understood her intentions with the school system. I also knew she could be a thorn in my side if she did not trust me.

I headed home after leaving Joan's house, feeling a little overwhelmed by the fast pace of the day on the job. Each day I usually started work at 9 a.m. and ended by 9 p.m. To see Rikki, I arrived home by 6 p.m. and ate dinner. By 7 p.m., I was back out coordinating or attending a neighborhood meeting. The only nights I did not work were Friday, Saturday and Sunday. "Hey, honey," said Rikki. "You're working pretty hard. Are you starting to get tired?"

"No, I'm not getting tired. I'm just trying to settle into my position to understand Decatur."

I was the typical Type A personality. I worked very hard and thought about work in my sleep. South Decatur was now my passion. It was a place I literally dreamed about.

I was beginning to worry Rikki. She did not want to bug me, but she was starting to lose her husband. After six months of the long days and nights, she decided to join me. Rikki talked to her thesis advisor about her quest. She wanted to work for the university as a liaison to the community. Her thesis advisor, who was one of the key confidants to the university president, suggested that the university needed a liaison to the new Metropolitan Project. The president of Georgia State University agreed to appoint Rikki to the position. Now, we could see each other almost every day professionally. It was a match made in heaven. I represented the people. Rikki represented the academy. I was often seen in khakis and a dress shirt, while Rikki wore polished suits. We were the model couple; winners in the minds of many. I led community revitalization meetings and worked on projects for at-risk youth. Rikki carried the responsibility of connecting higher education opportunities to Atlanta's rising communities. Rikki shared my passion and was able to get the university to sponsor a scholarship program that guaranteed a full ride for high school low-income students who graduated with B plus averages.

Lesson 25: Success comes with a price.

Chapter 26: The Emerging Leaders

Kids from the local community loved us because of our interest in their future and because we lent them an ear to air daily issues. They stopped by our house after school and on weekends. Often, when the two of us came home in the evenings, we would see the kids coming from our house. In fact, once the kids saw our cars coming, they would run up to catch us. We loved kids and it showed. We spent time guiding the young people to personal and academic success. Community members recognized our efforts and edged Rikki to run for office. At first she was amused by the offer, but then started to think about the possibility of representing the needs of many students. Politics was in her blood. Her father was a politico." He ran campaigns and was the machine behind D.C.'s government. He was known as the "king maker."

Rikki decided to call her Dad to get input on what to do.

"Daddy," said Rikki. "They want me to run for the school board."

"Are you serious?" asked her father.

"Yes, they are quite serious. There is no one else they want to run for the position, and the area manager of one of the banks wants to fund my campaign."

"It sounds like you have a good foundation for the campaign. I can come down to give you some help to lay out the plans."

"Okay, but this isn't the big city. It's a small town and if you start talking about laying out the crew for the grass roots campaign, it will scare the people in the town. They are still skeptical of northerners. It will alienate them if we come across as too slick."

"Got it. I know the right people to help you out. They are there in Georgia. I'll introduce you to them when I come down."

When Thelonius stepped off the plane from D.C., it seemed like everyone noticed. He wore a Burberry suit and pulled a Gucci garment bag. His air spoke command and control.

"Hey, kids, what's happening with the candidate? Have you scheduled any meetings where I can meet some of your key constituents? I want to get some key people to be the foot soldiers.

"Dad, we have meetings arranged for you," I said. "In addition, we've thought of people who could hold key positions like treasurer and field organizer."

Thelonius was glad he didn't have to start from square one. Although this was something he could do in his sleep, it was different with his own child. To him politics was fun but it was also a contact sport.

As we drove through Atlanta and through DeKalb County, Thelonius marveled at the Atlanta landscape.

"This country town has grown up."

"Yes, since we won the Olympics a whole lot has been going on daily," said Rikki. "You should see the construction near the Atlanta University Center and Georgia Tech."

As we headed down I-20, Thelonius recounted his days during the Civil Rights Movement when he flew into areas for a couple of days and organized communities around voting rights. This reminded him of those days.

"Rikki, have you called Joe? He said that he'll endorse you," said Thelonius.

"I'll give him a call while you're here," said Rikki.

Thelonius was going to pull out all the stops for his daughter. He had multiple connections in the city.

For the next two days, we towed Thelonius through the city. We met with people who would get out the vote, finance the campaign and volunteer their services. Rikki's campaign was becoming a machine and her fellow candidates were feeling the buzz. One of Thelonius's friends became the campaign manager. This really pleased him because he knew things would be done correctly. Just before he went back to D.C., Thelonius took Rikki shopping. He wanted Rikki to look the part of a winning candidate.

"Okay, honey," said Rikki. "Daddy is going to take me shopping. After shopping, I will drop him off at the airport."

"Sounds good, this will give you time to really catch up with your father."

I gave Rikki a smack on the lips and waved good-bye to Thelonius. They drove to Phipps Plaza, the upscale mall of Atlanta, to shop. This gave them an opportunity to catch up. As they drove to the mall, Thelonius asked her about married life and her future political position.

"You know that politics is hard on a marriage," said Thelonius. "I should know, it cost me two marriages and darn near the third. When you're in politics people think they own you or at least they feel they own your vote. Whatever you do, don't let your marriage fail because of politics."

Rikki let the words sink in before responding. It was the first time she heard her father speak about the negative impact of politics.

"Don't worry. You know I have no problem telling people no. I have allegiance to no one except myself when it comes down to protecting my marriage."

They both became a little silent. Thelonius knew it was more than just talking "stuff."

They shopped for a couple of hours. Most of the time was spent in Saks Fifth Avenue and the Bob Ellis Shoe Store. Thelonius purchased two pairs of shoes for himself, two pairs of shoes for Clementine and two pairs of shoes for Rikki. In addition, he purchased a couple of suits for Rikki that had interchangeable slacks and skirts. All were by Polo. Rikki looked like new money and a winning candidate. She liked when Thelonius came into town; it meant he would take care of her shopping needs. After they went shopping they had lunch at P.F. Chang's, an upscale Chinese eatery. Rikki lost track of time because she was having so much fun. It brought back memories of spending weekends shopping with her father. Rikki realized she had only an hour and a half to get her father across town to the airport. Her father was one to push the limit of catching a plane.

"Daddy, we have to go," said Rikki. "You're about to miss your plane."

"Rikki, you know I won't miss the plane. I've been doing this for years, and haven't missed a plane yet," said Thelonius.

Thelonius, however, had come perilously close to missing his plane several times. Rikki requested the food to go and starting packing up the clothes.

"Daddy, I'm going to get the car. Please be ready. I'll pick you up out front."

Rikki loaded the car and sped up front. She only had an hour to drop off her dad at the airport. They were an hour and a half away. Rikki decided they would make it.

"Buckle up Daddy, we're off to make your flight."

Rikki sped down GA-455 and then onto I-85. She flew past downtown and into College Park and East Point. "What airline are you on, Daddy?" Rikki inquired. "I'm on Delta and the flight number is 855," said Thelonius. Rikki swerved into the Delta departing flight space and popped open the trunk of her Audi. Her father pecked her on the check and gracefully exited the car. He hurried away but did not seem rushed.

Rikki was a bit relieved that her father was gone. He was a tremendous help getting her campaign on track and selecting the right people to move it forward. However, whenever he came to visit things got a bit out of whack. His confrontational style rubbed many people the wrong way. It didn't matter because he didn't care. As Rikki headed back home, she saw one of her friends from D.C. This was one of her hanging out buddies from back in the day when she drank and partied hard.

"Hey Binky," said Rikki. "It's good to see you. Have you seen any of the folks from D.C.?" "Hey Rikki, you're looking good. I heard you got married to some guy from California. So you had to go out West to get somebody. I guess the D.C. guys didn't fit the bill."

Binky's tone was playful yet direct. Rikki did not want to talk about the issue. Her past life was filled with dating guys from D.C. who treated her badly. She often minimized that part of her past so she did not have face her old friends.

"Nope, no one in D.C. could fulfill my needs." When Rikki said it, she was proud of her accomplishment. She rarely saw her buddies from D.C., but when she did, it was like a high school reunion.

"So Rikki," said Binky. "What happened to your boy Tim? I thought for sure you would marry him."

"No, I realized he wasn't committed to the relationship. He was committed to himself. I have a wonderful husband and a wonderful life. There's little confusion and my in-laws are wonderful people."

Rikki was happy with her marriage.

The next few weeks were hard, yet rewarding. Rikki campaigned like a veteran. Her campaign worked well. No one came remotely close to her in the polls. On Election Day, Rikki toured all the polls in the city. She shook hands and hugged babies. At the end of the evening she was declared a winner.

"I don't believe it. This won't set in for a while," she thought.

Rikki took pictures and gave a few interviews for the local papers. I stood by with glee. I was truly happy for her and watched Rikki work the room. She had style and charisma. Everyone she talked to wanted to be her new best friend. It was a memorable night. At 2 a.m. everyone left the school hall where Rikki had given her victory speech. Confetti was everywhere as were placards that read "Victory for Rikki." This is when it all sunk in.

"Wow, I'm now responsible for these kids," said Rikki. "The true work is about to begin."

I gave Rikki a reassuring hug. "No matter what, I'll be with you."

I held Rikki in my arms for awhile until she relaxed. It was time to go home. The glamour of being on the school board quickly wore off. Rikki was baptized by fire. All of the community people who had backed her wanted to be a thorn in the sides of all the other board members. It didn't matter that two of the board members were black men who did a good job of representing all students. In their minds, black men who came from corporate America had sold their souls.

"They're nothing more than figure heads," said Joan Liptrot, one of the staunchest advocates of poor children.

Rikki knew she was caught between a rock and a hard place. She represented the views of poor black families but she wasn't poor. She understood their issues but she was not going to represent them in a victimized manner. She was an outspoken critic of policies that did not support the poor children, but she was not going to alienate her colleagues who created those policies. No, Rikki was going to work this from the inside out where she would get some policies changed while building up the voice and support base for low-income children and their families.

Lesson 26: Sometimes we are placed into positions to lead the change.

Chapter 27: Slowing Down to Save the Marriage

While Rikki's career flourished, I started to realize that we could not keep up the pace. I knew that something had to give. I did a great job engaging the community members with the revitalization project. All the elements were in place for the physical development of the commercial area that had been abandoned for many years before I arrived. I pulled together the business, government and civic community so real issues could be resolved comprehensively. With all the elements in place, I started to search for another job. I found my new position with one of the most dynamic high profile women in Atlanta. She was Dr. Lavita Willson, also known as "Sista President." Dr. Willson served as an advisor to the revitalization project. One day at a meeting, I pulled her aside to mention my plans.

"Dr. Willson, I've done all that I can in my community. The people and structures are in place to carry out the vision of the revitalization project. I'm starting to look for my next act."

"Really?" said Dr. Willson with an inquisitive smile. "I think I have the perfect job for you at Spelman College. I'll give you $15K more than you make now, and you can start sometime next month."

I was ecstatic but kept a poker face. "Dr. Willson, I'm flattered. Can I get back to you tomorrow with an answer?"

Crossing the Bridge Over Troubled Water

That night we decided that working at Spelman would be a good thing. It would normalize my hours and I would work close to Rikki. There was only one catch—it was an all women's college. Rikki would not say it, but she had concerns about me working at the school. She did not worry about me; she was more concerned about the young women drooling over her husband. She had attended the school her first two years and remembered how her girlfriends would flirt with the men who worked at the school. She never heard of any students sleeping with the male faculty or staff. It was an unwritten rule that no one broke. I was aware of all the issues and was prepared to handle any distractions.

After accepting the offer from Dr. Willson, I prepared to wrap things up with the revitalization project. I held my last few community meetings and made sure the residents felt empowered. The residents had a few tricks up their sleeves. They had a surprise dinner planned for me at the local Spaghetti Factory. I arrived at the restaurant thinking it was a committee meeting and saw a parking lot filled with familiar cars. When I walked through the doors I heard "surprise!" I felt like a celebrity. The mayor, council members, city manager and the school superintendent were all there. It was a list of who's who in Decatur. I had participated in similar events for other people but never thought it would happen to me. As I greeted everyone, they all hugged me and thanked me for my service and commitment. After I grabbed a plate, the program began. Two community groups gave me a tribute along with a plaque and other memorabilia. The president of the chamber of commerce gave me a package from the business community. The final presentation came from the mayor. She gave me the key to the city and declared August 22 Bentley Johnson Day in the city. The declaration was laden with gold and it was framed. I kept reading it over and over before taking the podium to say a few words.

"When I began, I told my wife that I would treat this community like my family. I told her that I would take it personally. This is my home and you are my family. I have done all I could to improve the city and bring everyone in the community together. I knew I did something right when a mother from the community told me that because of me, her child would be a success." That statement really hit me. I knew I was on to something.

"I firmly believe that the success of the community can be measured by the success of children from low-income communities. It's a social issue that's tied to economic development." If I was a preacher everyone present would have said, "Amen" on that point. It was an appropriate way to end the celebration. Everyone came up to wish me the best of luck in my new gig. I accepted the kind words graciously and was glad to be out of the twenty-four-hour position. The long days and nights had finally caught up with me. I also knew that Rikki would need my help as she ventured on the school board.

As we returned home, we thought about the evening but also pondered the future.

"That was some party," said Rikki. "Those folks are going to miss you."

"I'm going to miss them too. I know if I kept at the pace I was going, a heart attack was around the corner. It was difficult for me to turn it off—especially when we had night meetings and weekend events. I'll focus my energy on supporting you on that board."

Rikki smiled and gave me a big hug. She felt good about the move. The regular hours would serve us well. No more answering the phone late at night and no more events in the evening or on the weekends. Rikki was glad to have me back.

When we arrived home, Rikki brushed her teeth, washed up and put on her silk pajamas. She knew these pajamas would arouse me.

I was watching the news when I saw Rikki enter the room. I was immediately aroused as I looked at Rikki's nipples peering through the silk top. I quickly went in the bathroom to wash up. I washed under my arms and in the groin area. I then put on my tight designer underwear. As I got out of the bathroom, I dimmed the bedroom lights. Rikki was watching the news when I slipped back into the bed. By now I was fully aroused and my body was hot. As I rubbed against Rikki she turned to kiss me. We kissed each other passionately as our hands explored each other's bodies. I was the aggressor. As I aroused Rikki, she then became aggressive making me even hotter until I couldn't take it anymore. I turned Rikki on her back and kissed her slowly from the back of her ears to her neck and all the way down to her ankles. As I kissed her thighs I gently eased off her pajamas bottoms slowly opening her thighs to kiss the inside of them. I then slowly eased up to her waist until Rikki couldn't take it any more. She grabbed me easing Mr. Johnson inside of her. I moved slowly yet forcibly until Rikki shuddered. Then I moved with the speed of a locomotive. Our bodies moved in syncopation. Rikki released all tension in her body, as she screamed with joy. I replied with a loud grunt. Both of us were drenched and exhausted. As we rested in each other's arms, we realized how wet we were.

"We better go wipe off," said Rikki.

"Better yet, why don't we take a shower?"

We took a quick shower washing each other's backs and rubbing each other's bodies. We had not made love like that for a while since we both were usually too tired. When we got back in the bed, Rikki fell fast asleep. She snored like a bear. I chuckled but finally went to sleep because I too was very tired.

The next day we hung out at Phipps Plaza. We window- shopped and strolled around the mall. I bought a couple of shirts for work while

Rikki bought a couple of scarves to add to her wardrobe. I felt relieved because there were no events planned for the weekend. It was the first time in a couple of years that I could truly enjoy the weekend with no cell phone or pager. The stress was lifted from my shoulders. While we were out, we saw a few of our friends and decided to have dinner at the mall. It was rather spontaneous, but it felt good. This was something we had not done in a long time.

Lesson 27: Community work is hard, but rewarding.

Chapter 28: EPT does not mean Exchange Personal Time

The next few weeks I adjusted to my new job at Spelman College. It was an incredible place to work. The most talented and beautiful women attended the school. As my brother-in-law told me, it was like being in a cookie jar but not being able to touch the cookies. I was okay with it. I was dedicated to my marriage and truly saw the students as little sisters. I quickly became a favorite on the campus. Faculty, administrators and students accepted my fresh perspective and ability to connect their interests to the outside community.

Rikki was doing okay with her transition to the school board. She cut out many of the night meetings associated with her day job to attend sub-committee meetings associated with the school board. Rikki was feeling lethargic, but her appetite was normal. She decided it was time to mention this to me.

"Honey, I've been feeling a little tired lately and it's not the type of tired that goes away. I can't quite describe it but for some reason, I think I'm pregnant."

I stopped in my tracks.

"Are you serious?"

"I think so," said Rikki.

We stood there for a while thinking about the gravity of what we were discussing. Then almost simultaneously we said, "Let's go to the drug store to get a test."

We put on our coats and headed to Kroger. On our way to the store, you could hear a pin drop. Both of us were anxious to know the results. Inside the store, we searched the aisles. We came upon the pregnancy tests near the feminine products.

"Okay, I believe this is it."

Rikki pulled the EPT from the aisle and put it in the basket. We left the drug store and picked up some ice cream from the local Highs. There were a lot of people enjoying the evening. I decided to ask Rikki how she *really* felt.

"So Rikki, if you are pregnant, would you be happy?" I was hoping she would say she's interested but I didn't know.

"I *know* I'm pregnant," said Rikki. "I've felt it before—remember I told you about my abortion many years ago." Those words made me shudder. I couldn't imagine anyone aborting a child.

"Yeah, I remember now, I guess I wanted to forget about it."

"That's something to forget about," said Rikki. "I never want to be in a position to do it again."

I did not bring up the topic again. We ate our ice cream, talked to a few friends and headed back home. By the time we pulled up in the driveway, Rikki was asleep. I gently nudged her and we headed into our place. While Rikki was getting ready for bed in the bathroom, she took the test. After washing her face and brushing her teeth, Rikki observed the color change of the test. It was positive. She hesitated to tell me but she knew I would eventually ask.

"Well dear, I'm definitely pregnant," said Rikki. I smiled and hugged her. We held each other for a few minutes.

Crossing the Bridge Over Troubled Water

"Let's go to bed, Mommy," I said. Rikki chuckled and got into bed. I cuddled Rikki and hugged her tummy. "I'm looking forward to the little one."

"So am I," said Rikki. "This will make everything complete."

With my new job I was able to commute with Rikki. I took her to Georgia State University before heading to Spelman. My day was pretty regular. I got to work by 8:30 a.m. and left by 5:00 p.m. The day consisted of meetings with faculty, administrators, students and community agencies. I was the liaison between the college and the community. Nearly all of the community agencies coveted my college students. My students were trained and oriented for agencies before stepping foot into the door. I believed I was responsible for training the next generation of leaders. I exposed students to real life situations but in a controlled environment. I had great relationships, on campus and off. Many of the local nonprofits asked me to serve on their boards. After a while, I selected two organizations that would enhance the work of my students.

Rikki continued to work with Georgia State University on The Metropolitan Project, connecting her university with community groups near Midtown. She paced herself so she wouldn't be too tired before her evening school-board meetings. Whenever possible, I made sure to attend the school-board meetings. I tried to always be there for my wife, especially if anyone tried to beat up on her. I carried snacks for her to nibble on and tried to make sure she didn't overdo it. The Christmas season was rapidly approaching and we were preparing for a trip to D.C. Rikki's mother and step-father were returning from London to a new home in a tony neighborhood in Maryland. This would be the first opportunity for us to see mom in two years and to stay at her mom's new home. It was also an opportunity for Rikki's mom to throw a baby shower.

Toward the end of the fall semester, we attended many of the "to be seen" holiday events. We sat in the front section of the Morehouse Glee Club holiday concert. Faculty, alumni, and only the well connected sat in this section. Everyone had heard that Rikki was pregnant, and they were genuinely excited for her.

"My, my," said Dr. Fortune, the director of the Glee Club. "I see we have the Johnson Family in attendance with a new addition on the way."

I chuckled and gave Dr. Fortune the thumbs up. Rikki smiled and blew him a kiss. Everything was going right and although our lives were busy, they seemed to be in balance.

After the concert, Rikki complained that she was getting a little tired.

"Wow, I think I'm going to stay home tomorrow," said Rikki. "Things are starting to catch up to me. I want to make sure I'm not too tired before the holidays begin."

"I totally understand. We've been doing a lot this semester and I'm sure by next semester you'll be ready to stop working by spring break."

Rikki chuckled, "You've got that right. That sounds like a good plan for me." As she said that Rikki felt the baby kick her. "See," said Rikki. "This baby wants me to stay at home too."

For the next two weeks, we slowed down and prepared for the D.C. trip. Rikki was feeling better because the night-time meetings were over and the semester was winding down. All the parties were over and most students were home for the holidays.

"Okay tomorrow we're off for D.C.," said Rikki.

I told the neighbors about the trip. On our way to the airport, I thought of the great time we would have in D.C.

"What's the first thing you want to do once we leave the airport?" I asked Rikki.

"I think I'm hungry for some Wings N' Things," said Rikki.

"Sounds like a plan to me," I responded.

∼

Lesson 28: Women really do glow during the early months of pregnancy.

∼

Chapter 29: An Eventful Christmas in D.C.

During our plane ride we saw a young couple navigating with their infant. It looked like they were laughing and playing. I pondered our future and admired the Dad's humor; yet he was firm when necessary. The children generally complied but they loved to challenge their Dad. For the remainder of the plane ride Rikki took a nap while I read *In Flight*. In the background, I admired the family and day dreamed of the day I would have a little one. Before I knew it, the captain mentioned we were beginning the descent to Baltimore-Washington Airport. I nudged Rikki so she could wake up.

"Hey dear, it's time to wake up."

I knew not to wake her up abruptly. She was not one to wake up in a pleasant mood. In fact, she could be down right grumpy. I kissed her on the cheek and then rubbed her leg. She woke up slowly but pleasantly.

"Hey, where are we?"

"We're almost to BWI; the plane is descending and we should be on the ground in 20 minutes."

Rikki started to wake up. Meanwhile, I gave her some water and a snack to eat. I also rubbed her tummy.

"How's the little one?"

"All is well, I feel some twitching."

As the plane descended Rikki let out the loudest burp. I was more embarrassed than Rikki.

"Oh excuse me," said Rikki. "I didn't mean to be a frog. In fact, I'll blame it on the baby." I shook my head and chuckled. The plane landed in and taxied to the terminal. We were excited. As the plane stopped, I popped up to assist Rikki. She was a little stiff but okay. We gathered our goods and headed off the plane. Rikki's mom and step father were waiting on us.

"Hi, sweetie," said Jane. "You look great."

"I don't feel great," said Rikki. "I feel like a stuffed turkey."

We all cracked up laughing.

"Let's get this stuffed turkey something to eat," I said. "I think the stuffed turkey wants some wings from Wings N'Things."

We all went down to the baggage claim. Meanwhile, Will picked up the car. Once the luggage came around, I picked it up and put it on a cart. While waiting, we saw a couple of our friends coming home. We exchanged numbers and told them about the baby shower.

We all piled into Will's new BMW. It had all the bells and whistles. It was a new model imported directly from Germany.

"Dag, what model is this?" I said. "It looks like something out of a James Bond movie." Will loved that kind of comment.

"Oh, it's the BMW 745ii with the tiptronic shift. It can go from zero to sixty in 6.3 seconds." With that comment, Will accelerated onto the Baltimore Washington Parkway. This straight shot from Baltimore to D.C. was a mini-Autobahn. The g-force of the car pulled us into our seat. Our heads and bottoms sunk into the deep leather seats while the car felt like it was floating on air. "Do you notice how the car's center of gravity pulls you closer to the road?" inquired Will. "This is how race cars accelerate off bank turns."

Jane was quiet. I could see the tension on her face and the whites of her knuckles clinging onto the door. She hated Will's driving. Although he was a masterful driver with training from the highest levels of law enforcement, it did not make a difference. She viewed his driving as reckless and immature. I knew what to say to diffuse the situation.

"Let's take the car for a spin later this evening. I think right now this baby needs some food."

"Oh yeah," said Jane. "Let's get that baby some food."

We went straight for a location of Wings 'N Things in Landover, Maryland. A few minutes later we were pulling up to the new subdivision where Jane and Will lived. The homes were immaculately maintained. The yards were trimmed and everything was orderly. There was no music, no off-beat colors and no beat up cars. The houses exuded confidence, character and cleanliness. It was a colonial style home with large columns, a hip roof and a side load garage. The downstairs had a full-sized apartment for Rikki's grandmother.

"This house is beautiful," said Rikki. "It looks much better than in the pictures."

We got out of the car. I walked around the back to pull in the bags while Rikki went inside with her mom. The inside looked better than outside.

"Wow, I forgot you had all those Lladros," said Rikki, looking into her Mom's dining room cabinet. The living room and dining room looked like something out of *Architectural Digest*. The paintings and collection of small statuettes alone were worth about $50K. Along the foyer were pictures of Will with Prince Charles and Jane talking to Princess Diana. The house exuded an air of royalty. It was impeccably decorated and exceedingly large.

The next day was the baby shower. I woke at the crack of dawn to assist Jane. I picked up the cake and bought flowers. I also picked up a few games for the participants. By 10 a.m., I had completed the errands and went back to the house. I helped Jane cook and clean. Before we knew it, it was time for the shower to begin. People started rolling in—Rikki's best friends, her cousins, aunts, stepmother and other friends. They all loved her mother's house. It was a showcase of her mother's travels around the globe as well as Rikki's baby shower. They played games and chatted about good times. Jane caught up on the lives of everyone. Since their tour to England, she did not have the opportunity to chat with Rikki's friends. As the afternoon wore on, Rikki started to tire. Jane realized Rikki was getting tired so she started winding down the activities and guiding people out.

"Are you okay, sweetie?" said Jane.

"Yeah, I'm okay but just a little tired. I think I did a little too much," said Rikki.

With her feet up, Rikki drank some lemonade, nibbled on some chips and said her good-byes. After everyone left, she and Jane debriefed. They laughed and talked about the people who attended.

I entered the room with Will and got the break down on the guests and all the activities of the baby shower. Rikki told us who attended the shower. I marveled at the number and type of the gifts. There were baby clothes, teddy bears, baby toys, baby safety devices and even a baby-mommy spa day! All of it was pretty amazing but it was also pretty draining. Rikki was tired. I propped her feet up and started to message them.

"It was a very special day," said Rikki. "All of my girls were here as well as my favorite relatives. We gossiped, played games, and laughed. I mean we laughed like we were in grade school. It was a trip. This party really made me miss home."

At that moment things got a little quiet. Rikki really wanted to return home. I was not too keen on moving to the D.C. area. I knew my best friends were there but there were also old friends who tried to get in your business. I had learned my lesson about friends. They were always there when you needed them, and sometimes when you didn't. This was particularly true of the men. After we talked, Rikki went to bed. Meanwhile, I stayed up to chat with Jane and Will. I also caught up on wrapping Christmas gifts.

Lesson 29: Nothing beats your true friends.

Chapter 30: Family Fun for Christmas

The next day was Christmas Eve. We had dinner at Thelonius's house in the District. Each time we went to his house, both of us needed to be mentally prepared. Thelonius had high standards, and he still did not really approve of me. It was all good though, I knew I was the best thing for Rikki. I respected her, gave her support and pushed her to excellence.

"Hey, baby," Thelonius said to Rikki as he answered the door.

"Hi, Daddy."

"What's up, Fella?" inquired Thelonius, as he gave me the grip.

As we walked into the house, I could smell the smoke. Thelonius and Clementine smoked like locomotives. Thelonius smoked cigars while Clementine smoked cigarettes. There was a mix of smoke, food and dogs in the air. Our loafers click clacked on the beautiful oak hardwood floors. We walked in and sat down in the T.V. room. The room had a fairly old leather couch and love seat. There was great original contemporary black artwork around the walls and plenty of books, music and tapes. Thelonius had been watching a basketball game.

"Come on in and watch the game," Thelonius motioned to me.

"Rikki, Clementine is in the kitchen." I sat on the love seat while Rikki strolled into the kitchen. The food smelled great and since she was eating for two, she needed a snack. Just as we started to settle into our seats, the door bell rang. Rikki's aunt and cousin had arrived. This cousin was like a younger brother to Rikki. He was just like Rikki's father—a fashion guru and quite vocal. I jumped up to get the door.

"Hey now," I said as I answered the door. Everyone greeted me warmly. They genuinely liked me and knew I was good for Rikki. They all walked in, gifts in tow.

By the time dinner started it was 8 p.m. Nothing was ever on time at Thelonius's house. They put the C in CP Time. After blessing the food, we guys broke into the T.V. room to watch the NBA game. The Bulls and the Lakers were on. This was the Michael Jordan era and everyone was enthralled. The women sat in the dining room and chatted about the latest books and fashions. They also talked about the previous day's baby shower. After the game at 10 p.m., we opened the gifts and gave a toast. I loved their gifts. Thelonius and Clementine gave clothes from the best retailers: Polo, Burberry, Barneys and Neiman Marcus, i.e., "Needless Mark-Up." They had recently found a second-hand store that packaged items for them that looked new. Rikki's aunt and cousins also bought high end gifts. I was absolutely amazed by the gifts. They were nice but beyond our budget. We bought gifts that were pretty practical and we could hear the commentary after we left.

"Hmmm, I could imagine them saying, "That Bentley is one boring soul. His gifts are always so 'useful' rather than stylish."

I didn't care. I rather liked being practical.

As we got into Granny's car we could smell the smoke from their clothes.

"My God, can you smell the smoke?" said Rikki.

"Yeah, it's pretty bad. I guess we're lucky that we come over here only a couple of times each year."

"The second hand smoke is pretty serious." Rikki said in agreement. She was rubbing her stomach with her head laid back and to the side. She was starting to drift off. Within minutes of getting on the Beltway, Rikki was in full REM. Her snore was becoming more pronounced. Meanwhile, I could only chuckle. I was amazed at how loud she snored.

"Well, at least I don't have to worry about drifting off to sleep," I said to myself. "Rikki is definitely keeping me up. Once the baby is born, I will make an appointment for Rikki with the ear, nose and throat specialist."

It took us thirty minutes to reach Rikki's mom's house. The streets were relatively quiet as everyone prepared for Christmas. As we drove up to Jane's house, we noticed that nearly everyone in the neighborhood was asleep. All lights were out and most neighbors were asleep except those kids waiting for St. Nick. I pulled into the driveway, but turned off the lights so I would not disturb anyone.

"We're here," I whispered in Rikki's ear.

"Really," Rikki said sleepily. "How long have I been asleep? It seems like forever."

"It's only been about thirty minutes. Let's head in and get you a bedtime snack."

I brought in the gifts and laid them near the Christmas tree. I then walked into the kitchen to pull down the cereal for Rikki.

"Thank you darling, you know how to treat your wife."

I smiled and held Rikki's hand. She ate her bowl of cereal while I took off her shoes and massaged her feet. Rikki drifted off to sleep.

"Okay sleepy head, the fun is over. It's time for bed."

I guided Rikki down the steps to bed. I took off her clothes and put on her gown. She was sound asleep as I tucked her into the bed. While she slept, I wrapped gifts and watched a little T.V. It was a quiet cold winter night.

The next day, we woke up to the smell of ham and greens. It smelled like Granny's southern cooking. As we stretched and yawned, I looked outside the window. "Hey, there's some snow outside," I yelled.

"I don't believe you," said Rikki with disbelief."

"Well, look for yourself." As she moved the shades, Rikki couldn't believe her eyes. A blanket of snow was on the ground. It felt officially like Christmas. The two of us put on our robes and headed up the stairs for breakfast.

"Well, look who's up," said Granny.

"Hey, Granny—Merry Christmas," I said.

"What do you want for breakfast, Sugar?" said Granny.

"Do you have any of your famous biscuits in the freezer?"

"Go for it," said Granny as she asked me to open the freezer. Granny's famous biscuits were in two containers. I pulled them out and heated up the oven. I then pulled out the eggs and bacon. Within fifteen minutes I whipped up biscuits, eggs and bacon. Rikki read the paper and rested her feet. She didn't look as tired as before and had not mentioned work or her school board activities. I noticed how relaxed she was near her mother and family. I knew moving to D.C. was the right thing to do. Before we knew it, company arrived. Rikki's uncles and cousins made their way. I helped Jane and Granny with the table while Will finished frying the turkey. The desserts were ready as was the stuffing. Rikki's uncles brought their specialties – sweet potato soufflé, red beans and rice, and ambrosia. Once everyone was ready, I blessed the food and we were off to the big meal. It was a feast. Everyone chattered away about the latest events and caught up on old people in the neighborhood. After dinner we exchanged gifts and sang Christmas carols. By the time we finished unwrapping gifts and eating dessert, it was past midnight. Everyone was quite happy. Rikki, however, looked tired again. I thought she had probably stayed on her feet too long, so I got her ready for bed.

"Okay Rikki, let's get you ready for bed. I think you may have overdone it."

"I'm okay—just a little tired."

"All right, everyone we're off to bed, good night."

As we headed down the stairs, I wondered what was going on with Rikki. The last time she looked tired like this, she had a bad case of the flu. I noticed once her body became totally stressed and tired, it shut down. It took Rikki little or no time to fall asleep. She started snoring within five minutes of hitting the pillow. The past two days caught up with me and I fell asleep within ten minutes of hitting the pillow.

I was in a deep sleep when I was awakened by Rikki moaning in the bathroom.

"Hey, are you okay?" I yelled.

"I don't think so," moaned Rikki. "My stomach hurts real bad, and blood is coming out." I was never one to delay my response to an emergency.

"I'm calling 911 to pick you up."

I ran upstairs to alert my in-laws and to call 911. By the time I headed back downstairs Jane had a cool pack on Rikki's head and was rubbing her back.

"How's she doing?" I inquired.

"About the same," said Jane. Her eyes said it all. She was worried and she pretty much knew what was going on. We all knew Rikki had a miscarriage. I ran back upstairs to check on the ambulance. Within five minutes, I could see the flashing lights coming down the street. I stood outside in the cold and directed them around the back so picking up Rikki would be easier.

"Come around back!" I shouted.

The guys heard me and headed around back with a quick pace as I explained what happened. Meanwhile, Will was downstairs preparing for the EMTs to enter. By the time I was back downstairs Jane had Rikki up off the toilet. She had on sweats and a robe and was lying down on the bed. Jane was wiping her brow and rubbing her back. I guided the EMTs into the room.

"Rikki, honey, it's time to head out," I said.

Rikki struggled to get up. The EMTs grabbed her and placed her onto the stretcher. Once on the stretcher, I covered her with a blanket. I knew she would be stunned once the cold air hit her. We all carried her up the steep back steps. By the time we hit the top of the steps, Jane had my coat, hat and gloves.

"Aren't you going with her in the back of the ambulance?" asked Jane.

"Uh, yeah." The question stunned me for a moment.

I had not really thought about it until that moment. I had never been in an ambulance and hoped it would be the last time. As they lifted Rikki into the ambulance, she mumbled something barely audible.

"I think we lost the baby." I repeated the words in my head.

"It's okay we'll get through it."

I didn't want to say I knew we lost the baby. I was pretty certain that was the case, but held a slight hope that it would be saved. Once inside the ambulance, I held Rikki's hand and stroked her head. The ride was bumpy and cold. It took no time to arrive to Doctor's Hospital in Lanham, Maryland. As the ambulance backed up, the EMT slid open the window.

Crossing the Bridge Over Troubled Water

"We called ahead Mr. Johnson, your wife will be seen by Dr. Cartwright. She's the OB-Gyn on call."

"Thank you," I replied.

As the ambulance stopped, I nudged Rikki.

"Okay, we're here." The EMTs opened the door. I jumped out and assisted them with Rikki. We then went through the emergency room doors and Rikki was immediately placed in a room full of monitors. It was a cold, impersonal room, much like an autopsy lab. It seemed like years until the doctor came. In my mind I recounted the many emergency room stories I had heard over the years. There was the case of the old man whose lungs were filled with fluid because of the exposure to cold. He hacked his way into the intensive care unit. There was also the teenager who had seizures from sniffing too much glue. His parents wondered out loud if this time he had suffered brain damage. The last case, which really got to me, was the toddler who choked from a Christmas tree needle. The Christmas tree seemed relatively harmless until the little one decided to taste the needle that had "frosting" on it. The child could breathe, but he complained that something sharp was in his throat. He had apparently thrown up several times until nothing else came up. His poor parents thought he swallowed some type of cleaner or a large object.

Lesson 30: Life can throw you a curve ball at any time.

Chapter 31: Our Loss

Dr. Cartwright was a tall elegant woman who had a no nonsense approach to medicine. When she came into the room, I smiled but she only acknowledged me by meeting my eyes with direct contact. She went quickly to Rikki with a very professional yet compassionate tone.

"Mrs. Johnson, can you tell me what happened?" Rikki was not very coherent and only moaned. She was still in pain and dazed from not sleeping. I then told Dr. Cartwright what happened. I used a very deliberative tone, explaining every detail. Dr. Cartwright did not interrupt. She made a mental note of all the details.

"Thank you, Mr. Johnson, I now have a good idea of what happened. Mrs. Johnson, I will now need to examine you. Please try to lift up your legs."

I assisted Rikki with getting her legs into the stirrups. Once she was positioned, Dr. Cartwright put on examining gloves and slid her hand into Rikki's vagina.

"Mrs. Johnson, this may hurt a little bit." I could tell Rikki was in pain.

"Okay," said Dr. Cartwright as she pulled her hand out of Rikki. "Unfortunately, you had a miscarriage. I will need to come back in about fifteen minutes to complete the DNC."

"DNC?" I asked.

"Yes," said Rikki who was now fully awake. "That's when she clears out the remains of the fetus. It's essentially the same procedure that's used for abortions."

I was numb. Just the day, before we were celebrating at a baby shower and now Rikki had the miscarriage. The dramatic change was a bit much for both of us. We sat in the room quietly until Dr. Cartwright returned. Dr. Cartwright took all of five minutes to complete the procedure. Once it was finished, she briefly counseled us on letting Rikki's body and emotions recover. After Dr. Cartwright left the room, Rikki broke down.

"Why, did this happen? I just don't understand," Rikki cried uncontrollably.

There were only a few times that I saw Rikki cry and each time it happened I felt powerless. She wept for about five minutes. It seemed like an eternity. I could not bring myself to cry. The gravity of the events had not hit me yet. I was more concerned with Rikki's feelings than my own. After the tears subsided Rikki became quiet. I stroked her hand and head.

"Everything will work out fine. We'll be okay."

"I don't want to go back to Georgia," said Rikki. "I want to be closer to home."

I did not want to get into a debate with Rikki. I did not feel a fight would be worth it. As we both thought about the gravity of Rikki's words, a nurse came in to release Rikki and gave her a prescription for the pain. Jane and Will then came in to assist with the check out.

"I'm sorry sugar," said Jane. Will also came forward to give her a hug. I left the room to get a wheel chair.

"How is Bentley handling this?" asked Jane.

"I think he's shell shocked and numb. He really did not respond. Bentley is more concerned about my feelings than his own."

Rikki knew me pretty well. I had a steady stream of consciousness—not too sad but not too happy. Overall, my outlook was pretty positive.

I returned with the wheel chair while Will warmed up and moved the car. As I eased Rikki into the wheel chair, I could tell she was in a daze. I did not say much as I covered Rikki from head to toe with a warm blanket. I knew the winter air would shake loose the cobwebs. Jane came back to the room to tell us the car was ready.

"Okay, let's go, sweetie. The car is ready."

As we headed out the door, the winter air hit our faces. Rikki shook her head and mumbled a few words. I lifted her up into Will's car and covered her up. I held her tightly and gently rocked her back and forth. The only sound in the car was the sounds the saxophone of Grover Washington. It only took a few minutes to get to the house. Before she knew it, I had her back in the bed, wrapped up. She fell asleep within minutes. I then went upstairs to chat with Jane and Will. Both were seated in the family room. I got a bite to eat and sat at the kitchen table. The three of us discussed how to get Rikki back on her feet and how to make her slow down. I was concerned about Rikki's high blood pressure and pace of activities. Her school board duties and university job were too much. I vowed to slow her down. Part of my strategy was to drop Rikki off and pick her up every day from work. I would also prepare her meals and snacks so she would not have to think about it. This would keep both of us on schedule to balance our lives. We stayed at Jane's for the next two days and prepared for our trip back to Atlanta.

When we returned to Atlanta, we had to deal with explaining the miscarriage. As we talked to people, it became evident that miscarriages were quite common—especially for two-career families. I told my office mates. They were stunned. Nedra Jackson, my officemate who also worked at Morehouse School of Medicine, did research on the impact of two-career families on pregnancies. I had no idea that she studied this issue. According to Nedra's research, as women became busier with their careers, the stress on their bodies became more pronounced. This is what I felt happened to Rikki. I knew we had to get control of our lives. Our positions at the universities were not stressful, but they were time consuming. Our extracurricular activities also took up the time.

I was on two nonprofit boards and was mentoring a homeless young man from New York who attended the local high school. Rikki was on the school board and was an active board member of a nonprofit organization dedicated to working with troubled teenage girls. I quickly resigned from one of the boards and was scheduled to end my term on another board. Meanwhile, Rikki quit one of her boards and stayed on the school board until her term ended. As our lives became less busy and less confusing, we became more comfortable with each other. Although the wounds of the miscarriage were fresh in our minds, Rikki's body recovered well. Within eight weeks, Rikki was back to herself physically. She attended community meetings for the university during the day and her school board meetings once every two weeks in the evenings.

Although we did not talk about it, trying to get pregnant again was on our minds. With the emergence of spring, we made passionate love for the first time in six months. We felt like high school sweethearts, giggling and cuddling one another. That night was the best night of sleep in a while for both of us. We were exhausted but ecstatic at finally feeling comfortable enough to make love. Early the next morning, I felt aroused again. I rubbed up against Rikki and she rubbed back. Before we knew it, we had used what little energy we had left to make love one more time. With each rapid motion, we came closer and closer to climax—until gasping our last bit of energy into each other's arms. We slept well into the mid-morning. I woke up first as the sun peered through the windows and the hunger shot through my stomach.

"Hey, sweetie, do you want to grab a bite to eat at The Flying Biscuit?"

"Sure," said Rikki. "Let me catch a few more winks."

While Rikki slowly woke up, I got up to get the paper and make coffee. When I returned to the room, Rikki was ready. We headed out for my favorite meal at my favorite restaurant. While at "The Biscuit," we saw our friends Debbie and Dawson. We spent a while catching up on old times. Both Debbie and Dawson were heavy into the Atlanta scene. Debbie had a circle of friends at the Atlanta University Center while Dawson had friends at Emory and Georgia Tech. Between the two of them, the black social scene was covered. We listened and laughed. Debbie and Dawson gossiped and speculated like two gypsies. It made for good breakfast fun. After we finished, Rikki excused herself to the ladies' room. Debbie went with her.

"So how do you feel?" asked Debbie as they freshened up in front of the mirror.

"I feel good girl," said Rikki. "I'm pretty much back to myself."

"I bet you are," chuckled Debbie. "I think you've got your groove back."

Crossing the Bridge Over Troubled Water

Rikki smiled because she knew Debbie could tell she had "the glow." Somehow sex could do that to you.

~

Lesson 31: A setback is a set up for a comeback.

~

Chapter 32: Pregnancy, Take Two

Rikki did have her groove back. In fact, by next month she had missed her period. She wanted to be absolutely sure before she told me. She waited another two weeks, during which we were pretty silent on the issue. One day at dinner, Rikki brought up the issue.

"Hey dear, I missed my period last month."

"Well congratulations," I said.

We gave each other half smiles.

"We'll get through this just fine."

I gave Rikki a long hug. We embraced for a long time. Rikki's eyes started to well up with tears.

"I hope everything will be okay," said Rikki. "If something happens this time, I don't know what I would do."

"It doesn't do any good to speculate on what *could* happen," I said. "We can only deal with what we've got, which is a wonderful baby on the way and a healthy mommy."

Over the last few weeks, I started to attend a neighborhood AME church. The services were rather long, but the fiery sermons by the pastor inspired me. I wanted to eventually join but Rikki was rather noncommittal. I did not wait on her and joined the church for spiritual balance. It was not the Catholic Church that we had grown up with.

The AME church *moved* me. It had the spiritual grace of the Bible Belt. I was also moved by the prophetic sermons and the choir. Moreover, the church was walking distance from our home. Each Sunday, I prayed for a healthy baby. I also took being a family man quite seriously.

I bought an Extended Cab Ford pickup so that my family could fit in the cab comfortably. I also opened an Education Savings Account to start off the little one's education fund. I cautiously began to prepare for the little one's arrival in other ways too like figuring out child care and the eventual move to D.C.

As an educator and mother-to-be, Rikki began to voice concern about the education system in Georgia.

"I can't imagine raising a child in this system," said Rikki. "There is so much inequality. Why should we raise our children in this system?"

I understood the issue, but also knew that Rikki missed her family. Once her mother returned from London, Rikki had an urge to live closer to her.

"So, where would you like to live?" I asked rhetorically. "Perhaps you would like to move to D.C.?" Rikki smiled because she knew the answer.

"Of course I would like to live in D.C.," she said. "So would our baby. In fact, if we move back, my grandmother will assist with childcare."

I did not automatically agree, but I knew the move would be a good idea.

"Let's weigh the options and then make an informed decision," I said.

As a product of a family that raised kids with and through relatives, I knew that we would eventually move. In fact, I set a personal deadline to be in D.C. by the end of the year but I did not tell Rikki. It was a man thing and I did not want to raise her expectations.

Both of us were biding time on our boards and our jobs. Things were pretty mundane and in fact we were waiting for the summer when we would spend two weeks in D.C. with her mom. The one thing we would do before heading to D.C. was attend the Johnson Family Reunion. This year, the reunion was in Atlanta. My brother and sister and their families were staying with us. Although our house was not big, it had just enough space so people could have some privacy.

By the time the Johnson Family Reunion arrived, Rikki was five months pregnant. She was starting to waddle and was definitely hypersensitive.

"I don't have anything that fits me," yelled Rikki. "We need to go to the mall for some casual wear."

There was a sense of urgency in Rikki's voice that indicated she was serious.

"Okay, I understand, let's head down to the mall"

We hopped into the car and headed to South DeKalb Mall. Although Rikki preferred Phipps Plaza, the South DeKalb Mall was much closer and was the black people's mall" As we approached the mall, I saw one of my former colleagues.

"Hey, there's Mary Brown in the silver Volvo. Do you remember her from the Metropolitan Project?" Rikki nodded.

She was a little perturbed because she was hungry and did not want to socialize. I got a sense that something was wrong because of her coldness.

"Let's get a bite to eat."

Rikki nodded and smiled because she knew I understood. After spending the larger part of the evening at the mall, Rikki was ready to go home. She purchased a couple of linen pant suits and an African motif dress. All were loose fitting and quite comfortable. I took the shopping bags and watched her waddle back to the car. When we returned home, we were surprised to see my siblings and their families in the drive way.

"Oh no, I wonder how long they've been waiting," I said.

We got out of our cars at the same time. My niece and nephews nearly tackled me as they hugged me. I picked them all up and tumbled on the grass. Meanwhile, Rikki hugged and kissed my sister Denise, brother Silas, and their spouses.

"We'll let the kids play," said Denise as she looked at me wrestling the little ones.

All the grown-ups went into the house lugging the suitcases. By the time they hit the door, Rikki remembered our newly adopted dog Shadow was inside. Our Labrador-Rottweiler mix greeted Rikki at the door with excitement. Shadow was only a year old but he was huge. In fact, I nicknamed him Marmaduke.

"Wait Shadow, don't jump up on me," yelled Rikki.

Shadow backed off but then realized there were strangers present. By this time I was right behind Rikki.

"Hi Shadow," I said as I grabbed his collar and leash. "Come with me buddy."

As I took the huge dog outside, he jumped up to lick my face. I then patted his huge chest and rubbed him like a polar bear. Shadow then rubbed against my leg like a big baby. As he heard the kids at the door, his ears perked up and his tail started to wag. I knew it was time to move him out of the house. Just as I started to cart Shadow off, I heard a low growl. Shadow was looking right at my brother-in-law, who was at the front door.

"No Shadow, it's okay, he's okay."

I never saw a dog roll his eyes like Shadow did just then. Shadow turned, and then rolled his eyes as if to say, "Okay, I'll let him off the hook this time but next time I'll take a chunk off his a_ _."

Shadow slowly went to the back porch, peering periodically at my brother-in-law.

Everyone slowly settled down for a bite to eat. The kids played games while the parents caught up on current happenings in the family and the schedule of activities for the next few days. By 11 o'clock, everyone was tired and ready for bed. The bathroom became a revolving door where kids ran to and fro. Even Shadow tired from seeing people move back and forth. By 1am the house was as still as a church mouse. We were all sound asleep.

The next day, the house came to life by 8 a.m. The kids played inside and out while the adults sat at the kitchen counter laughing and talking about old times. Denise and Silas went to high school in the Seventies so they laughed about the styles of the time and the people in their classes. Although Rikki and I enjoyed the conversation, we were more focused on the kids. We watched the kids play and enjoy themselves making Shadow do goofy things. We both imagined having a little one who could hang with his or her cousins. It would make the picture much more complete.

"In a little time," I thought to myself.

Rikki rubbed her tummy. She knew the baby could hear the children playing. I could see the smile on Rikki's face and knew what she was thinking about. I couldn't wait to spend the next Christmas with the family, knowing our little one would be there.

Lesson 32: Being near family is best for everyone.

Chapter 33: The Family Reunion

Since our house was small, our parents stayed at a hotel in downtown Decatur. After picking up our parents at the hotel, we caravanned to Stone Mountain. As we entered the gate, signs were posted indicating the location of the reunion. As we got closer, my stomach started to flutter. I had not seen a number of my cousins for years. As we approached the picnic site, we saw a big sign with a DJ, balloons and a stage. There were four grills cooking up food and a game of volleyball going on.

"This is it," I said.

"Yep," said my father. "We have arrived to the promised land."

I saw cousins that I had not seen since childhood. My aunts from Texas were present as was my uncle from Louisiana. I saw little kids who were spitting images of their parents. The old folks were sitting at one table playing cards while the younger folks with kids sat near the end of the playground. The high school and college students hung out near the DJ, who was spinning sounds of some of the old school rappers like Doug E. Fresh and KRS One. Rikki stayed close to Denise, who introduced her to all the cousins. After the meet and greet, Rikki sat down in some shade. She sipped a tall glass of lemonade and watched the children play.

"You'll be yelling at your little one by the next family reunion," said Pam, my cousin from California.

Rikki and I smiled and concurred.

Everyone had a great time. The younger group exchanged numbers and vowed to stay in touch. The older set tried to keep the memories going by electing a new state to have the Johnson Family Reunion. Rikki and I hoped that by the next family reunion, our little one would be chasing their older cousins around. The out of town crew headed back to the house. We dropped off our parents and said good-bye. When we returned home, it was a free-for-all to get in the bathroom. The adults made the kids take quick baths and get ready for bed. While the kids bathed, the adults packed all the belongings for the next day's travel.

Rikki sat in the breakfast room with her feet propped up. She was tired from being out in the sun. I messaged her feet and shoulders so she could relax. Rikki was always stressed in crowds and the pregnancy made it worse. Once the kids settled down and the adults were clean, Rikki and I took a shower together. I scrubbed her back and shoulders while simultaneously massaging her arms. I then worked the kinks out of her neck and shoulders. Rikki's eyes were closed, which meant she was relaxed.

"Okay, sweetie, it's time to dry off and go to bed."

I quickly got out of the shower and dried myself. I then dried off Rikki, who was so tired, she was sleep-walking. I helped her put on her night gown and led her to bed. I then slipped out of the room to chat briefly with my siblings before they went to bed.

The next day I got up early to make coffee and breakfast. Rikki was so tired that she slept through breakfast and everyone's morning ruckus. I woke her up just before we said our good-byes. She brushed her teeth and washed her face while everyone loaded up the cars.

"It was a fun-filled couple of days," I thought. "But there were too many people for our little house."

I stood in the driveway waving to the two cars that pulled out of the driveway. While I waved, Shadow barked because he missed the children who played with him during their stay.

Once the families departed, we took a collective sigh of relief. We had a great time but it took a lot out of us. The presence of my siblings confirmed that we had to move to D.C. Rikki was going to be even more vigilant in getting me to agree to relocate. In fact, she found that with their departure, now would be the perfect time to broach the subject.

"Honey, did you see how well your nieces and nephews acted with their relatives around?" "Yeah, I'm sure they would act even better if we lived by them."

Although that was not Rikki's point, she did agree with me.

"Well, honey, I was actually thinking about how nice it will be for our baby to grow up with its cousins in D.C. You know my mom is thinking about retiring early. If we move now, we'll still have Granny's support. After a few years my mom can take over."

That was music to my ears. I believed that family was everything. Just as I grew up with extended family, I wanted to make sure my child experienced the same.

"Okay, dear, let's really talk. We've avoided directly talking about this issue for a while. It seems like we need to make a move to D.C."

"I agree," said Rikki. "You know, I've always wanted to return home."

For the next two hours, we talked about our plans. We would sell our home in Georgia and live with Jane and Will for a short time. This would give Rikki the chance to have direct help in the house. In many ways it would be like having a live-in nanny. I would immediately find a job. That was our plan and we vowed to stick by it. For the next few weeks, we worked our D.C. connections and each Sunday, we purchased the Washington Post from Barnes and Noble. I saw many opportunities. After a month, I received a call from a higher education association. My interview was scheduled the end of September. While waiting for the interview, we decided that by the end of the semester, we would move to D.C. regardless of the employment outcome. We also decided to test the real estate market.

"With the Olympics coming to Atlanta, people will want a nice home like ours to rent out. There will be athletic events at the nearby colleges—Agnes Scott and Emory University. I have a couple of colleagues who already rented out their houses for next summer."

Rikki smiled and nodded. Usually she would say something that would temper my ideas. This time she thought I was right, particularly around the Olympic housing. We decided to sell the house. I asked around for agents and interviewed three. I was most impressed with a friend of a neighbor who sold their house in two weeks. We agreed to use him and put our house on the market when I returned from my interview in D.C.

The atmosphere in Atlanta and around the nation was buzzing with excitement about the Million Man March. The March, with the mission of connecting and catalyzing black men to be responsible stewards of their communities, was gaining a groundswell of support. Locally, the men of my AME church and several other churches competed on how many men we would send. At the Atlanta University Center, Morehouse College boasted their aim to send virtually the whole school as a testament to their historic mission. Even at Spelman College, where I worked, several of the students and staff encouraged me to attend. Without much convincing, I decided to stay a few more days in D.C. for the Million Man March.

Rikki was both happy and sad that I was traveling to D.C. She was glad that I had a job opportunity and would attend the Million Man March. However, this would be the first doctor's appointment she would attend without me. The date of the trip quickly arrived as we prepared to put our house on the market.

"Well, when I return, the house will be ready for showing. The only thing we'll need to do is to vacate."

My tone had a certain finality to it. The gravity of the move started to sink in. Rikki's mind drifted as she imagined Jane and Granny looking after our child. Rikki rubbed her stomach. She was so happy as she thought about being near her family. It would make our life complete. Meanwhile, I started to pack away my clothes in a garment bag and a duffle bag. After I finished packing, the two of us went to bed. My plane left at 8 a.m.

Lesson 33: Listen to your spouse's needs.

Chapter 34: The Life Changing Trip to D.C.

The next day as I prepared to leave, I woke Rikki with a kiss.

"Bye, baby, I'll call you once I get to D.C."

"Okay," said Rikki. "I love you."

I kissed Rikki again and rubbed her stomach. She gave me a big hug and held onto me for a while. Rikki hated being alone, especially when I had to travel. I fed and walked Shadow before I left.

"Take care of Mommy. Okay, boy?" I whispered as I hugged my pet. Shadow gave me a slobbery lick on the face.

I left the house and got into my truck. The morning air was crisp and I felt the newness of the day. As I turned on the radio to NPR, I listened to a story on the Million Man March.

"This will be the largest gathering in D.C. since the March on Washington," said Ben Jones, the executive director of the NAACP.

"Nothing in modern history will match its magnitude," he said.

I started to get excited. I sensed a kinship growing among brothers from around the Diaspora. When I arrived at the airport, I parked the car on the first level of the garage. As I headed toward the ticket gate, I saw a number of brothers with custom made T-shirts with slogans indicating their support for the Million Man March. I went through security, got on the train and approached my gate. As I got closer to the gate, the crowd got thicker. The majority of people present were black men. It was an incredible sight to see. The white people around clearly did not have a clue as to what was going on. In fact, they looked rather paranoid with the large crowd of black men enjoying themselves and showing solidarity.

Being on the plane reminded me of my days on the varsity track team. Everyone had butterflies as the plane taxied down the runway. There was a buzz in the air but it was not disorderly. The chatter was constant but not loud.

"What's the occasion?" inquired a white middle-aged woman sitting next to me.

"I'm sorry, what do you mean?" I responded.

The white woman was now clearly nervous as I looked at her dead in the eye.

"Oh, it appears there's a team event or something," she said nervously.

"You mean, what's going on with all the black men? Well we're all headed to the Million Man March in D.C. That's where at least a million black men from across the country will get together for the sake of rebuilding our communities."

"That's really positive," said the woman. She appeared relieved.

The hour and a half flight to D.C. went by quickly. The pilot asked all passengers to return to their seats and put on their seat belts. The plane circled Alexandria, Virginia and then D.C. I looked down at Georgetown University, the Kennedy Center and the Jefferson Memorial. My stomach started to get butterflies as I heard the landing gear pull out from under the plane. The plane felt like it was accelerating as it descended. The tires touched down and everyone lurched forward just a bit. The plane taxied down the runway quickly and turned almost instantly into its gate.

"Wow, that was quick," said the woman seated next to me.

"Yes, it was," I replied.

The open seat belt light came on as the ramp connected to the plane. I unlatched my seat belt and gazed around me. I could feel the excitement. I pulled my garment and duffle bags from the overhead bin and disembarked. National Airport was especially crowded due to the March. I saw more brothers greeting each other and talking about the March. I left the baggage claim area and looked for Will's silver Beamer. Within minutes I heard the horn and saw the impeccably clean car pull up. The car stopped while Will opened the trunk and window simultaneously. As the window came down, the familiar sound of Grover Washington filled the air. People waiting for their rides immediately turned to watch the exchange.

"What's up son," said Will. "Put your things in the back. We're headed to Pentagon City and then we'll come back this way to pick up Tim and his buddy Erickson."

Will showed me his office at the Justice Department in Pentagon City and we grabbed a quick bite at the mall. I always felt good about hanging with Will. He was a man's man. He knew how to fix everything, could play any sport well, and had cool manly toys. Most importantly, Will was super dependable and knew how to listen.

While waiting on Tim and Erickson, Will and I watched women and talked shit. We mixed in serious talk to keep the balance.

"So when are you thinking about moving," inquired Will.

"I anticipate being back here by Christmas. We decided to put the house on the market a few days ago and I feel pretty confident that it will sell quickly because of the Olympics."

Will decided to head back to the airport around the time Tim and Erickson's plane landed. Once at the airport, we slowed down near

Crossing the Bridge Over Troubled Water

the baggage claim area. I saw two young men walking out of baggage claim.

"There they go!" I yelled. I remembered what Tim looked like as a teenager.

Will beeped his horn. Tim and Erickson knew who it was and started heading in the direction of the car.

"What's up, fellas?" I asked as I rolled down the power windows.

"Hey, Bentley," yelled Tim, who was Will's son from a previous marriage... "This is my boy Erickson."

"What's up, man," I said giving Erickson the grip from the window. "Welcome to D.C." We greeted each other while Will popped the truck. Will then greeted Tim and Erickson.

"Dad," said Tim. "When do I get a chance to take your ride out for a spin?"

"Never," Will said in a curt tone. "You know I don't let anyone drive my main ride. You can drive the old Beamer any day."

Will was very particular about his car. He waxed it and kept it clean as if it were a retired piece of art.

The four of us headed down to The Pier to get a quick bite and a drink. This was the D.C. version of Cheers. As we walked into The Pier, where Will was a regular, we heard the crowd at the door.

"Damn, look at that line," said Tim. "How are we going to get in there?"

Will smiled. "Follow me, youngin's."

Within minutes, we were in the restaurant mingling with Will's crew and talking to beautiful women. It seemed that the women knew that all the brothers would be out for the Million Man March. They sought out brothers that traveled near and far to support the cause. After leaving The Pier and finally arriving home around midnight, we crashed. I went downstairs to the basement apartment where Granny usually slept. She let me sleep in her bedroom while she slept upstairs in one of the extra rooms. Tim and Erickson also slept upstairs in the other bedrooms. Memories of the miscarriage were still fresh in my mind. I replayed the scene where the paramedics carried Rikki up the steps and the groans of Rikki in pain. I quickly dismissed those memories as something of the past. I pulled out my suit for the next day. I then touched base with Jane who was still up.

"What time is your interview?" asked Jane as I walked into the kitchen.

"I'm scheduled for 9 a.m. at One Dupont Circle."

"Okay, this is the plan," said Jane. "You can drive with me to Metro and that way we can ride in together."

"That sounds like a good plan. I'll see you in the morning."

I then proceeded to call Rikki.

"Hey, sweetie, I made it and everything is okay," I whispered.

"Okay, good luck tomorrow, call me after the interview," said Rikki sleepily.

"Thanks, I will."

I hung up the phone and stared at the ceiling. The air smelled of mothballs, and I could hear the multiple clocks ticking as I finally drifted off to sleep.

I was awakened by Will getting his coffee and preparing his oatmeal. I jumped up and looked at my watch. It was 6 a.m. and time for me to get up. I stretched and then turned on the light. The daylight peeked through the basement window. I dragged myself up and pulled my suit out of the closet. As I opened the closet door, the strong scent of mothballs hit my nose.

"Whew, that's enough to wake me up."

I then took my suit and underwear with me to the bathroom. After a quick shower and shave I was ready to dress. As I put on my clothes,

I rehearsed answers to questions about my experience. I then put on my shoes and socks before heading up the stairs. While upstairs I was greeted by my mother-in-law.

"Good morning Bentley," said Jane.

"Hi Mom," I replied.

We exchanged morning pleasantries and ate breakfast. During this time we listened to the morning news and traffic conditions.

"Well, it sounds like we'll be okay heading in," said Jane. "I'll let you drive us in."

Jane hated driving. If she could catch the train everywhere, she would be a happier lady.

"Sounds good, when do you want to leave?"

"How about in ten minutes?" said Jane.

I smiled then walked downstairs to brush my teeth. After giving myself the once over in the mirror, I then walked back upstairs.

"Mom, I'm heading out to warm up the car." I grabbed the keys from the closet and walked out the door. As I stepped outside, I saw the relatively new Mercedes sedan. I got in and turned on the radio. Before I realized it, Jane was there.

"Let's go," said Jane. I put the car in reverse and headed out the development. As we got on route 50 heading into the District, the traffic started to slow as we approached Cheverly.

"So, Bentley, what do you think are your chances of getting this job?"

"Oh, I'm at about ninety percent." My reply was quick yet firm. "I have a pretty good chance since working for the former president of the United States and the esteemed Sister President of Spelman College."

"That's good. Keep that positive attitude and self-confidence."

I smiled as I focused on the road. People were starting to shift lanes as they entered the District.

We listened to the Tom Joyner morning show as we proceeded down New York Avenue. I glanced at the new BET office building constructed by millionaire Bob McHenry.

"This is why I want to live in D.C.," I thought. "Atlanta is progressive, but D.C. is cutting edge."

We made a left near the McDonalds at New York and Florida Avenues. I was amazed at all of the lots for sale in the area.

"We're coming close to Union Station," said Jane. "You can catch the Red Line to Dupont Circle from this stop."

I edged the car through traffic and double parked near the American Psychological Association in back of Union Station.

"Thanks for the ride, Mom."

"Good luck, honey."

I jumped out the car and headed to the Metro station to catch the Red Line. I felt the beat of the workers commuting to their final destinations. It was unlike any metro transportation system in the country- clean, efficient and dependable. I smiled at the sisters sitting on the cars while hearing everyone talk about the March. Before I knew it, the operator announced Dupont Circle. I followed the crowd of people heading out and walked up the endless steps on the escalator. This escalator appeared to shoot straight up into the sky. At the top of the escalator I made a U-turn and headed toward One Dupont Circle, the epicenter of U.S. higher education. I arrived at the front desk where I was greeted by a guard.

"May I help you, sir?" asked the guard in an authoritative tone.

"Yes, I have an appointment with Dr. Lori Sanders of the American Association of State Universities," I said.

"Who shall I say is waiting?" asked the guard. "Mr. Johnson," I replied. The guard called up to Dr. Sanders' Office. He exchanged pleasantries with Dr. Sanders' assistant. I sat intently while the guard made a temporary badge and wrote down the combination for the bathroom.

"They are ready for you," said the guard. "Good luck on your interview."

The guard said this as he handed me the pass and the piece of paper with my name on it. He then quickly buried his face in paperwork before I could reply. As I picked up the pass and piece of paper I thought about the impact of the Million Man March. The effect of it was already being felt. I smiled because I had the support of the guard and countless other brothers who went through the same thing.

"Thank you," I said, heading into the elevator.

As I got off the elevator on the floor of AASU I looked up at the Wall of Fame. The Wall featured all former presidents of the Association. The Wall looked like most of the corporate world – all white men. As I turned around, I was greeted by an attractive black woman.

"Hello, Mr. Johnson, I'm Alicia Youngblood, the director of personnel." She shook my hand firmly. "I will be your first interview."

I smiled and for the next hour I explained my views on higher education issues and my views for the future.

"Mr. Johnson, I am most impressed with your ability to communicate with people of the highest authority and people who they ultimately serve," said Ms. Youngblood.

For five hours, I interviewed with Ms. Youngblood and various people in the association. By the end of the four interviews, I felt energized. As I left the last interview with Sam Kirkpatrick, president of the association, I reiterated my experience working with all types of people.

"Education is the key," I said. "But higher education is what breaks the cycle of poverty. If we establish partnerships between elementary and secondary schools and AASU institutions, we can create pathways to vocational success."

Mr. Kirkpatrick smiled as we wound up the interview.

"I like that a lot. In fact, I think I'll incorporate it in a speech I'm doing with the AASU Schools of Education."

I gave him a firm handshake and a wink. I then said good-bye to the people I met during the interviews. The last person to walk me out was Alicia Youngblood.

"Well, how did it go?" said Alicia incredulously.

"I think it went well."

"I'm sure we'll be in contact with you, Mr. Johnson, and thank you for interviewing with us."

I shook her hand firmly and headed out the office. Riding down the elevator I quietly thought about all the conversations I'd had. As I headed past the guard's desk, my new found friend asked me the big question.

"How did it go?"

"I feel good about it. In fact, I feel great."

The two of us exchanged brotherly handshakes before I departed. I was confident. This was mine to claim. I displayed charm as well as a shrewd understanding of higher education issues.

I left the building and walked down Connecticut Avenue to Filene's Basement. While at Filene's I picked up a couple of sweaters and hats. With my anticipated move up north, my wardrobe would have to change.

The Million Man March was in the air. Every conversation I heard or participated in was about the March. I decided to call Rikki's uncle.

"Hey George, what's up? Do you have time for an afternoon snack?"

George made the time to meet with me. He worked downtown for the FAA. We met at a small café near L'Enfant Plaza.

"So what's up, fella?" asked George. "I heard you had a job interview."

I spent the next thirty minutes talking about the interview and our upcoming move. George had a close connection to me. He knew my brother Silas from his years living in California. We wrapped up lunch in time for George to head home. I decided to walk past the Mall to watch the set up for the March. Huge movie screens that looked like bill boards were placed in key areas along the Mall. Vendor booths were being erected and police barricades were moved in. As I sat down on a bench to observe history in the making, my phone rang. It was Rikki.

"Hey, sweetie. How are you?" I answered enthusiastically. "The interview went great. They will call me Monday morning with an answer one way or another. The office and the people seemed really nice. Other than that, I'm chilling out on the Mall watching the set up until your Mom gets off work."

We talked about Rikki's day and her check up with the doctor the next day. Rikki seemed generally happy but she did not like me being away from home.

"I'll call you after my appointment," said Rikki. "I know you'll be at the March, but I want to give you the results."

"Sounds good, sweetie, I'm sure everything will be okay."

We hung up feeling pretty good about everything. The move would be coming soon and a new beginning was on the horizon. I left the Mall to pick up Jane from the Department of Commerce. Jane was already in the lobby by the time I arrived. We picked up her car and talked about my interview and her day at work. When we finally arrived to Jane's house, a group of visitors greeted us at the door.

"What's up Bentley, you want to buy a shirt?" asked Tim. His buddies were putting together shirts they would sell at The March. They had catchy phrases with Afro-centric designs and colors.

"How much are you charging?" I asked.

"For you, my brother," said Tim, "only $5.00 but for most people $10."

"I'll take it before you change my price due to demand," I quickly pulled out my wallet. We all laughed. I put down my briefcase and suit jacket and rolled up my sleeves to help pack the shirts.

"This is what the March is about," I thought. "I hope this catalyzes other brothers to work together after the March."

Before we knew it, 9 o'clock was upon us. We ate dinner and watched a little basketball.

I called it a night and dragged myself downstairs. I was a little tired due to the constant movement of the day, but I kept thinking about the future possibilities. I washed my face, brushed my teeth and said a long prayer for Rikki and the baby. Before I knew it, I was off to sleep dreaming about playing patty cake with the baby.

Lesson 34: A positive attitude and strong base of support can get you everything.

Chapter 35: The Ride to the Mall

The next day, I woke up bright and early. The sun shone brightly through the window and even though I was in the basement I could tell the weather was unseasonably warm for October. I put on my jogging clothes and departed from the basement door. I ran around the new development. It felt like a spring morning. There was stillness in the air. The development's enclave of black professionals was ready for the March. In fact, it felt like a holiday. No one rushed around. No cars were pulling out for the early morning rush hour. Even the children were home from school. I waved to the neighbors as they stepped out to get their papers.

By the time I finished the run and returned to my in-laws' house, the place was bustling. The fellas were up eating breakfast while Will paced from the media room to the kitchen drinking coffee and watching the morning news. The top story in the news was the March. Although only a few people were present by 8 a.m., organizers and passersby were being interviewed.

"All right yo," boomed Tim. "Are you coming with us or what, sweat man?"

"I'll be with you before the car is loaded up."

I quickly took a shower and returned before they finished breakfast.

"See, that's what an Alpha man can do," I chided, knowing I was in a house full of Ques.

"Awww don't even go there," yelled Tim. "You just didn't want to get left."

We all laughed and slapped each other five. This would be the day when black men would unite into one big fraternity. We all loaded up in two cars and parked at the New Carrollton Metro station. Each person took a box of T-shirts to sell. We would divide the proceeds at the end of the day.

The true impact of the March was seen at the Metro. It looked like game day. All the parking lots were filled and brothers were streaming in from everywhere. Since the New Carrollton stop was also a stop for Greyhound and Amtrak, the station was extra crowded. Brothers from New York, Philadelphia and Baltimore were well represented. The vibe was extremely positive. There were no stare downs or loud music. No one appeared worried about an outbreak of violence or gang retaliation. This was the one day when the black man did not feel threatened. Everyone in my car was silent but thinking the same thing. If this was the Metro stop, what would the Mall look like? As the cars stopped Tim yelled out,

"What's up brothers---Chicago is in the house!"

Almost simultaneously, brothers from throughout the parking lot started yelling the names of their hometowns.

Meanwhile, me, Tim, Will and the crew pulled out the boxes of T-shirts and backpacks. We then filled the backpacks with lunches, cameras and water. We followed the stream of other black men heading into the trains. Each train was filled to capacity. I heard a couple of brothers complementing me on the design of my T-shirt.

"Hey bro," I spoke up, "You can buy a T-shirt for $10 or pick up two for $17."

"I'll take two," said the brother, who was from New York. I started to pull out the change and before I knew it, a few more people wanted T-shirts.

"Well damn Bentley," said Tim. "You're beating us to the punch. I'm going to slide you some more T-shirts to sell."

I had just about finished selling my T-shirts before entering the train. While on the train, I asked people if they wanted to purchase a shirt. This was because I started to assist Tim with his box. Within 20 minutes, Tim's box was sold out. As I was heading off the train, an older brother approached me.

"Do you have a card? I want to buy some T-shirts for my church youth members who could not be here."

I pulled out a card and jotted down my cell number and email address.

"Just give me a call and I'll get some out to you at $7 a piece."

We exchanged numbers and gave each other the grip. A few more people bought shirts from me, all the while talking about where they came from and why the March was important. Before I knew it, we were exiting at the Smithsonian Metro Station. There was a massive exodus from the train. Only a few commuters stayed on the train looking befuddled at the large number of black men. I chuckled at their wide eyes.

"History is in the making," I said as I picked up my empty T-shirt box and followed the crowd. I met Will, Tim and the crew near the escalator.

"Are you guys ready?" I asked.

"Hell yea," said Tim. "I've got to sell the rest of my shirts." We all gave out a laugh while looking at my empty box.

As we emerged from the station, we could not believe our eyes. There was a sea of men from the Capitol to the Washington Monument. Along each side of the Mall, there were vendors along with the huge billboard-sized screens.

"Damn," I exclaimed. "This is deep—real deep."

All the men in my group were dumbfounded. Will shocked everyone into reality.

"Okay, fellas, let's meet back here by 5 p.m. If anyone gets separated just call me on the cell phone. Program my cell number into your phone. The number is 202-378-2581."

We all pulled out our cell phones and typed in Will's number.

"Okay," said Tim. "We're off to sell some shirts."

Tim and his boys took off. Meanwhile, I stayed with Will and George to walk up closer to the stage. As we weaved in and around the crowds of brothers greeting each other, we each saw people we knew. It was similar to a high school reunion. The time quickly went by with each speaker giving a different perspective on economic, spiritual, or voluntary efforts for community empowerment. One of the most dynamic speakers was a 12-year-old boy from the Bronx who described his upbringing in a single-parent home. He was unapologetic about his environment. In fact, he thought of his upbringing as an asset. After his speech, everyone gave a thunderous applause. I understood why this young brother was opening for Minister Farrakhan.

When Minister Farrakhan came on stage he was given a thunderous applause. He had everyone's attention. I had attended one other sermon by Minister Farrakhan so I was ready for his fiery speech. The minister articulated each point with a cadence that was reminiscent of Martin and Malcolm. His point by point description of responsibility of black men as fathers and stewards of the community resonated with everyone. In fact, brothers were jotting down notes from his speech

Crossing the Bridge Over Troubled Water

because it hit home. The mood was joyful, yet eerily quiet. The Minister had captured not only the imagination of the participants but also our sense of manhood.

"Damn, this is deep," I whispered to Will. "Every brother is taking this to heart."

The Minister spoke for nearly two hours without notes. Upon his conclusion, we gave a thunderous round of applause.

"Okay, let's go before we get stuck in the crowd," said Will.

With that, we took off for the Smithsonian Metro station. Although we tried to get ahead of the crowd, it was nearly impossible. Other brothers had the same thing in mind. They wanted to get home. The exit was orderly and un-rushed. Brothers were exchanging the grip and promising to start a program or a "continuation group" in their communities. This March marked a new beginning for a lot of brothers.

"Wow," said Will. "I haven't felt this type of power since the March on Washington. I think we're onto something."

Lesson 35: A million black men can be a positive force.

Chapter 36: The Call Home

I was feeling really good, so I decided to give Rikki a call to share the results of the March. The phone rang several times until Rikki finally answered. She sounded groggy—almost sedated.

"Hey, honey, you must have been taking a nap. I can call you later."

There was a pause from the line.

"What's wrong, baby?"

I could tell something was wrong—Rikki was crying.

"Hey, baby, did someone upset you? Was it the doctor's appointment?"

My mind raced as I tried to ask the right questions to pull out the problem.

"The doctor said the baby is very sick. He said the baby has about a month to live."

The words hit me like a ton of bricks. For a moment I was speechless. After I regained my composure, I was able to respond.

"Dear when I get home, we'll try every avenue to help our baby."

I tried everything in my power to calm down Rikki. I felt powerless and totally out of control. After coaxing Rikki off the phone and to sleep, I talked at length with Jane. We decided that she would go down to Atlanta once we heard more from the doctor.

I slept very little that evening. In fact, I came down from the emotional high of attending the Million Man March only to sink into the uncertainty surrounding the possible death of my baby.

I got up early the next morning, ran four miles and soaked a long time in the tub. I then prepared myself for the difficult task of telling the rest of the family members about the latest development. Will, Tim, and the other guys were sitting at the table eating breakfast as I emerged from the basement with my bags.

"Good morning, fellas," I said.

"Hey man," said Tim. "We heard the bad news. We're going to set up a prayer circle for you and Rikki."

"Thanks," I said. "I don't know a lot about what's going on, but Rikki said the baby has a thirty percent chance to survive."

"Well," said Tim "We'll focus on the odds in our favor."

We all hugged and I departed to Atlanta. While I was on the on the plane, my mind wandered, and I thought about what I would say to ease Rikki's pain. I also wondered about the health of the baby. As the plane edged further into the sky, I closed my eyes for a brief respite. The chatter of colleagues talking about a recent trip and the babbling of a baby filled the air. Before I knew it, I had drifted off to sleep. My neck tilted and shoulders relaxed. The sleep was deep. And I didn't dream. My mind was in a total state of darkness. When I awoke, we were descending over the northern part of Atlanta. I quickly regrouped and popped a piece of gum into my mouth and looked outside the window. As the plane slowly descended, my mind raced quickly to the problem of easing Rikki's fears. Within a flash I thought of one of my colleagues doing research on pregnancy risk factors.

"Of course," I thought. "Freida's doing research on the subject. She can help us better understand what's going on. In fact, she could probably refer us to someone doing important research on our issue."

I began to feel much better. As the plane touched down and taxied onto the runway, I decided to call Frieda as soon as I got off the plane.

When the plane reached the gate, I departed and found Frieda's number in my address book. I dialed the number hoping she would answer. The number rang several times. She was not in the office, so I left a message. I then decided to check in with Rikki, who was at home resting.

"Hey dear, how are feeling today?"

Rikki had been melancholy since hearing about the bad news. She did, however perk up once she heard my voice.

"Hey, baby, you must be at the airport." Rikki said.

"Yes, I'm here and I'll be at home in about forty-five minutes. Do you need anything from the store?" I said.

"Yeah, you better get some of the staples from the store. I have not been in the mood to do much shopping."

We exchanged small talk then hung up. I was left with a feeling of powerlessness.

"Damn," I thought. "This may be harder than I expected."

After buying a few groceries from the Publix supermarket, I headed down Candler Road to our house. Everything looked the same as I observed the stores along the commercial corridor. As I got closer to home, I started to get nervous.

"What should I say to make things right?" I thought. "What if she breaks down and sobs uncontrollably?" These were all issues I could not control. I did my best to calm down. I pulled into the driveway and was welcomed by the bark of Shadow. As I emerged from the truck, Shadow started to whine.

"Hey, big fella."

I reached under the gate to rub Shadow's nose. "I'm coming inside buddy."

I knew I would have to clean the yard and take Shadow for a long run. It had been three days since he had been walked. Before I could open the door, Rikki opened it up and waited for my entry. She hugged me the minute I crossed the door. We embraced for about five minutes without saying a word. It seemed like eternity.

"Please promise that you won't leave me again," Rikki said as she started to sob. "That was the hardest seventy-two hours of my life."

"I understand, baby," I replied. "We are going to work it out. I'm home and the good news is that we are moving to D.C." That was music to Rikki's ears. "We will have the support of your family with whatever happens to the baby."

More than ever, Rikki wanted to be with her mom and grandmother.

"Our baby will have everything we both had growing up. You don't have to worry about being isolated in Georgia."

Rikki cried both tears of happiness and tears of fear. For now, I said the right things to allay her fears. After spending quality time caressing Rikki, I put my bags away and then played with Shadow. I gave him a few treats and then went for the dog chain. Shadow jumped and wagged his tail uncontrollably. He was ready to go for his walk. Rikki cooked dinner while Shadow and I were out. When we returned, I took a shower and pulled out my gift to Rikki. While in D.C. I had picked up a sweatshirt from Georgetown Visitation, her alma mater, and an old framed picture of the U Street corridor. Before we ate dinner I gave Rikki her gifts. She absolutely loved them.

"Thank you, honey, I love these gifts and I can't wait to put that picture in our new house."

During dinner, we talked about the upcoming week. The items on our agenda included reviewing the strategy of the real estate agent and meeting with additional medical specialists. Talking through the weekly schedule helped both of us. We knew there was only so much we could do. The rest was in God's hands. Monday morning came quickly.

Lesson 36: Don't leave a pregnant woman alone for an extended period of time.

Chapter 37: Meeting with Specialists

We both took off the day to meet with the specialists at Emory University. As we stepped into the office of Dr. Joseph Keller, a perinatologist, we were given a brochure on genetic testing. "Good morning Mr. and Mrs. Johnson," said the receptionist. "We're glad to have you. Dr. Keller will be with you in about five minutes. In the meantime, please take a few moments to review this information on genetic testing. By the way, may I get you both something to drink?"

The office had a warm feel to it and the receptionist was well trained in customer service. I knew that this was not fully covered by the health insurance. I didn't care. Our child's welfare was on the line.

"I'll take some water," said Rikki.

I'll take some water too, I said.

The young lady came back with a small tray.

"Here you go and Dr. Keller is ready for you. Please follow me."

We traveled through a colorful corridor filled with smiling faces of young children. It was definitely uplifting. We entered an office of a well dressed middle-aged white man who was quite warm and affable.

"Mr. and Mrs Johnson, I'm Dr. Keller, chief of perinatology. I've reviewed your records and have come up with a couple of scenarios. Please take a seat so I can explain everything to you."

For the next hour, Dr. Keller took us through a mini-seminar on the latest technology in research on genetic testing to confirm any abnormalities. By the end of his presentation, our heads were spinning but we did feel somewhat better about our options.

"Okay," said Dr. Keller. "Do you have any questions?"

"Yes," I replied. "What are the chances of any of this being successful?"

"We won't know that until we start to rule out certain things. The key is to get in there quickly before your little one gets any sicker."

"Can we get started today?" asked Rikki.

"Indeed," said Dr. Keller. "We'll obtain a bit of amniotic fluid for the genetic testing and set up an appointment with my colleagues at Crawford Long for the percutaneous umbilical cord blood sampling (PUBS) procedure. Please follow my PA to get started."

Rikki followed the physician's assistant into a nice room that was warm and fuzzy. It had a sonogram and a table with a syringe and a few test tubes.

"Mrs. Johnson," said the PA, "Please change into this gown so Dr. Keller can obtain some of the amniotic fluid."

Rikki switched into her gown and when she came out, Dr. Keller was ready for her. I was also waiting for her.

"Okay, Mrs. Johnson, I'm going to place a topical numbing cream on your stomach so I can insert the needle. My PA will place the sonogram on your belly so we can view everything inside. There will be a little discomfort with the needle. You'll start to feel the needle inside your tummy."

Everything happened just as Dr. Keller explained. As the needle went inside her stomach, Rikki flinched a little because she thought the needle would poke the baby. It didn't.

Dr. Keller was very gentle and exact. He extracted enough amniotic fluid for two vials. Meanwhile, Rikki and I viewed the sonogram. We could see the little fingers, toes and big head. We could also tell it was a boy. He was resting but twitching every now and then.

"Hang in there little buddy," I said.

Before we knew it, the procedure was over.

"How did it go?" asked Dr. Keller.

"It was okay," replied Rikki.

Dr. Keller smiled and pulled out some literature.

"In about a week's time we'll have your results. That coupled with your appointment with my colleagues at Crawford Long Hospital, should give us a better determination."

Rikki put on her clothes and thought about everything that was happening. It was a bit overwhelming but she did not let her concerns overwhelm her. After the appointment Rikki and I got a bite to eat. During lunch we reviewed the literature received from Dr. Keller.

"I wonder if he has Downs Syndrome," asked Rikki.

"I don't think so," I replied. "We don't have a family history of it. Let's hope this new procedure works out."

It all seemed so foreign, but we gathered all the information we could to understand what was going on. After leaving the hospital, we stopped off at Barnes & Noble to get a book on genetic testing.

While perusing the bookstore, I saw a book on selling your own home.

"Hey Rikki, are you satisfied with our real estate agent? This guy has not produced any real leads. I think I can do better than him."

"Bentley what happens if you don't sell the house before we leave? We will then be left with selling a house from D.C."

"It's all about pricing and marketing," I said. "I'm going to use 4 Sale By Owner."

I had my mind made up. I needed something to distract my attention and channel my nervous energy. I called the "4 Sale By Owner" company and ordered my signs and called the paper to place an open house ad in the Sunday paper.

"Time to fire our trifling agent," I said.

Within minutes of returning home, I did just that. Rikki was a bit skeptical but that was the last thing on her mind. After dinner she read up on the genetic testing and the new in-utero procedure called PUBS. Both things provided promise but nothing was assured. For the next couple of days, we both went to work to stay busy. In addition, I started to receive inquiries about the house. Things picked up quickly until Friday, the day of the next doctor's appointment. That morning at breakfast Rikki expressed her concern.

"What happens if he lives?" asked Rikki. "He will probably be a really sick kid."

"Honey, we can't control that. The good news is that we'll be with relatives who will help out. If, heaven forbid, God takes our son from us, we have to ask ourselves: Did we do everything we could do to save him? The answer to that is a resounding yes. In essence, this is out of our hands and we need to pray on it."

As we finished breakfast, there was an eerie quietness in the air. The ride to Crawford Long Hospital was also very quiet. We took the scenic route down Ponce de Leon Avenue. We went past Fernbank Museum, the old Sears Building, and the famous restaurant Pitty Pat's Porch. I loved Atlanta and knew I would miss it once we left to start a new beginning in D.C. As my mind drifted, I navigated the car into the parking lot at Crawford Long Hospital. After parking, we took our time heading up to the doctor's office. Rikki was now seven months pregnant. Our baby was at least six pounds and could survive a C-section but before they attempted it more tests had to be run. The big test was today. By the time we arrived at the doctor's office, Rikki was winded.

"Okay, I am now officially ready for a nap," gasped Rikki.

"Well, dear, hopefully you'll be able to rest during the procedure."

The receptionist greeted us and within minutes we were called into the doctor's office. A tall young doctor named Dr. Stein came to greet us. He was kind yet distant. His approach was much like a researcher.

"Mrs. Johnson we are going to draw blood from your umbilical cord and listen to the heart beat of your baby," said Dr. Stein. "Based on my conversations with your doctor, we believe the best course of action is to examine the blood of your baby and then determine if there is an infection. By the end of the day, we will call you with the results. Time is of the essence."

By now, Rikki knew the drill. She would be hooked up to the sonogram while the doctor examined her and the baby. The special sonogram cream was rubbed on her large tummy. Our baby kicked a few times as the crème was applied.

"I guess he knows we're going to look at him again," said Rikki dryly. Within a few seconds, we saw him. Dr. Stein rubbed a topical analgesic on Rikki's stomach to numb the pain of the needle penetrating her stomach.

"Okay here we go," said Dr. Stein.

Rikki flinched for a moment as the needle entered her stomach and went directly into her umbilical cord. Dr. Stein extracted three large vials of blood from Rikki.

"Okay that's it," he said. "Let's see what we have so we can get you the results this afternoon."

Rikki could feel the edge of the needle in her stomach. While the blood was extracted, she could feel the baby moving.

"It's hurting him," Rikki said to Dr. Stein.

Dr. Stein assured Rikki that everything was going to be okay. As the doctor finished up, we listened intently.

"Mrs. Johnson, you can put your clothes back on. I'll be sure to meet you later this afternoon. Susan up front will give you an exact time."

Rikki slowly took off the gown. Meanwhile I helped her put on her pants and shoes. "Are you hungry, honey?" I asked. "We can run up to the Sunshine Café in Buckhead and just hang out for a couple of hours."

"Sure," said Rikki. "I actually like that idea."

When we left the room, Susan the receptionist had the appointment ready.

"Mr. and Mrs. Johnson, Dr. Stein will see you at 4 p.m."

As we left the office, we saw other couples with eyes filled with concern and anxiety.

"Wait here in the lobby and I'll pull the car around." I ran to get the car. Once I picked Rikki up we then headed up Peachtree to Buckhead. On the way, we could see the city transforming into a destination for Olympic travelers. There were more billboards than ever before. In addition, new restaurants and hotels were being constructed. This led to a somewhat slower ride to our destination. When we arrived at Sunshine Café, it was virtually empty. I parked right at the front door.

"Okay, we're here, honey." I gently nudged Rikki.

"Okay," said Rikki with a great stretch. We sat near the window and gazed outside.

"Can you believe this is happening?" asked Rikki.

"It's pretty damn crazy," I replied.

We both ate slowly and deliberately and tried to take our minds off of what was going on. After lunch, we went to Publix to get something for dinner and to get some Goobers, which were a craving of Rikki's.

By the time we finished shopping, it was time to head back to Crawford Long. The traffic crawled down Peachtree, so I hopped on the freeway. After parking the car, I tried to rush but remembered that Rikki could not move any faster than a turtle.

When we arrived upstairs to Dr. Stein's office, the receptionist waved us back to see Dr. Stein. When he opened the door, another physician was with him.

"Hi Mr. and Mrs. Johnson, this is my good friend Dr. Kessler whose specialty is pediatric cardiology. Please sit down so we can explain."

Rikki did not like the seriousness of his tone. She could feel her eyes welling up. Instinctively, I grabbed her hand and started to rub her back. Immediately, Rikki felt better.

"Mr. and Mrs. Johnson," said Dr. Stein. "Your baby has a really bad infection that has caused the pericardial cavity to fill with fluid. For some reason, your baby's body is fighting off an infection by creating an over abundance of antigens to kill it. To counteract it, we suggest doing a blood transfusion. This will give the body new blood and thus a reason to stop producing the antigens. We would like to schedule the transfusion for Monday morning."

We were stunned. However, we knew there was little time to waiver.

"We'll be ready for Monday morning. Is that okay, honey?" Rikki nodded.

She squeezed my hand.

"Thank you Mr. and Mrs. Johnson," said Dr. Kessler. "We'll be with you all the way through."

Rikki tried to produce a little smile but it was not genuine. She looked out the window and thought about the last few days. She felt like she had aged by at least twenty years.

"Are we finished?" Rikki whispered, looking straight through Dr. Stein. Her reply threw Dr. Stein off balance. He expected more questions and wanted to provide a detailed explanation. As a researcher, he cherished a challenge.

"Okay, since you don't have any questions, we'll see you Monday morning. The overall procedure should take no longer than a couple of hours."

We left the hospital feeling an even greater sense of uncertainty.

"They have no idea what they're dealing with," I said to myself. "I could stand this a little more if they would admit it."

Lesson 37: Sometimes illnesses are unexplainable.

Chapter 38: A Friend in Need

We headed home in silence letting the gravity of events sink in. After going roughly half-way to our house, I headed through downtown Decatur.

"Let's stop by Payt and Morgan's." Payt and Morgan were friends we met while working on the Metropolitan Project. They had just bought a new house with all the bells and whistles. As I drove up to the house, Payt was pulling into his driveway.

"What's up, newlywed?" I bellowed.

"Nothing much, old wise one," Payt replied.

"We were in the neighborhood and just wanted to say hi."

Payt motioned for us to come into the house. As we all entered the house, Payt called Morgan on his cell phone.

"Hey, Dear, guess who stopped by---Bentley and Rikki. Can you stop and get some Chinese food?"

Before I could say anything, Payt told Morgan we were staying for dinner. I had only stopped by their house to get Payt's opinion on the baby's condition. Payt was a pediatrician by training but he worked for the international health organization called Cooperative for Assistance and Relief Everywhere or CARE. Payt placed his work bag near their library and headed upstairs to change his clothes.

"Why don't you guys make yourselves at home? We have juice and water in the fridge and Bentley I have a new CD by Dave Coz sitting on the CD player."

I took the hospitality to heart and grabbed some juice for myself and a bottle of water for Rikki. By the time Payt returned to the living room, we had our feet propped up and were listening to Dave Coz.

"So what's up, fella?" asked Payt. "You guys look like you have something on your minds."

"Well, I do have something to ask you…"

I looked for the opening and Payt gave it to me. I talked non-stop for about an hour. Rikki had little chance to chime in, but she did make sure that I did not miss important details. After I finished, Payt sat for a while letting it all sink in.

"Wow, that's pretty heavy," Payt said solemnly. "I've heard of similar problems only a couple of times in my career. I'm going to need to do a literature review and check with a couple of my friends who are researchers at the medical school.

Rikki's eyes started to well up.

"What could it be?" asked Rikki. "It just came on so fast."

"There are several possibilities," said Payt. "And what we do in the medical field is narrow down the possibilities to something that is remotely similar to what we can recognize."

For the next two hours, we discussed factors with Payt and he gave us specific implications. Rikki was starting to feel better – not about the situation, but about our ability to understand the range of options and implications.

Morgan arrived midway through the conversation. She laid out the Chinese food and quickly changed her clothes. Although she was not deeply involved in the conversation, she was a quick study and knew the situation was rather grave.

"Come on, guys. Let's eat dinner here in the dining room."

Throughout dinner, we changed subjects and focused on life as newlyweds. We told Payt and Morgan funny stories of our first few years. After dinner, Rikki and Morgan talked at the table while Payt and I watched the basketball game. It was 10 o'clock by the time the game ended.

"Oh my," I said. "We've stayed way beyond our welcome and must head home to feed Shadow."

"Oh boy," said Rikki. "Poor Shadow has probably disturbed our neighbors. He starts to bark when he's mad."

We exchanged hugs and pleasantries. Morgan and Rikki hugged for a long time while Payt and I promised to keep each other informed of the situation. The evening was exactly what we needed.

"Wow, that was great," said Rikki. "We've got to hang with them more often. Did you know that Morgan experienced something similar with her son?"

"Her son?? I didn't know she had a son."

"Yep, and he's coming to live with them in a couple of weeks."

By the time we finished talking about Payt and Morgan, we arrived home. As we pulled into the driveway, we could see Shadow's big head peering through the gate. He was barking loudly because he was hungry and mad.

"Okay boy," I said as I got out of the car. "Let's get you something to eat."

After feeding and walking Shadow, I was ready for bed.

Around 7 a.m. on Saturday, Shadow walked into the room and nudged me with his nose. I knew Shadow was there before his big nose touched my face. Shadow usually stared at me for a couple of minutes before touching me.

"Hey buddy," I said as I touched Shadow's head.

"Are you ready for your walk?" Shadow jumped up and down. I quickly put on my sweats and headed out of the bedroom. I washed up and proceeded to make coffee. As the coffee brewed, I fed Shadow. Within minutes, Shadow's bowl was clean. I placed my coffee in a portable mug and grabbed Shadow's leash. We headed out the back door and gate. Before heading out the gate, I remembered to put a couple of tennis balls in my pockets. For the next hour we had fun. Shadow sniffed through bushes and explored the leaves. I, on the other hand, let my mind wander from selling the house to our baby's future. The latter was really on my mind because there was no clear outcome. When we returned from the walk, I decided to check on Rikki. As I walked into the room, Shadow tip toed behind me. Shadow's toenails click clacked on the hardwood floor. I was certain this would wake up Rikki. It didn't. Rikki slept soundly for the next two hours. By the time she awoke, I had straightened up the house and cooked her brunch.

"What's up sleepy head," I bellowed. Rikki rubbed her eyes and her stomach.

"That food woke me up. The two of us are hungry."

"Well, why don't you have a seat my dear?" I replied while holding the seat for Rikki.

I prepared a southern style breakfast that consisted of grits, eggs, turkey sausage and biscuits. I got the Saturday paper and decided to have another cup of coffee while Rikki ate her food.

"Don't you want to join me for this feast?" said Rikki.

"I'm not hungry. You know it's always hard for the chef to eat his own food."

We read the paper and considered going to the movies. Meanwhile, Shadow sat on our enclosed back porch, waiting for the next squirrel to run into our yard.

We decided to go to the movie theater near Emory University. Right before the movie, I copied flyers advertising our house. In addition I bought a few "open house Sunday" signs. When we arrived at the movie theater, it was packed. I dropped Rikki off at the box office while I parked the car. I arrived just in time. Inside the theater, Rikki bought raisinettes and a bag of popcorn. She had to have that sweet and salty mixture. After the movie ended, we went to the all-you-can-eat soup and salad place. This was one of our favorite places to eat. With our minds focused on the open house, we decided to get a few knick knacks and a guest book for a sign in. When we finally returned home, it was about 9 p.m. We were tired. As we drove into the driveway, we could see Shadow's eyes reflecting the headlights. He was pacing back and forth, waiting for us to get out of the car. I got out and acknowledged Shadow. I then went to the door to help Rikki out of the car. We headed to the front door and both took a look at the house. It was clean and very inviting. The hardwood floors and open floor plan made it a great entertainment house. The added bonuses were the side sun room and rear enclosed porch.

"Let me feed that dog before he tears something up," I said.

I headed off to the back to feed Shadow. Meanwhile, Rikki got ready for bed. After feeding Shadow, I washed up and heated up the tea kettle. Rikki was in the tub relaxing her nerves.

"Bentley!" screamed Rikki. "Come here."

I quickly ran into the bathroom.

"What's wrong?" I asked while catching my breath.

"The baby is getting weaker!" Rikki screamed.

"How do you know?"

"His kicks are getting weaker." The two of us looked at each other. This raised the stakes significantly for a successful blood transfusion.

Tears streamed down Rikki's cheeks. I was speechless. There was not much I could say without sounding ridiculous.

"We're going to work through this," I said as I knelt down to scrub Rikki's back. "God's going to take care of us and our baby."

I heard the whistling of the tea kettle and hurried out of the room. I returned with two cups of tea. By the time I returned, Rikki put on her gown and was sitting up in the bed. We watched the evening news and by the time "Saturday Night Live" came on, Rikki was asleep. I, on the other hand, did not fall asleep until after "Showtime at the Apollo." My mind raced through everything I had to do. The first thing was to sell the house. The second was to relocate to the D.C. area. I was confident the baby would survive. I finally drifted off to sleep at 1:00 a.m.

Lesson 38: In times of uncertainty, appreciate the little things in life.

Chapter 39: The Procedure

At 7 a.m., I was awakened by the wet cold nose of Shadow. As I tried to turn away, Shadow moved his large head into the bed and nudged me on the back.

"Okay boy, I'm getting up."

Shadow, seemingly satisfied, led the way into the kitchen to get his food. I fed and walked him. When we returned, I took a shower and got ready for church. My church's service began at 9 a.m. and the time was 8:30 a.m. I did all I could to wake Rikki up. She was too tired and did not want to attend.

"This is a losing battle," I thought. "Only God can get us through this and I'll have to be the one that carries the load."

I gave Rikki a kiss and headed out the door. At church I sat in the balcony because the church was already full when I arrived. The choir rocked the church with a rendition of "How Great He Is." I was starting to be filled with the Spirit. All the tension and anxiety subsided, while tears streamed down my cheeks. By the time the sermon began I was totally focused. Rev. Brooks, the senior pastor gave the sermon. He was an old school southern gentleman from Alabama. His sermons tended to be a bit unfocused and rambling but this day it was different. Rev. Brooks used a contemporary example of the singer Teddy Pendergrass who lost focus, but not faith. It was a great sermon for me to hear. I felt strongly about my faith, and that it would guide me through the storm. When Rev. Brooks ended his sermon, I felt energized and more hopeful. Apparently, so did quite a few other folks.

"Wow, Rev. Brooks pulled out a special one today," said a young lady sitting next to me. "Yes he did," I replied.

The young woman smiled at me. I smiled back but knew the look was not one I could acknowledge.

"Damn, she looks good," I thought. "But I'm not trying to get in trouble."

At the end of the service, I headed out and then went to the store to get some balloons to hang on my signs and on the front porch. When I returned home, Rikki was up eating her breakfast.

"Hey, sweetie, how do you feel?"

"Not bad."

"So, how long are we going to stay out of the house?" inquired Rikki.

"Hmmm, let's hang out until 6 p.m." Rikki finished her breakfast and took her shower. By the time she finished and dressed, our good friend Lynn had arrived to show the house. We had removed all signs of race in the house. No one could tell the race of the owners.

The idea of having Lynn show our house came through me. I figured the South was still the South so with Lynn, I hoped to get better movement. When we returned at 6 p.m. the outcome was positive. We had one contract and two prospects interested in writing a contract. The couple who wrote the contract was ready to close in two weeks—most likely because, they lost out on another house in South Decatur.

"Lynn," I said. "You are worth your weight in gold. Have you thought about getting into real estate on the side?"

I was really teasing Lynn but she didn't realize it.

Crossing the Bridge Over Troubled Water

"Well, I might think about it now," she said. "Especially if every deal is this easy."

We all chuckled and hugged. I had $200 ready to put in Lynn's hands.

"Don't you even try to give me that money," Lynn said with an evil eye.

"Well, I don't want you to think I don't value your time. I was taught to respect people's time and pay them for what they're worth."

"Well," said Lynn. "Just keep that money for the baby's scholarship fund."

"Thank you," I said while giving Lynn another hug.

By the time Lynn left the house, it was 7:30 p.m.

"Whew, it's time to eat and then go to bed. I'll heat up the leftovers while you feed Shadow," said Rikki.

By the time I finished, Rikki was at the table with our meal.

"It's always better the second day," I said. "Thanks for heating the food."

"You're welcome, sweetie," said Rikki. "You know what? I'm getting excited about moving to D.C."

I smiled and reached for Rikki's hand. I squeezed it, acknowledging her wishful thinking. I also knew we had a long road ahead. After dinner, we watched a little T.V. and read our books. Shadow gnawed on a pig ear and tried to get me to play tug of war. We all finally went to bed around 11:30 p.m. Rikki drifted off into a deep sleep. I, on the other hand, drifted in and out of sleep wondering what the next day would bring.

The next day we woke up at 7 a.m. I quickly fed and walked Shadow. I said barely one word to Rikki after returning from the walk.

"Sweetie, are you okay?" asked Rikki.

"Yes, I'm just thinking."

"What are you thinking about?"

"Oh, I was just thinking about how the baby is feeling."

"Well, I don't think he's in pain."

The answer was sufficient for the moment and I let it go. Rikki put on her clothes, washed up and brushed her teeth. Meanwhile, I heated up the car. Rikki waited at the door for me to assist her in walking down the steps.

"Alright, sweetie, let's take these one at a time."

Once in the car, I turned on Arrested Development. They were a rap group with members from Emory University. Their motto was "rappers with a conscience."

"Hey, I like this song," said Rikki.

I smiled while Rikki looked at the CD cover.

"I like the lyrics and they actually make sense." By the time the CD completed the songs, we were at Crawford Long Hospital. The parking attendant, who now knew me, waved me into the spot. At 9 a.m., we were in the doctor's office. We did not have to wait; in fact the receptionist waved us into the outpatient surgery suite.

"Well, hello, Mr. and Mrs. Johnson. We will get started in a moment. Please change into the surgical gown and then lie on the table," said Dr. Keller. "My colleague Dr. Stein will be in shortly."

Within minutes, Rikki returned. Almost simultaneously, Dr. Stein appeared.

"Good morning Mrs. Johnson let's begin this procedure with the sonogram."

Dr. Stein was an efficient man. While the radiology tech prepared the sonogram, he pulled out a long needle and laid it close to the table.

"Don't let the size of the needle scare you. It won't hurt a bit."

While Dr. Stein prepared the syringes, Dr. Keller pulled out the B negative blood that would be used for the transfusion.

"Let's give your little guy strength with some new blood because he's getting weaker." The words "getting weaker" stuck in my head. Rikki already knew that was happening because of the infrequent movement.

"Hold on little guy," said Rikki to herself. "Please hold on."

Dr. Stein rubbed the topical anesthetic on Rikki's stomach. Within a couple of minutes it was numb. Dr. Stein then eased the needle with the first pint of blood into Rikki's stomach near the umbilical cord. Once he got the needle into Rikki's stomach, he guided the tip of the needle into the umbilical cord. The sonogram served as his second set of eyes.

"Okay, Mrs. Johnson, we are now going to start the transfusion," said Dr. Stein.

As he exchanged syringes filled with fresh blood, I looked at the long needle in Rikki's stomach. Meanwhile, Rikki just stared at the sonogram praying for the baby to get better. Within thirty minutes, the procedure was done.

"Okay," said Dr. Stein. "We've completed the procedure. Let's hope that your little guy takes to the fresh supply of blood."

Dr. Stein voice sounded moderately positive. As he pulled off his gloves and his assistants took over, I summoned Dr. Stein.

"Hey Dr. Stein, do you have quick minute?"

"Sure."

We walked into the empty nurses' station.

"What's on your mind, Mr. Johnson?" asked Dr. Stein.

"What are the real chances for success?'

"The real chances are unknown but if you're looking for my personal opinion, I would say fifty-fifty," replied Dr. Stein.

"I see," I said. "What about induced labor?"

"The truth is," said Dr. Stein. "The best environment to care for the infant is in the mother's womb. She provides protection and nutrients. In the exterior world we would need to mimic the womb plus try to solve the problem."

We gave each other a blank stare. I was convinced for now that there were no other alternatives. I thanked Dr. Stein and headed back to Rikki. Back in the outpatient suite, Rikki was chatting with Dr. Keller.

"Mr. Johnson, we were just talking about next steps. We're going to let the blood transfusion take its course and then schedule a follow-up visit for a week from now. In the interim make sure you see your ob/gyn."

"Will do," replied Rikki.

I gathered Rikki's goods and put them in the duffle bag. Rikki put the bag in her lap as she stepped into a wheelchair. I then pushed Rikki down to the car. We were glad to get a breath of fresh air and feel the openness of outside.

"Are you hungry, honey?" I asked.

"Not really," replied Rikki. "I'm just a little numb right now."

I tried to sooth Rikki's nerves. Everything I suggested was denied. I knew she was not rejecting me. It was just that I did not want Rikki to drift into depression. On the way home, we passed by Payt and Morgan's house. We were surprised to see a "For Sale" sign in the front yard. "What in the world is going on?" asked Rikki. "We were just there a few days ago."

"This is a good diversion," I thought.

"You know, dear, I don't know, but we're going to find out."

It had been about two weeks since we had hung out with Payt and Morgan.

"I'm going to knock on their door."

I pulled up near the house and got out and rang the door bell a couple of times. Just as I was leaving the porch, Payt answered.

"What's up, cool daddy?"

"Hey man," I said. "What's up with the sign?"

"We're moving to South Africa," replied Payt.

"What?!"

Rikki heard the whole conversation and was in total disbelief. We sat on the porch talking to Payt for two hours. Payt gave us the lowdown on his new position with the World Health Organization while we explained the procedure that took place with Dr. Stein. We also mentioned our upcoming move to D.C. By the time we finished, it was 8 p.m. We stopped by J.R. Cricket's to get hamburgers. We also stopped at the pet store to get a crate for Shadow's transportation to D.C.

As we headed home from the store, I wondered what was next. Rikki wondered the same thing. For the next week we packed boxes. Rikki did as much as she could from the bed and from her lounge chair. She did not feel well physically or emotionally.

"He's not getting better," she said to herself.

It was a mother's premonition that she did not want to share with me. On the D.C. side of things, Jane prepared Granny's basement apartment and got a referral for the doctor to deliver the baby if everything went as planned. Rikki was now thirty weeks pregnant. She was close enough to have the induced labor—if the doctors agreed. Jane questioned the expertise of the Emory doctors. In fact, she questioned their motives—it was still the Deep South. Jane paced nervously around their house, getting things just right.

"Jane, you need to sit down," said Granny. "Nothing you do now is going to change the outcome of that child's pregnancy. You know that when the Lord calls, you've got to answer."

"Well, Mom," said Jane. "If the Lord calls, you need to have a phone to answer. I'm just trying to make sure Rikki has everything."

Jane knew Granny was right. There was nothing she could do to change the situation. As any mother would, she wanted to fix the problem for her child.

Meanwhile, back in Georgia, a week had passed. We went back to Dr. Stein for a check up. The outcome of the visit was inconclusive. The baby's condition was about the same.

"Let's give it until the end of the week," said Dr. Stein. "In the meantime, I will call a few of my colleagues across the country."

When we returned home, I completed packing the boxes. My last day at work was coming up and soon my father would fly in to assist us in moving.

"Bentley," said Rikki. "I think our little guy is sicker than we think. His movement is down to twitching."

Rikki's words stunned me. I immediately got the phone.

"We should call your OB-GYN."

Rikki thought about saying "no" for a hot second.

"I think we should call her."

I dialed the number and talked to Dr. Sweeney's assistant.

"Hi Rachel, this is Mr. Johnson. My wife needs to see Dr. Sweeney as soon as possible. She thinks the baby's movement is down to nothing."

"Hold on for a moment," said Rachel. "I'm going to check in with Dr. Sweeney."

The smooth jazz of David Benoit blared over the phone. Just as I was getting into the rhythm, Rachel returned.

"Can you guys see her first thing in the morning?"

"Yes," I said. "We'll be there at 9 a.m."

When I got off the phone Rikki was crying.

"I don't want to lose my baby."

Rikki tried desperately to keep it together, but it didn't work. She started to sob uncontrollably.

"Honey, we don't know what's happening. Let's make it to Dr. Sweeney's office before we jump to any conclusions."

I held Rikki and just rocked her. I knew that what she needed most was a hug to calm her down.

"I know this is difficult, honey. God will only give us as much as we can take."

Rikki pulled herself together. We decided to go to the movies. After the movie, we got some dessert at a small café near Emory. We marveled at how quickly things had changed in our lives.

Lesson 39: The bond between child and mother is metaphysical.

Chapter 40: The Outcome

The next morning as we drove down Ponce de Leon Avenue, Rikki thought about the pleasantries of being in Atlanta.

"I love this town," she said. "One day we'll be back after all this is over."

Within minutes, we were at Dr. Sweeney's front door. I buzzed the door bell twice. Rachel answered the door.

"Hi, Mr. and Mrs. Johnson," said Rachel. "Dr. Sweeney will be right with you, she's finishing up with a patient."

We waited for about five minutes. Rikki was on pins and needles.

"Hi, Mr. and Mrs. Johnson, please come in," said Dr. Sweeney. "Can you please slip into the gown while I get the sonogram?"

Rikki knew the drill. She took off her clothes and waited for the inevitable. When the sonogram came into the room, she laid back and stared at the ceiling.

"Can you tell me the last time you felt movement?" asked Dr. Sweeney.

"Oh, a couple of days ago," replied Rikki.

By now, Dr. Sweeney had placed the stethoscope on Rikki's stomach and was trying to detect a beat. She moved the scope horizontally, vertically and diagonally. Although she was poker faced, her actions told the outcome.

"Let's see what can be seen via the sonogram."

Dr. Sweeney rubbed the hand held device against Rikki's stomach. We viewed the baby lying there with no movement and no beat.

"Mr. and Mrs. Johnson, I'm sorry but your little one has passed away."

The words pierced through Rikki's ears. Tears welled up in her eyes.

"My baby," weeped Rikki, "Why my baby…."

I felt numb. The gravity of everything made me react slowly.

"Dr. Sweeney, what next? Will they have to induce labor?"

"First, let me express my sincere condolences," said Dr. Sweeney. "In very rare cases, something like this occurs. I know it does not make the situation better, but just know that this rarely happens."

We still could not fully understand what happened. I put my arm around Rikki and let her sob uncontrollably. The series of events ran through my head.

"Dr. Sweeney, can we have a moment alone?"

I needed time to focus on next steps. As Rikki cried, I tried to figure out the best thing to say. I decided rather than saying more, I would resort to the lowest common denominator.

"Honey, we're going to get through this. I know it seems unbelievable at this time, but we'll get through it together. I'm going to call back Dr. Sweeney so we can move on to the next steps."

I called down the hall for Dr. Sweeny. She was with another patient so she couldn't come immediately. Meanwhile, Rikki put on her clothes. By the time she was finished, Dr. Sweeney had returned.

"Mr. and Mrs. Johnson, I talked to my colleagues at Crawford Long and they will be ready to induce labor at 3 p.m. today."

Rikki had regained her composure, but was not quite ready for Dr. Sweeney's news.

"What do you mean by induced labor?" asked Rikki as she stared incredulously into Dr. Sweeney's eyes.

"Mrs. Johnson, I know you've been through a very traumatic experience but you must deliver your son," replied Dr. Sweeney. "We don't want to further complicate matters associated with your pregnancy."

Rikki couldn't believe the conversation. Never in her wildest dreams did she think that she would have to deliver a still born child. I decided to step in to change the subject.

"So, Dr. Sweeney what's the healing process after the delivery?"

"Well," said Dr. Sweeney. "Mrs. Johnson should be okay but more than anything, the two of you should take your time and perhaps take a long vacation to the Bahamas."

I tried to get a smile out of Rikki.

"That's the best advice we've heard yet!" I exclaimed. Rikki stared into space completely oblivious of the conversation.

"Honey let's call our parents," I said as I gathered our belongings and headed out of the examining room." Since we had a lot of time to spare, I wanted to take Rikki somewhere to call our parents in peace.

"I'm going to head up to Buckhead. In the meantime, please call your mom while I'm driving."

Rikki pulled out her cell phone as I headed out the driveway and up Peachtree Street.

"Hi Mom, yeah, I don't sound too good because we just came from the doctor's office. Our baby boy died."

Rikki cried quietly as she listened to her mom's consolation. She shook her head and listened intently. They talked for about twenty minutes and ended with Rikki saying she would see her mom the next day. I then called my parents.

"Hey Mom," I said. "Hmmm, I'm not doing too good. We just returned from the doctor's office and they said our baby passed away. Yes, I'm really sorry too. I'm doing as best as I can but more importantly I'm trying to keep Rikki's spirits up. By the way, Dad is still on for early next week, right?"

While my conversation was calm and controlled, inside the whole situation was tearing me up. My stomach churned and I could hardly concentrate on driving. After I got off the phone, Rikki called her best friends.

Rikki spent at least a half an hour with each friend. Her girl friend Leeza was driving down from D. C. after work. Rikki tried to convince her otherwise, but she was not having it. Leeza would be in town around the same time as Jane. By the time they ended their calls and getting a small bit to eat, it was time to return to Crawford Long. When we arrived at the Birthing Center, we were greeted by Dr. Stein, Dr. Keller and Dr. Sweeney.

"Hi Mrs. and Mrs. Johnson," said Dr. Stein. "We want to express our deepest sympathy for your loss."

"Thanks doctors," I said. "We appreciate all your efforts through this ordeal. I know this is difficult for you as well."

Once I said this, the eyes of the doctors started to well up.

"We have a birthing suite for you, Mrs. Johnson," said Dr. Keller. "I will induce the labor and deliver your son. If it's okay, let's head up to your suite."

We all headed down the hall to an area that was serene and surreal. The Crawford Long Birthing Center was filled with happy families who seemed to be in their own bedroom communities.

"I can't believe this is happening," Rikki said to herself. "What a nightmare."

Rikki followed the doctor with me in tow. When we arrived to her suite, a nurse was there. Rikki went into the bathroom to change into her gown. She rubbed her stomach and said a prayer. Meanwhile, I talked to the doctors about follow-up care and indicators of depression. When Rikki emerged from the bathroom, everyone got quiet.

"Okay, I'm ready," she said softly.

Dr. Keller directed her to a warm table with fluffy pillows and cotton sheets. The room was painted in a series of earth tones and the sound of classical music could be heard.

"Mrs. Johnson, just relax and in a moment you're going to feel your uterus start to contract."

Rikki drifted off to almost a state of sleep when her uterus started to contract.

"Okay, Mrs. Johnson in a moment you will need to start pushing." Rikki placed her legs in the warm stirrups. I positioned myself behind her and placed my hands on her shoulders. I started to give her a light massage which eased her tension. Rikki automatically grabbed my arms. As she started to push, she felt the sharp pain of the baby's movement down her uterus. His head was starting to push through her vagina. The pain was nothing Rikki had ever experienced. Slowly but surely our baby started to emerge. Rikki pushed and puffed. Tears of pain streamed down her face as she wished for a sound or scream of a baby coming out. The room was filled with a deafening silence and the pain of a mother birthing a lost child. Tears streamed down my cheeks as I questioned God's decision to take my only son.

"Push, Mrs. Johnson," said Dr. Keller, "He's coming out."

Rikki contracted her abdomen and hip muscles and out came our baby. He was blue as the ocean. As the nurse pulled him out, Rikki looked up and cried. Tears of joy and sadness overcame her.

"Here, honey," said the nurse. "You must hold him." Rikki cupped him in her arms and rocked him.

"He's beautiful," I said. "And he's in God's hands."

Rikki extended her arms for me to take him. I rocked him briefly as tears streamed down my cheeks.

"I'm sorry," I said to myself. "I don't know why you had to die."

Just then, the social worker came in with a folder.

"Hi, I'm Mrs. Cunningham and I'm the social worker and grief counselor. I'm here to explain options for your son. I know this may seem to be a bad time but it's better now than later. There are a couple of options for you to consider for your son. This has to do with burying him or having him cremated here at the hospital. Why don't you take a few hours to think about it and I'll be around later this evening."

We nodded our heads—in disbelief. When everyone departed, we stared at our baby.

"If they had only found out earlier, he'd be alive," said Rikki. "I still can't believe he's dead."

"I know, honey," I said. "I can't believe it either."

"So what do you want to do?" asked Rikki.

I thought about the question for a while and then responded.

"Honey, we will be moving to D.C. in a week and I just don't think we can handle burying him."

Rikki thought about it for a while.

"I'm just too tired to think about it. It's just too much to think about it. Can you please handle it?"

I made the hardest decision of my life and had my son cremated.

∼

Lesson 40: Make sure you have a way to memorialize your loved one.

∼

Chapter 41: Released from the Hospital

Later in the evening I talked to the social worker, who gave us a packet about our decision and promised to check in with Rikki before we departed from the hospital. The nurse practitioner came to pick up our baby about an hour after the decision.

"Mr. and Mrs. Johnson, I'm nurse Hathaway and I'm here to take your baby boy away." We shook our heads and acknowledged the inevitable. Nurse Hathaway reached for the infant I held. Rikki glanced at me and the nurse. Both of us were careful to read Rikki's body language. Rikki bent down her head and said yes. Streams of tears flowed down her cheeks.

"Bye, baby, I love you and will always miss you," wept Rikki.

We were numb and held each others hands. The T.V. was on, but it was only background noise.

"I'm going to get a soda, would you like anything?" I asked.

"Yes, I'll take a ginger ale."

While I was out, Rikki's father called. The normally stoic Thelonius chattered nervously as he tried to figure out the best words to express his grief.

"Hey, honey," said Thelonius. "I talked to your mother and she gave me your information at the hospital. I'm sorry. I thought things were getting better."

Rikki explained the circumstances and the ultimate outcome. On the other end of the line Thelonius wept quietly for Rikki and the baby.

"How long will you be in the hospital?" asked Thelonius.

"They'll probably discharge me tomorrow."

"I've got to run to a meeting, honey. Clementine wants to talk to you."

Clementine offered her own condolences. I walked in while Rikki was getting off the phone with Clementine.

"Well, I'll see you guys in about a week," said Rikki. "We've got to finish boxing up our house."

Rikki shook her head as Clementine offered words of encouragement. She then said her good-byes.

"How are the folks?" I asked as I handed Rikki her ginger ale.

"Not bad, but of course they are shocked and saddened. My father was pretty shaken up."

"I can understand that. I'll call my folks later on this evening."

We took a little nap and were awakened by a dinner call and a visit by Dr. Keller.

"Mrs. Johnson, how are you feeling?"

"Oh, okay, I'm still a little sore."

"Let's see how you're doing," said Dr. Keller.

Dr. Keller examined Rikki and noted minor spotting.

"I think you'll be able to leave tomorrow morning."

"Thanks, Dr. Keller," I said. "We appreciate your care."

Dr. Keller reached out to give me a hand shake. He then shook Rikki's hand and gave her a hug. Just as Dr. Keller left, in came the social worker Mrs. Cunningham.

"Hi, Mr. and Mrs. Johnson, I hope this isn't a bad time. I will be short. Here's a package of material for you and inside of it is a picture of your little one and the clothes from birth."

Rikki took the packet and stared at the contents. She smiled at the picture and leaned the clothes against her chest. The packet also contained information on grief counseling and signs of depression.

"Please feel free to call me if you have any questions or feelings of grief."

"Thanks Mrs. Cunningham, we appreciate your efforts," I said.

Mrs. Cunningham recognized the signals time and time again.

"Mrs. Johnson, you can call me anytime or we can set up an appointment. Just know I'm here for you."

I knew my wife would never call Mrs. Cunningham, but I acknowledged her effort.

"I'll take your card with me just in case we need to talk."

As Mrs. Cunningham headed out the door, I decided to escort her.

"I'm watching her closely, Mrs. Cunningham. If I have questions, I'll call you."

"Mr. Johnson, you're a good man, but don't forget to take care of yourself."

I shook her hand and headed back to the room. By the time I came back, Rikki was back on the phone with her mom and stepmother. I watched T.V. and looked outside the window. Time seemed to pass by slowly, but I knew we had little time to fool around. I had to finish packing the house and Shadow had to be shipped off to D.C.

"Bentley, my Mom is on the phone with Clementine. They want to talk to you."

I walked over to the phone, but wondered what was going on.

"Hello Mothers, what's going on—am I in trouble?"

I chuckled a little bit, but before I could say anything, I was bombarded with rapid fire questions about what happened. They asked about Rikki's condition and how she was feeling. I was very calm and deliberate in my diction so they knew precisely what happened and the sequence of events. "Bentley you don't have an ounce of emotion in your voice," said Clementine. "Are you okay? You're not getting ready to kill someone are you?"

"No! I'm just trying to keep things together."

"Well damn," exclaimed Clementine, "You've got to express yourself. I don't want you to explode or something."

"Clementine, I don't have the energy or the time to even think about that. I need to finish packing up the house and ship Shadow up to D.C. We'll be okay. Rikki just needs to be there as soon as possible. Mom, we'll see you tomorrow, right?"

"Oh yes, sweetie," said Jane. "I'll be there to help out while Rikki rests."

"Sounds good," I said. "I'll see you in the morning.

I felt relieved that my mother-in-law was coming, but I still had a lot to do around the house. We then watched the news and fell asleep. I took the position on the lounge chair next to Rikki. I then held her hand and had the baby's folder on my lap.

The next day we were awakened by breakfast and a brief visit by Nurse Hathaway.

"Good morning, Mrs. Johnson, I'm here to check your spotting."

Nurse Hathaway checked Rikki's bandage and wrote a few notes on her chart.

"Looks pretty good—I'm sure the doctor will release you today. I anticipate he'll be here by 9 a.m."

Within the next forty-five minutes, the resident on call came through to release Rikki. After he left, we gathered Rikki's belongings and made our way out of Crawford Long Hospital. I loaded up the car before bringing Rikki down in the wheelchair. When Rikki finally exited the front door, the fresh air hit her face.

"Wow, it feels good to be outside," said Rikki. "I was getting a little claustrophobic in there."

As we walked across the street, we spotted a young couple cross the street with their infant. It was a painful reminder of what we had just gone through.

"Will it ever end?" said Rikki dryly.

"Yes, one day it will," I replied. "One day it will."

I loaded up Rikki into the car and turned on the smooth jazz of Kenny G. As we headed down Ponce de Leon, we noticed the landscape starting to change in preparation for the Olympics. The signage on the streets looked large and bright. In addition, storefronts received face lifts and consistent colors. The southern flavor of Atlanta was starting to meld into Madison Avenue. Within a half an hour, we were home. Rikki went straight to the bed. Shadow followed her and lay by her side quietly. His presence soothed Rikki's nerves. Meanwhile I prepared lunch. After taking Rikki her lunch and giving Shadow pig ears, I delved into packing boxes. Shadow walked slowly into the living room to observe me in action.

"Hey buddy, I'm getting us ready for our trip to D.C. In a couple of days, I'll be shipping you as well."

Shadow dropped down on the floor and stared at me with sad eyes. It was as if he knew what had happened.

"Hey boy—come here."

I petted Shadow on the head and gave him a big bear hug. Just then the doorbell rang. Shadow jumped up and let out a thunderous bark. I looked outside and saw a Super Shuttle van departing. I then glanced out the door and saw Jane.

"It's Mom!"

Shadow's ears shot up and his tail started to wag. I then opened the door for Jane. I gave her a big hug and grabbed her bags. Meanwhile, Shadow jumped in front of her, looking to be petted. Jane gave him a big hug. Jane then made a bee line to see Rikki with Shadow in tow. After greeting Rikki and catching up on her needs, Jane sat in the room reading a book as Rikki went to sleep.

In three hours Rikki finally woke up.

"Hey, honey, how are you feeling?" asked Jane. Rikki gave a big smile.

"I'm feeling much better now."

Although the pain of delivery had subsided, Rikki felt weak and had a low-grade fever. Jane and Rikki talked for hours, and during the time they talked, Rikki's best friend Leeza arrived from D.C. Emotionally Rikki felt much better with the moral support of her Mom and best friend. She ate a little, but still felt feeble. By 7 p.m. her temperature had elevated to 102.

"Honey," I said. "I'm going to call Dr. Sweeney's twenty-four-hour emergency line. I think your body has some virus."

Within 10 minutes Dr. Sweeney called.

"Hi Mr. Johnson, can you give me a run down on what's going on with Mrs. Johnson?"

I told Dr. Sweeney the story in full detail. After hearing the story, Dr. Sweeney surmised that Rikki's body was fighting off an infection.

Crossing the Bridge Over Troubled Water

"Please have her check back into Crawford Long Hospital as soon as possible," said Dr. Sweeney.

I knew Rikki would be devastated. As I walked back to the bedroom where Rikki and her Mom were watching T.V., I rehearsed my speech in his head. My palms sweated as I anticipated a barrage of questions.

"Hey, honey, I just got off the phone with Dr. Sweeney. She said we need to check you back into Crawford Long."

"What?! What do you mean?" exclaimed Rikki.

"Based on your symptoms, Dr. Sweeney suggested that I bring you in."

Rikki gave me a stiff eye. She was disappointed but understood she was sick.

"I hope they can figure this out. I don't want to end up like my baby."

I nodded my head but did not say a word. I avoided an argument because I knew where her frustrations originated.

"Mom, can you please help Rikki prepare a bag? She's got to return to the hospital. Dr. Sweeney thinks she's got an infection."

Jane, Leeza and Rikki looked at each other as they sat in the living room chattering.

"Bentley, please tell us what's going on," said Jane. I repeated the story three times before it sunk in. Meanwhile, Rikki was moving slowly preparing herself to leave. When Jane realized it, she jumped into action.

"Bentley, is there anything I can help you do around here?" asked Leeza.

"No," I said. "I need you to watch over your friend while I finish up here. If not, we'll probably kill each other."

259

As the ladies prepared to leave, I continued to package boxes while Shadow sat on the floor wondering what in the hell was going on. After they got Rikki ready, I drove her back to Crawford Long with Jane and Leeza in tow.

For the next three days, Rikki stayed in the hospital battling a fever of 102. Meanwhile, I completed the packaging and got ready to ship off Shadow for a Saturday flight to D.C. This was also the flight Rikki and her Mom would take. Since Rikki was somewhat out of it, Jane, Leeza and I decided it was best to get her to D.C. as soon as she got out of the hospital. In addition, the Weather Service announced that within a week a major storm was headed toward the East Coast.

By Friday morning Rikki was discharged, but she was extremely weak. Jane decided it would be best to stay at a hotel close to the airport to minimize the stress on Rikki. Meanwhile, Leeza left to head back to D.C.

"Hey, honey, it's almost all over. You'll be in D.C. tomorrow morning."

Rikki smiled and squeezed my hand as we walked across the street to the familiar parking lot. As we approached Rikki's car, the attendant who I talked to over the weeks wished us good luck.

"Mrs. Johnson, you are a very strong woman," said the attendant in a thick Middle Eastern accent. "Allah has a special plan for you."

The comment struck Rikki as somewhat prophetic.

"I hope he does," replied Rikki. "I hope he does."

We departed Crawford Long and headed down 75/85S. Rikki realized this would be the last time she would see Atlanta for a while.

"Bye downtown," said Rikki. "It's been fun living down here. I'll be back as a tourist one day."

Tears streamed down her face as she reminisced on her first visit to Atlanta as a freshman at Spelman. Jane, who was in the back seat, knew what Rikki was thinking.

"Yeah, honey, you were pretty green back then."

We both chuckled and talked about Rikki's first year in Atlanta. We all laughed at the past and marveled how fast the times had changed. I pulled up to the Marriott and let them out.

"Honey, I'll see you guys in the morning when I drop off Shadow at the airport."

I gave Rikki a big hug and a kiss. I then headed back home to tie up a few loose ends.

Lesson 41: Leave the hospital on your terms, not theirs.

Chapter 42: The Departure

The next morning, I took Shadow for a long run to tire him out. When we returned, Shadow sprawled his legs out on the floor and put his head down to rest.

"Okay buddy, you're going to head out on a flight today. It's going to be a while before you to see me again, but just know you will see me again."

Shadow's eyes followed me wherever I went and it appeared he understood what I said. "It's going to be okay boy," I said as I walked by Shadow and patted him on the head. "It's going to be okay boy. We're all going to a new home."

I walked outside to place the huge portable kennel into the back of my truck. I then returned to the house to get Shadow.

"Okay boy—let's go."

Shadow jumped into the crate and was ready for the journey.

I called Rikki and Jane at the hotel and gave them an estimated time of arrival to the hotel. Within twenty minutes I pulled up to the front door, Shadow barked at the hotel workers who jumped way back. Once he saw Rikki and Jane, Shadow became excited. His tail wiggled with joy shaking the whole back of the truck.

"Good morning, Shadow," said Rikki.

Crossing the Bridge Over Troubled Water

"Hi Shadow," replied Jane.

The two women stroked Shadow's head and gave me their bags to load up. The ladies climbed into the truck while I loaded up the luggage. On the way to the airport, we talked logistics. Jane would get a wheelchair for Rikki while I unloaded the truck and gave the luggage to the Skycaps.

"Okay, honey, this is it," I said as I unloaded the luggage. "I'll see you in D.C."

I helped Rikki out of the truck and into the wheelchair. Before getting into the wheelchair, we embraced and kissed. Rikki was reluctant to leave, but knew it was in everyone's best interest that she departed for D.C. When Jane returned with the skycap, she whisked Rikki away before she could become upset.

"See you guys next week," I said.

"You be careful driving," replied Rikki as she waved from a distance. "I know we'll talk a hundred times before you leave."

We blew each other kisses as Rikki entered the airport doors. I then jumped into the truck to take Shadow to the cargo area. Once I arrived to the area I let Shadow out of the crate to use the bathroom.

"Okay Shadow, come get your snack!"

Shadow galloped over to me to get a large ball of cheese. Inside the cheese were two tablets that were the pet equivalent of motion sickness pills. As Shadow munched on the pills I tried to explain the plane ride to Shadow.

"Everything is going to be okay, boy. You'll be in your new home in no time."

I then loaded up the crate onto a four-wheel dolly and had Shadow jump inside. I pushed the crate into the loading area for processing. The men in the shipping area were amazed at Shadow's size.

"What is he, a jaguar?" asked one of the workers. As the man looked inside the crate, Shadow let out a low growl.

"I think it would be best if you put a light blanket over the cage as you load him."

The man complied and Shadow calmed down.

"Alright, Shadow, I'll see you in D.C.," I said as I looked at the men whisk Shadow away to be loaded onto the plane.

For the next few hours I drove around Atlanta to see some of the sites for the last time. My first stop was at the west end to pick up sweatshirts and hats from the Atlanta University Center. I also stopped by the Jamaican food outlet to get meat patties and coco bread. My other stops were Emory University and The Presidential Center to get a signed edition of the former president's latest book. I reminisced about my days as a student and working on the Metropolitan Project. I was happy about our accomplishments, but sad about leaving. We had built a strong network in Atlanta and I was proud that we did it on our own. I departed for the airport with thirty minutes to spare and arrived just as my father emerged from an airport door. I beeped my horn for Dad to look up. He threw his bags in the rear of the truck and entered in the cab.

"Hey Brat," said Dad. Brat was my dad's term of endearment for me.

"Hey, Dad, I'm glad you made it."

We talked all the way to my house. I gave my father the run down of everything.

"Boy, you've been through quite a bit. I hope you take a little break before you begin your new job."

"I will Dad. The first thing on my mind is to get my family settled."

We ate an early dinner at 3 p.m. and picked up the moving truck and trailer. Once we finally returned to the house, we started to load the truck.

"Hey Dad, tomorrow afternoon I've been invited to attend an awards ceremony. Would you like to go?"

"Are you getting an award?" asked dad.

"I think so. They are making it a surprise for all guests."

Meanwhile my Dad was starting to slow down. He finally called it quits at 7:30 p.m. and was sleep by 8:30 p.m. I continued to load up the truck as my Dad slept. The phone rang around 10 p.m

"Hello," I said.

"Hey, sweetie, how are you?" Rikki's voiced sounded tired but cheery.

I was glad she sounded better.

"So how was your flight?" I asked.

"It was great. The fun came after the flight because Will called an ambulance to pick me up and transport me to the outside gate where his car was waiting. What was even funnier was when I added a few grunts and groans so people thought I was really sick."

"Wow," I said. "That's what happens when you know the Man."

We chuckled at what happened, but it was indicative of the types of connections we had in D.C.

"There was one glitch to the trip," said Rikki. "Our dear Shadow got sick on the plane and laid in his poop and vomit. When the baggage handlers tried to take him off the plane he became really agitated and tried to bite them. Will had to go to the cargo area to give him another dose of the motion sickness medicine, which made him sleepy."

"How's he doing now?" I asked.

"Oh, he's doing fine. He woke up at Leeza's and she immediately fed him some hot dogs. She and the girls then gave him a shampoo and walked him. They are now friends for life."

I was relieved that Rikki felt better. She sounded more like herself.

"Okay, baby, I'll talk to you tomorrow. If we can make it all the way, I'll see you late tomorrow."

"I love you."

"I love you too," replied Rikki.

I let out a sigh of relief. The toll of the events and moving were wearing me down. However, I knew there was a long road ahead. I brushed my teeth and went to bed for a deep long sleep. The next day I woke up at 10AM. My father had already exercised, read the paper and eaten a bowl of cereal.

"Hey Brat, I think that's the longest you've ever slept."

"Yea, I needed the refueling."

I then got up to eat a quick bowl of cereal. We then loaded up the last few items onto the truck. By 12:30 p.m., we were finished. We both took quick showers and quickly ate sandwiches. Once we completed lunch, it was time to depart for the awards ceremony.

The Young Atlanta Civic Awards took place at the Civic Center. The mayor spoke as did Andrew Young, the former ambassador of the United States. Both men emphasized the important role of young civic leaders in shaping the landscape of Atlanta, the state of Georgia, the nation and ultimately the world. After the speakers, it was time for the distribution of awards. None of the awardees were aware of their receipt of an award. It was totally a surprise. My hands were sweaty as each person was announced. Each honoree was presented an award and was given a brief opportunity to speak. I knew each person personally or professionally. By the time they called the seventh name, I felt I was not going to receive an award. Although I thought it was an honor, I did not get my hopes up.

The moderator then announced, "Last but not least, we honor Bentley Johnson." My heart raced. I looked at my father who beamed proudly.

"Head on up, superstar," cheered my Dad with a big smile. I got up to approach the stage. My legs felt a little weak. I shook hands with the mayor and former ambassador before receiving the award. As I approached the podium I looked over the audience where I saw my two former office mates from The Metropolitan Project. I also saw my former boss from Spelman College.

"I'd like to thank my nominator and the selection committee for this honor. This award is a testament to my parents who laid my foundation—thank you Dad who is here from California." I then became a bit overwhelmed by the recent loss of the baby.

"I would like to dedicate this award and my continued work in the country to my son who passed away last week."

Everyone was stunned. The room was quiet. I then walked off the stage. Tears welled-up in the eyes of many attending the ceremony. I, on the other hand, was somewhat relieved. It was something I had to publicly acknowledge. As I sat down, my dad extended his hand. I grabbed it and we embraced.

"I'm really proud of you, son."

The moderator came back to close out the ceremony and acknowledge the corporate sponsors. My Dad and I stayed for a few minutes to chat with friends and other awardees.

"Okay Dad, let's roll out."

We headed back to Decatur to pick up the moving truck and Rikki's car. I passed through downtown Decatur and Agnes Scott College. I beeped the horn at some of my soon-to-be former neighbors. As we arrived at my sold home, I took one more walk through the house.

"Wow, there are so many memories in this house. Now it's time to leave them behind."

I locked the door and placed the key through the door mail slot. I then waived to my neighbors who were peeking out their windows. They were sad but they understood.

We headed out I-285 and then I-85, around 4 p.m. As we hit 7 p.m., I knew we would need to stop overnight in Durham. I called Rikki's stepmother Clementine, whose parents lived in Durham. After talking to her Dad, she called me back to say the beds would be ready. By 11p.m., we pulled into Durham and by 11:30, we were eating a light snack.

"Bentley you better call your wife," said Clementine's dad. "She's called here three times looking for you."

"Yes, sir," I said. "It's not like I'm going anywhere."

The three men chuckled—especially the elders.

"Hey, honey, how are you?"

"I'm better now," said Rikki. "Much better. Did you hear about the winter storm that's coming? They are anticipating two to six inches of snow by tomorrow afternoon. It's coming from the Midwest."

I was totally surprised. Snow should not be coming this early.

"Oh well, I guess we won't be lounging in Durham," I said. "We'll head out of here by nine tomorrow morning. That will get us to your mother's by at least 2 p.m."

We talked about Shadow and the plan to move everything into a storage facility. Rikki had lined up cousins and a few friends to help unload.

"Alright dear, it's time for me to go to bed," I said.

"Okay, drive safely," said Rikki.

Crossing the Bridge Over Troubled Water

I went to bed and slept like a rock. The next day, we ate a hearty breakfast and thanked the Smiths profusely. Mr. Smith and my Dad had hit it off.

"Please come visit us in California," said my dad. "One day I'll bring my wife out here to Durham."

We were given a huge box lunch filled with fried chicken, biscuits, pound cake and sweet tea.

"Wow!" exclaimed Dad. "I really appreciate your hospitality. It reminds me of my days back in Louisiana when I traveled to California. We would get big meals from cousins and friends along the way."

I chuckled. I loved to hear Dad reminisce about his early years. I stepped into the truck and cranked it up. The big diesel engine roared. We headed out of Durham onto I-85 North and drove all the way to D.C. with only one stop for gas. As we rolled past Andrews Air Force Base at 2 p.m., I called Rikki.

"We're here, sweetie; in fact we're about twenty minutes away."

Rikki's heart raced. She was so relieved I made it.

"Okay, honey," said Rikki. "I'll make sure everyone can assist us."

As we pulled into the driveway, I could see Rikki seated at the window. As the truck pulled up, she popped out of her chair to greet me.

"Hey, honey."

"Hi, baby," I said as I got out of the truck.

I gave Rikki a big long hug. We swayed back and forth with our heads bowed in each other's shoulders.

"I'm glad to be home," I said.

"I'm glad you're home, sweetie. We can now start our life anew."

The chill of the winter ran down our backs as soft snow flakes dropped out of the sky. "Hey you love birds," said Dad. "Let's go inside, it's starting to snow."

We clasped hands and walked slowly toward the front door. The move to D.C. marked a fresh chapter in our lives. We could leave our troubles behind and start anew with the circle of family and friends in a nest of support and love.

~

*Lesson 42- Through tragedy and triumph,
focus on family, friends and faith*

~

When you're weary, feeling small,

When tears are in your eyes, I will dry them all;

I'm on your side, when times get rough

And friends just can't be found,

Like a bridge over troubled water

Bridge Over Troubled Water – Simon & Garfunkel